DISCOVERY
OF THE MIDIANITES!

Out of the clouds floated a strange apparition—a terrifying thing—a great, white thing above, below which there swung to and fro a tiny figure. At the sight of it dropping gently toward them, a dozen of the watchers collapsed, frothing, in convulsions.

Abraham, the son of Abraham, dropped to his knees, raising his hands in supplication toward the heavens. His people, those of them who were still upon their feet, followed his example. From his lips issued a torrent of strange sounds—a prayer perhaps, but not in the same language as that in which he had previously spoken to his people.

His followers knelt in terrified silence.

Closer and closer floated the mysterious apparition, until at length, expectant eyes recognized in the figure floating beneath the small white cloud . . . the outline of a human form!

The *Authorized Editions* of
Edgar Rice Burroughs'
TARZAN NOVELS
available in Ballantine Books Editions
at your local bookstore:

COMPLETE AND UNABRIDGED!

TARZAN TRIUMPHANT

Edgar Rice Burroughs

BALLANTINE BOOKS • NEW YORK

Tarzan Triumphant was first published serially in *The Blue Book Magazine,* October 1931, to March, 1932, under the title "The Triumph of Tarzan."

ISBN 0-345-28688-X

This authorized edition published by arrangement with Edgar Rice Burroughs, Inc.

Manufactured in the United States of America

First U.S. Edition: March 1964
Ninth U.S. Printing: March 1984

Cover painting by Neal Adams

CONTENTS

TIME is the warp of the tapestry which is life. It is eternal, constant, unchanging. But the woof is gathered together from the four corners of the earth and the twenty-eight seas and out of the air and the minds of men by that master artist, Fate, as she weaves the design that is never finished.

A thread from here, a thread from there, another from out of the past that has waited years for the companion thread without which the picture must be incomplete.

But Fate is patient. She waits a hundred or a thousand years to bring together two strands of thread whose union is essential to the fabrication of her tapestry, to the composition of the design that was without beginning and is without end.

A matter of some one thousand eight hundred sixty-five years ago (scholars do not agree as to the exact year), Paul of Tarsus suffered martyrdom at Rome.

That a tragedy so remote should seriously affect the lives and destinies of an English aviatrix and an American professor of geology, neither of whom was conscious of the existence of the other at the time this narrative begins—when it does begin, which is not yet, since Paul of Tarsus is merely by way of prologue—may seem remarkable to us, but not to Fate, who has been patiently waiting these nearly two thousand years for these very events I am about to chronicle.

But there is a link between Paul and these two young people. It is Angustus the Ephesian. Angustus was a young man of moods and epilepsy, a nephew of the house of Onesiphorus. Numbered was he among the early converts to the new faith when Paul of Tarsus first visited the ancient Ionian city of Ephesus.

Inclined to fanaticism, from early childhood an epileptic, and worshipping the apostle as the representative of the Master of earth, it is not strange that news of the martyrdom of Paul should have so affected Angustus as to seriously imperil his mental balance.

Conjuring delusions of persecution, he fled Ephesus, taking ship for Alexandria; and here we might leave him, wrapped in his robe, huddled, sick and frightened, on the deck of the little vessel, were it not for the fact that at the Island of Rhodus, where the ship touched, Angustus, going ashore, acquired in some manner (whether by conversion or purchase we know not) a fair haired slave girl from some far northern barbarian tribe.

And here we bid Angustus and the days of the Caesars adieu, and not without some regrets upon my part for I can well imagine adventure, if not romance, in the flight of Angustus and the fair haired slave girl down into Africa from the storied port of Alexandria, through Memphis and Thebae into the great unknown.

1
Gathering the Threads

A S FAR as I know the first Earl of Whimsey has nothing to do with this story, and so we are not particularly interested in the fact that it was not so much the fine grade of whiskey that he manufactured that won him his earldom as the generous contribution he made to the Liberal party at the time that it was in power a number of years ago.

Being merely a simple historian and no prophet, I cannot say whether we shall see the Earl of Whimsey again or not. But if we do not find the Earl particularly interesting, I can assure you that the same may not be said of his fair daughter, Lady Barbara Collis.

The African sun, still an hour high, was hidden from the face of the earth by solid cloud banks that enveloped the loftier peaks of the mysterious, impenetrable fastnesses of the forbidding Ghenzi Mountain range that frowned perpetually upon a thousand valleys little known to man.

From far above this seeming solitude, out of the heart of the densely banked clouds, there came to whatever ears there might be to hear a strange and terrifying droning, suggesting the presence of a preposterous Gargantuan bumblebee circling far above the jagged peaks of Ghenzi. At times it grew in volume until it attained terrifying proportions; and then gradually it diminished until it was only a suggestion of a sound, only to grow once again in volume and to again retreat.

For a long time, invisible and mysterious, it had been describing its great circles deep in the concealing vapors that hid it from the earth and hid the earth from it.

Lady Barbara Collis was worried. Her petrol was running low. At the crucial moment her compass had failed her, and she had been flying blind through the clouds looking for an opening for what now seemed an eternity of hours to her.

She had known that she must cross a lofty range of mountains, and she had kept at a considerable altitude above the clouds for this purpose; but presently they had risen to such heights that she could not surmount them; and, foolishly, rather than turn back and give up her projected non-stop flight from Cairo to the Cape, she had risked all in one effort to penetrate them.

For an hour Lady Barbara had been indulging in considerable high powered thinking, intermingled with the regret that she had not started thinking a little more heavily before she had taken off, as she had, against the explicit command of her sire. To say that she was terrified in the sense that fear had impaired any of her faculties would not be true. However, she was a girl of keen intelligence, fully competent to understand the grave danger of her situation; and when there loomed suddenly close to the tip of her left wing a granite escarpment that was lost immediately above and below her in the all enveloping vapor, it is no reflection upon her courage that she involuntarily caught her breath in a quick gasp and simultaneously turned the nose of her ship upwards until her altimeter registered an altitude that she knew must be far higher than the loftiest peak that reared its head above any part of Africa.

Rising in a wide spiral, she was soon miles away from that terrifying menace that had seemingly leaped out of the clouds to seize her. Yet even so, her plight was still as utterly hopeless as it well could be. Her fuel was practically exhausted. To attempt to drop below the cloud banks, now that she knew positively that she was among lofty mountains, would be utter madness; and so she did the only thing that remained to her.

Alone in the cold wet clouds, far above an unknown country, Lady Barbara Collis breathed a little prayer as she bailed out. With the utmost meticulosity she counted ten before she jerked the rip cord of her chute.

At that same instant Fate was reaching out to gather other threads—far flung threads—for this tiny fragment of her tapestry.

Kabariga, chief of the Bangalo people of Bungalo, knelt before Tarzan of the Apes many weary marches to the south of the Ghenzi Mountain.

In Moscow, Leon Stabutch entered the office of Stalin, the dictator of Red Russia.

Ignorant of the very existence of Kabariga, the black chief, or of Leon Stabutch or Lady Barbara Collis, Lafayette Smith, A.M., Ph.D., Sc.D., professor of geology at the Phil Sheri-

dan Military Academy, boarded a steamship in the harbor of
New York.

Mr. Smith was a quiet, modest, scholarly looking young
man with horn rimmed spectacles, which he wore not because
of any defect of eyesight but in the belief that they added a
certain dignity and semblance of age to his appearance.
That his spectacles were fitted with plain glass was known
only to himself and his optician.

Graduated from college at seventeen the young man had
devoted four additional years to acquiring further degrees,
during which time he optimistically expected the stamp of
dignified maturity to make itself evident in his face and bearing; but, to his intense dismay, his appearance seemed quite
as youthful at twenty-one as it had at seventeen.

Lafe Smith's great handicap to the immediate fulfillment
of his ambition (to occupy the chair of geology in some
university of standing) lay in his possession of the unusual
combination of brilliant intellect and retentive memory with
robust health and a splendid physique. Do what he might he
could not look sufficiently mature and scholarly to impress
any college board. He tried whiskers, but the result was
humiliating; and then he conceived the idea of horn rimmed
spectacles and pared his ambition down, temporarily, from
a university to a prep school.

For a school year, now, he had been an instructor in an
inconspicuous western military academy, and now he was
about to achieve another of his cherished ambitions—he was
going to Africa to study the great rift valleys of the Dark
Continent, concerning the formation of which there are so
many theories propounded and acclaimed by acknowledged
authorities on the subject as to leave the layman with the
impression that a fundamental requisite to success in the
science of geology is identical to that required by weather
forecasters.

But be that as it may, Lafayette Smith was on his way to
Africa with the financial backing of a wealthy father and
the wide experience that might be gained from a number of
week-end field excursions into the back pastures of accom-
modating farmers, plus considerable ability as a tennis player
and a swimmer.

We may leave him now, with his note books and seasick-
ness, in the hands of Fate, who is leading him inexorably
toward sinister situations from which no amount of geological
knowledge nor swimming nor tennis ability may extricate him.

When it is two hours before noon in New York it is an
hour before sunset in Moscow and so it was that as Lafe

Smith boarded the liner in the morning, Leon Stabutch, at the same moment, was closeted with Stalin late in the afternoon.

"That is all," said Stalin; "you understand?"

"Perfectly," replied Stabutch. "Peter Zveri shall be avenged, and the obstacle that thwarted our plans in Africa shall be removed."

"The latter is most essential," emphasized Stalin, "but do not belittle the abilities of your obstacle. He may be, as you have said, naught but an ape-man; but he utterly routed a well organized Red expedition that might have accomplished much in Abyssinia and Egypt but for his interference. And," he added, "I may tell you, comrade, that we contemplate another attempt; but it will not be made until we have a report from you that—the obstacle has been removed."

Stabutch swelled his great chest. "Have I ever failed?" he asked.

Stalin rose and laid a hand upon the other's shoulder. "Red Russia does not look to the OGPU for failures," he said. Only his lips smiled as he spoke.

That same night Leon Stabutch left Moscow. He thought that he left secretly and alone, but Fate was at his side in the compartment of the railway carriage.

As Lady Barbara Collis bailed out in the clouds above the Ghenzi range, and Lafayette Smith trod the gangplank leading aboard the liner, and Stabutch stood before Stalin, Tarzan, with knitted brows, looked down upon the black kneeling at his feet.

"Rise!" he commanded, and then; "Who are you and why have you sought Tarzan of the Apes?"

"I am Kabariga, O Great Bwana," replied the black. "I am chief of the Bangalo people of Bungalo. I come to the Great Bwana because my people suffer much sorrow and great fear and our neighbors, who are related to the Gallas, have told us that you are the friend of those who suffer wrongs at the hands of bad men."

"And what wrongs have your people suffered?" demanded Tarzan, "and at whose hands?"

"For long we lived at peace with all men," explained Kabariga; "we did not make war upon our neighbors. We wished only to plant and harvest in security. But one day there came into our country from Abyssinia a band of *shiftas* who had been driven from their own country. They raided some of our villages, stealing our grain, our goats and our people, and these they sold into slavery in far countries.

"They do not take everything, they destroy nothing; but

they do not go away out of our country. They remain in a village they have built in inaccessible mountains, and when they need more provisions or slaves they come again to other villages of my people.

"And so they permit us to live and plant and harvest that they may continue to take toll of us."

"But why do you come to me?" demanded the ape-man. "I do not interfere among tribes beyond the boundaries of my own country, unless they commit some depredation against my own people."

"I come to you, Great Bwana," replied the black chief, "because you are a white man and these *shiftas* are led by a white man. It is known among all men that you are the enemy of bad white men."

"That," said Tarzan, "is different. I will return with you to your country."

And thus Fate, enlisting the services of the black chief, Kabariga, led Tarzan of the Apes out of his own country, toward the north. Nor did many of his own people know whither he had gone nor why—not even little Nkima, the close friend and confidant of the ape-man.

2

The Land of Midian

ABRAHAM, the son of Abraham, stood at the foot of the towering cliff that is the wall of the mighty crater of a long extinct volcano. Behind and above him were the dwellings of his people, carved from the soft volcanic ash that rose from the bottom of the crater part way up the encircling cliffs; and clustered about him were the men and women and children of his tribe.

One and all, they stood with faces raised toward the heavens, upon each countenance reflected the particular emotion that the occasion evoked—wonder, questioning, fear, and always rapt, tense listening, for from the low clouds hanging but a few hundred feet above the rim of the great crater, the floor of which stretched away for fully five miles to its opposite side, came a strange, ominous droning sound, the like of which not one of them had ever heard before.

The sound grew in volume until it seemed to hover just above them, filling all the heavens with its terrifying threat;

and then it diminished gradually until it was only a suggestion of a sound that might have been no more than a persistent memory rumbling in their heads; and when they thought that it had gone it grew again in volume until once more it thundered down upon them where they stood in terror or in ecstasy, as each interpreted the significance of the phenomenon.

And upon the opposite side of the crater a similar group, actuated by identical fears and questionings, clustered about Elija, the son of Noah.

In the first group a woman turned to Abraham, the son of Abraham. "What is it, Father?" she asked. "I am afraid."

"Those who trust in the Lord," replied the man, "know no fear. You have revealed the wickedness of your heresy, woman."

The face of the questioner blenched and now, indeed, did she tremble. "Oh, Father, you know that I am no heretic!" she cried piteously.

"Silence, Martha!" commanded Abraham. "Perhaps this is the Lord Himself, come again to earth as was prophesied in the days of Paul, to judge us all." His voice was high and shrill, and he trembled as he spoke.

A half grown child, upon the outskirts of the assemblage, fell to the ground, where he writhed, foaming at the mouth. A woman screamed and fainted.

"Oh, Lord, if it is indeed Thee, Thy chosen people await to receive Thy blessing and Thy commands," prayed Abraham; "but," he added, "if it is not Thee, we beseech that Thou savest us whole from harm."

"Perhaps it is Gabriel!" suggested another of the long bearded men.

"And the sound of his trump," wailed a woman—"the trump of doom!"

"Silence!" shrilled Abraham, and the woman shrank back in fear.

Unnoticed, the youth floundered and gasped for breath as, with eyes set as in death, he struggled in the throes of agony; and then another lurched and fell and he, too, writhed and foamed.

And now they were dropping on all sides—some in convulsions and others in deathlike faints—until a dozen or more sprawled upon the ground, where their pitiable condition elicited no attention from their fellows unless a stricken one chanced to fall against a neighbor or upon his feet, in which case the latter merely stepped aside without vouchsafing so much as a glance at the poor unfortunate.

With few exceptions those who suffered the violent strokes

were men and boys, while it was the women who merely
fainted; but whether man, woman or child, whether writhing
in convulsions or lying quietly in coma, no one paid the
slightest attention to any of them. As to whether this seeming
indifference was customary, or merely induced by the excitement and apprehension of the moment, as they stood with eyes,
ears, and minds focussed on the clouds above them, only a closer
acquaintance with these strange people may enlighten us.

Once more the terrifying sound, swollen to hideous proportions, swept toward them; it seemed to stop above them
for a moment and then——

Out of the clouds floated a strange apparition—a terrifying
thing—a great, white thing above, below which there swung to
and fro a tiny figure. At sight of it, dropping gently toward them,
a dozen of the watchers collapsed, frothing, in convulsions.

Abraham, the son of Abraham, dropped to his knees,
raising his hands in supplication toward the heavens. His
people, those of them who were still upon their feet, followed
his example. From his lips issued a torrent of strange sounds
—a prayer perhaps, but if so not in the same language as
that in which he had previously spoken to his people nor in
any language known to man, and as he prayed, his followers
knelt in terrified silence.

Closer and closer floated the mysterious apparition until,
at length, expectant eyes recognized in the figure floating
beneath the small, white cloud the outlines of a human form.

A great cry arose as recognition spread—a cry that was a
mingling of terror born wail and ecstatic hosanna. Abraham
was among the last to recognize the form of the dangling
figure for what it was, or, perhaps, among the last to admit
the testimony of his eyes. When he did he toppled to the
ground, his muscles twitching and jerking his whole body
into horrid contortions, his eyes rolled upward and set as in
death, his breath expelled in painful gasps between lips
flecked with foam.

Abraham, the son of Abraham, never an Adonis, was
at this moment anything but a pretty sight; but no one
seemed to notice him any more than they had the score or
more of lesser creatures who had succumbed to the nervous
excitation of the experiences of the past half hour.

Some five hundred people, men, women and children, of
which thirty, perhaps, lay quietly or writhed in convulsions
upon the ground, formed the group of watchers toward which
Lady Barbara Collis gently floated. As she landed in, if the
truth must be told (and we historians are proverbially truth-
ful, except when we are chronicling the lives of our national

heroes, or living rulers within whose grasp we may be, or of enemy peoples with whom our country has been at war, and upon other occasions)—but, as I was recording, as Lady Barbara landed in an awkward sprawl within a hundred yards of the assemblage all those who had remained standing up to this time went down upon their knees.

Hastily scrambling to her feet, the girl disengaged the harness of her parachute and stood gazing in perplexity upon the scene about her. A quick glance had revealed the towering cliffs that formed the encircling walls of the gigantic crater, though at the time she did not suspect the true nature of the valley spreading before her. It was the people who claimed her surprised attention.

They were white! In the heart of Africa she had landed in the midst of a settlement of whites. But this thought did not wholly reassure her. There was something strange and unreal about these prone and kneeling figures; but at least they did not appear ferocious or unfriendly—their attitudes, in fact, were quite the opposite, and she saw no evidence of weapons among them.

She approached them, and, as she did so, many of them began to wail and press their faces against the ground, while others raised their hands in supplication—some toward the heavens and others toward her.

She was close enough now to see their features and her heart sank within her, for she had never conceived the existence of an entire village of people of such unprepossessing appearance, and Lady Barbara was one of those who are strongly impressed by externals.

The men were particularly repulsive. Their long hair and beards seemed as little acquainted with soap, water and combs as with shears and razors.

There were two features that impressed her most strongly and unfavorably—the huge noses and receding chins of practically the entire company. The noses were so large as to constitute a deformity, while in many of those before her, chins were almost nonexistent.

And then she saw two things that had diametrically opposite effects upon her—the score of epileptics writhing upon the ground and a singularly beautiful, golden haired girl who had risen from the prostrate herd and was slowly approaching her, a questioning look in her large grey eyes.

Lady Barbara Collis looked the girl full in the eyes and smiled, and when Lady Barbara smiled stone crumbled before the radiant vision of her face—or so a poetic and enthralled admirer had once stated in her hearing. The fact that he lisped, however, had prejudiced her against his testimony.

The girl returned the smile with one almost as gorgeous, but quickly she erased it from her features, at the same time glancing furtively about her as though fearful that some one had detected her in the commission of a crime; but when Lady Barbara extended both her hands toward her, she came forward and placed her own within the grasp of the English girl's.

"Where am I?" asked Lady Barbara. "What country is this? Who are these people?"

The girl shook her head. "Who are you?" she asked. "Are you an angel that the Lord God of Hosts has sent to His chosen people?"

It was now the turn of Lady Barbara to shake her head to evidence her inability to understand the language of the other.

An old man with a long white beard arose and came toward them, having seen that the apparition from Heaven had not struck the girl dead for her temerity.

"Get thee gone, Jezebel!" cried the old man to the girl. "How durst thou address this Heavenly visitor?"

The girl stepped back, dropping her head; and though Lady Barbara had understood no word that the man spoke, his tone and gesture, together with the action of the girl, told her what had transpired between them.

She thought quickly. She had realized the impression that her miraculous appearance had made upon these seemingly ignorant people, and she guessed that their subsequent attitude toward her would be governed largely by the impression of her first acts; and being English, she held to the English tradition of impressing upon lesser people the authority of her breed. It would never do, therefore, to let this unkempt patriarch order the girl from her if Lady Barbara chose to retain her; and, after glancing at the faces about her, she was quite sure that if she must choose a companion from among them the fair haired beauty would be her nominee.

With an imperious gesture, and a sinking heart, she stepped forward and took the girl by the arm, and, as the latter turned a surprised glance upon her, drew her to her side.

"Remain with me," she said, although she knew her words were unintelligible to the girl.

"What did she say, Jezebel?" demanded the old man.

The girl was about to reply that she did not know, but something stopped her. Perhaps the very strangeness of the question gave her pause, for it must have been obvious to the old man that the stranger spoke in a tongue unknown to him and, therefore, unknown to any of them.

She thought quickly, now. Why should he ask such a question unless he might entertain a belief that she might have understood? She recalled the smile that the stranger had brought to her lips without her volition, and she recalled, too, that the old man had noted it.

The girl called Jezebel knew the price of a smile in the land of Midian, where any expression of happiness is an acknowledgment of sin; and so, being a bright girl among a people who were almost uniformly stupid, she evolved a ready answer in the hope that it might save her from punishment.

She looked the ancient one straight in the eye. "She said, Jobab," she replied, "that she cometh from Heaven with a message for the chosen people and that she will deliver the message through me and through no other."

Now much of this statement had been suggested to Jezebel by the remarks of the elders and the apostles as they had watched the strange apparition descending from the clouds and had sought to find some explanation for the phenomenon. In fact, Jobab himself had volunteered the very essence of this theory and was, therefore, the more ready to acknowledge belief in the girl's statement.

Lady Barbara stood with an arm about the slim shoulders of the golden haired Jezebel, her shocked gaze encompassing the scene before her—the degraded, unkempt people huddled stupidly before her, the inert forms of those who had fainted, the writhing contortions of the epileptics. With aversion she appraised the countenance of Jobab, noting the watery eyes, the huge monstrosity of his nose, the long, filthy beard that but half concealed his weak chin. With difficulty she stemmed the involuntary shudder that was her natural nervous reaction to the sight before her.

Jobab stood staring at her, an expression of awe on his stupid, almost imbecile face. From the crowd behind him several other old men approached, almost fearfully, halting just behind him. Jobab looked back over his shoulder. "Where is Abraham, the son of Abraham?" he demanded.

"He still communeth with Jehovah," replied one of the ancients.

"Perhaps even now Jehovah revealeth to him the purpose of this visitation," suggested another hopefully.

"She hath brought a message," said Jobab, "and she will deliver it only through the girl called Jezebel. I wish Abraham, the son of Abraham, was through communing with

Jehovah," he added; but Abraham, the son of Abraham, still writhed upon the ground, foaming at the mouth.

"Verily," said another old man, "if this be indeed a messenger from Jehovah let us not stand thus idly staring, lest we arouse the anger of Jehovah, that he bring a plague upon us, even of flies or of lice."

"Thou speaketh true words, Timothy," agreed Jobab, and, turning to the crowd behind them; "Get thee hence quickly and fetch offerings that may be good in the sight of Jehovah, each in accordance with his ability."

Stupidly the assemblage turned away toward the caves and hovels that constituted the village, leaving the small knot of ancients facing Lady Barbara and the golden Jezebel and, upon the ground, the stricken ones, some of whom were evidencing symptoms of recovery from their seizures.

Once again a feeling of revulsion gripped the English girl as she noted the features and carriages of the villagers. Almost without exception they were disfigured by enormous noses and chins so small and receding that in many instances the chin seemed to be lacking entirely. When they walked they ordinarily leaned forward, giving the impression that they were upon the verge of pitching headlong upon their faces.

Occasionally among them appeared an individual whose countenance suggested a much higher mentality than that possessed by the general run of the villagers, and without exception these had blond hair, while the hair of all the others was black.

So striking was this phenomenon that Lady Barbara could not but note it almost in her first brief survey of these strange creatures, yet she was never to discover an indisputable explanation, for there was none to tell her of Angustus and the fair haired slave girl from some barbarian horde of the north, none who knew that Angustus had had a large nose, a weak chin and epilepsy, none to guess the splendid mind and the radiant health of that little slave girl, dead now for almost nineteen centuries, whose blood, even now, arose occasionally above the horrid decadence of all those long years of enforced inbreeding to produce such a creature as Jezebel in an effort, however futile, to stem the tide of degeneracy.

Lady Barbara wondered now why the people had gone to their dwellings—what did it portend? She looked at the old men who had remained behind; but their stupid, almost imbecile faces revealed nothing. Then she turned to the girl. How she wished that they might understand one another.

She was positive that the girl was actively friendly, but she could not be so sure of these others. Everything about them repelled her, and she found it impossible to have confidence in their intentions toward her.

But how different was the girl! She, too, doubtless, was an alien among them; and that fact gave the English girl hope, for she had seen nothing to indicate that the golden haired one was being threatened or mistreated; and at least she was alive and uninjured. Yet, she must be of another breed. Her simple, and scant, apparel, fabricated apparently from vegetable fibre, was clean, as were those parts of her body exposed to view, while the garments of all the others, especially the old men, were filthy beyond words, as were their hair and beards and every portion of their bodies not concealed by the mean garments that scarce half covered their nakedness.

As the old men whispered among themselves, Lady Barbara turned slowly to look about her in all directions. She saw precipitous cliffs completely hemming a small circular valley, near the center of which was a lake. Nowhere could she see any indication of a break in the encircling walls that rose hundreds of feet above the floor of the valley; and yet she felt that there must be an entrance from the outer world, else how had these people gained entrance?

Her survey suggested that the valley lay at the bottom of the crater of a great volcano, long extinct, and if that were true the path to the outer world must cross the summit of those lofty walls; yet these appeared, insofar as she could see, utterly unscalable. But how account for the presence of these people? The problem vexed her, but she knew that it must remain unsolved until she had determined the attitude of the villagers and discovered whether she were to be a guest or a prisoner.

Now the villagers were returning, and she saw that many of them carried articles in their hands. They came slowly, timidly nearer her, exhorted by the ancients, until at her feet they deposited the burdens they had carried—bowls of cooked food, raw vegetables and fruits, fish, and pieces of the fibre cloth such as that from which their crude garments were fabricated, the homely offerings of a simple people.

As they approached her many of them displayed symptoms of great nervousness and several sank to the ground, victims of the convulsive paroxysms that marked the seizures to which so many of them appeared to be subject.

To Lady Barbara it appeared that these simple folk were either bringing gifts attesting their hospitality or were offering their wares, in barter, to the stranger within their gates; nor did the truth once occur to her at the moment—that the villagers were, in fact, making votive offerings to one they believed the messenger of God, or even, perhaps, a goddess in her own right. When, after depositing their offerings at her feet, they turned and hastened away, the simple faces of some evidencing fear caused her to abandon the idea that the goods were offered for sale; and she determined that, if not gifts of hospitality, they might easily be considered as tribute to appease the wrath of a potential enemy.

Abraham, the son of Abraham, had regained consciousness. Slowly he raised himself to a sitting position and looked about him. He was very weak. He always was after these seizures. It required a minute or two before he could collect his wits and recall the events immediately preceding the attack. He saw the last of those bringing offerings to Lady Barbara deposit them at her feet. He saw the stranger. And then he recalled the strange droning that had come out of the heavens and the apparition that he had seen floating down toward them.

Abraham, the son of Abraham, arose. It was Jobab, among the ancients, who saw him first. "Hallelujah!" he exclaimed. "Abraham, the son of Abraham, walketh no longer with Jehovah. He hath returned to our midst. Let us pray!" Whereupon the entire assemblage, with the exception of Lady Barbara and the girl called Jezebel, dropped to its knees. Among them, Abraham, the son of Abraham, moved slowly, as though in a trance, toward the stranger, his mind still lethargic from the effects of his seizure. About him arose a strange, weird babel as the ancients prayed aloud without concord or harmony, interrupted by occasional cries of "Hallelujah" and "Amen."

Tall and thin, with a long grey beard still flecked with foam and saliva, his scant robe ragged and filthy, Abraham, the son of Abraham, presented a most repulsive appearance to the eyes of the English girl as, at last, he stopped before her.

Now his mind was clearing rapidly, and as he halted he seemed the to note the presence of the girl, Jezebel, for the first time. "What doest thou here, wanton?" he demanded. "Why are thou not upon thy knees praying with the others?"

Lady Barbara was watching the two closely. She noted the stern and accusing attitude and tones of the man, and she saw the appealing glance that the girl cast toward her. Instantly she threw an arm about the latter's shoulders. "Remain here!" she said, for she feared that the man was ordering the girl to leave her.

If Jezebel did not understand the words of the strange, heavenly visitor, she could not mistake the detaining gesture; and, anyway, she did not wish to join the others in prayer. Perhaps it was only that she might cling a few brief minutes longer to the position of importance to which the incident had elevated her out of a lifetime of degradation and contempt to which her strange inheritance of beauty had condemned her.

And so, nerved by the pressure of the arm about her, she faced Abraham, the son of Abraham, resolutely, although, withal, a trifle fearfully, since who knew better than she what a terrible man Abraham, the son of Abraham, might become when crossed by anyone.

"Answer me, thou—thou—" Abraham, the son of Abraham, could not find an epithet sufficiently excoriating to meet the emergency.

"Let not thy anger blind thee to the will of Jehovah," warned the girl.

"What meanest thou?" he demanded.

"Canst thou not see that His messenger hath chosen me to be her mouthpiece?"

"What sacrilege is this, woman?"

"It is no sacrilege," she replied sturdily. "It is the will of Jehovah, and if thou believest me not, ask Jobab, the apostle."

Abraham, the son of Abraham, turned to where the ancients prayed. "Jobab!" he cried in a voice that arose above the din of prayer.

Instantly the devotions ceased with a loud "Amen!" from Jobab. The old men arose, their example being followed by those others of the villagers who were not held earth-bound by epilepsy; and Jobab, the apostle, approached the three who were now the goal of every eye.

"What transpired while I walked with Jehovah?" demanded Abraham, the son of Abraham.

"There came this messenger from heaven," replied Jobab, "and we did her honor, and the people brought offerings, each according to his ability, and laid them at her feet, and she did not seem displeased—nor either did she seem pleased," he added. "And more than this we knew not what to do."

"But this daughter of Satan!" cried Abraham, the son of Abraham. "What of her?"

"Verily I say unto you that she speaks with the tongue of

Jehovah," replied Jobab, "for He hath chosen her to be the mouthpiece of His messenger."

"Jehovah be praised," said Abraham, the son of Abraham; "the ways of the Almighty passeth understanding." He turned now to Jezebel, but when he spoke there was a new note in his tones—a conciliatory note—and, perhaps, not a little of fear in his eyes. "Beseech the messenger to look upon us poor servants of Jehovah with mercy and forgiveness; beg of her that she open her mouth to us poor sinners and divulge her wishes. We await her message, trembling and fearful in the knowledge of our unworthiness."

Jezebel turned to Lady Barbara.

"But wait!" cried Abraham, the son of Abraham, as a sudden questioning doubt assailed his weak mind. "How can you converse with her? You speak only the language of the land of Midian. Verily, if thou canst speak with her, why may not I, the Prophet of Paul, the son of Jehovah?"

Jezebel had a brain worth fifty such brains as that possessed by the Prophet of Paul; and now she used it to advantage, though, if the truth were known, not without some misgivings as to the outcome of her rash proposal, for, although she had a bright and resourceful mind, she was none the less the ignorant child of an ignorant and superstitious people.

"Thou hast a tongue, Prophet," she said. "Speak thou then to the messenger of Jehovah, and if she answers thee in the language of the land of Midian thou canst understand her as well as I."

"That," said Abraham, the son of Abraham, "is scarce less than an inspiration."

"A miracle!" exclaimed Jobab. "Jehovah must have put the words in her mouth."

"I shall address the messenger," said the Prophet. "O angel of light!" he cried, turning toward Lady Barbara, "look with compassion upon an old man, upon Abraham, the son of Abraham, the Prophet of Paul, the son of Jehovah, and deign to make known to him the wishes of Him who sent you to us."

Lady Barbara shook her head. "There is something that one does when one is embarrassed," she said. "I have read it repeatedly in the advertising sections of American periodicals, but I haven't that brand. However, any port in a storm," and she extracted a gold cigarette case from a pocket of her jacket and lighted one of the cigarettes.

"What didst she say, Jezebel?" demanded the Prophet— "and, in the name of Paul, what miracle is this? 'Out of his nostrils goeth smoke' is said of the behemoth of holy writ. What can be the meaning of this?"

"It is a warning," said Jezebel, "because thou didst doubt my words."

"Nay, nay," exclaimed Abraham, the son of Abraham, "I doubted thee not. Tell her that I did not doubt thee, and then tell me what she said."

"She said," replied Jezebel, "that Jehovah is not pleased with thee or thy people. He is angry because thou so mistreat Jezebel. His anger is terrible because thou dost make her work beyond her strength, nor give her the best food, and that thou dost punish her when she would laugh and be happy."

"Tell her," said the Prophet, "that we knew not that thou wert overworked and that we shall make amends. Tell her that we lovest thee and thou shalt have the best of food. Speak to her, O Jezebel, and ask if she has further commands for her poor servants."

Jezebel looked into the eyes of the English girl, and upon her countenance rested an expression of angelic guilelessness, while from her lips issued a stream of meaningless jargon which was as unintelligible to Jezebel as to Lady Barbara or the listening villagers of the land of Midian.

"My dear child," said Lady Barbara, when Jezebel eventually achieved a period, "what you say is as Greek to me, but you are very beautiful and your voice is musical. I am sorry that you can understand me no better than I understand you."

"What saith she?" demanded Abraham, the son of Abraham.

"She says that she is tired and hungry and that she wishes the offerings brought by the people to be taken to a cave—a clean cave—and that I accompany her and that she be left in peace, as she is tired and would rest; and she wishes no one but Jezebel to be with her."

Abraham, the son of Abraham, turned to Jobab. "Send women to make clean the cave next to mine," he commanded, "and have others carry the offerings to the cave, as well as clean grasses for a bed."

"For two beds," Jezebel corrected him.

"Yea, even for two beds," agreed the Prophet, hastily.

And so Lady Barbara and Jezebel were installed in a well renovated cave near the bottom of the cliff, with food enough to feed a numerous company. The English girl stood at the entrance to her strange, new abode looking out across the valley as she sought to evolve some plan whereby she might get word of her predicament and her whereabouts to the outside world. In another twenty-four hours she knew the apprehension of her friends and her family would be aroused and soon many an English plane would be roaring over the Cape to Cairo route in search of her, and, as she pondered her unfortunate situation, the girl called Jezebel lay in luxurious idleness upon her bed of fresh grasses and ate from a pile of fruit near her head, the while a happy smile of contentment illumed her lovely countenance.

The shadows of night were already falling, and Lady Barbara turned back into the cave with but a single practical idea evolved from all her thinking—that she must find the means to communicate with these people, nor could she escape the conviction that only by learning their language might this be accomplished.

As darkness came and chill night air replaced the heat of the day, Jezebel kindled a fire at the mouth of the cave. Near it the two girls sat upon a soft cushion of grass, the firelight playing upon their faces, and there the Lady Barbara commenced the long and tedious task of mastering a new language. The first step consisted in making Jezebel understand what she desired to accomplish, but she was agreeably astonished at the celerity with which the girl grasped the idea. Soon she was pointing to various objects, calling them by their English names and Jezebel was naming them in the language of the land of Midian.

Lady Barbara would repeat the word in the Midian language several times until she had mastered the pronunciation, and she noticed that, similarly, Jezebel was repeating its English equivalent. Thus was Jezebel acquiring an English vocabulary while she taught the Midian to her guest.

An hour passed while they occupied their time with their task. The village lay quiet about them. Faintly, from the distant lake, came the subdued chorus of the frogs. Occasionally a goat bleated somewhere out in the darkness. Far away, upon the opposite side of the valley, shone tiny, flickering lights—the cooking fires of another village, thought Lady Barbara.

A man, bearing a lighted torch, appeared suddenly, coming from a nearby cave. In low, monotonous tones he voiced a chant. Another man, another torch, another voice joined him. And then came others until a procession wound down toward the level ground below the caves.

Gradually the voices rose. A child screamed. Lady Barbara saw it now—a small child being dragged along by an old man. Now the procession encircled a large boulder and halted, but the chanting did not cease, nor did the screaming of the child. Tall among the others Lady Barbara recognized the figure of the man who had last interrogated her. Abraham, the son of Abraham, the Prophet, stood behind the boulder that rose waist high in front of him. He raised his open palm and the chanting ceased. The child had ceased to scream, but its broken sobs came clearly to the ears of the two girls.

Abraham, the son of Abraham, commenced to speak, his eyes raised toward the heavens. His voice came monotonously across the little span of darkness. His grotesque features were lighted by the flickering torches that played as well upon the equally repulsive faces of his congregation.

Unaccountably, the entire scene assumed an aspect of menace in the eyes of the English girl. Apparently it was only the simple religious service of a simple people and yet, to Barbara Collis, there was something terrible about it, something that seemed fraught with horror.

She glanced at Jezebel. The girl was sitting cross legged, her elbows on her knees, her chin supported in the palms of her hands, staring straight ahead. There was no smile now upon her lips.

Suddenly the air was rent by a childish scream of fear and horror that brought the Lady Barbara's gaze back to the scene below. She saw the child, struggling and fighting, dragged to the top of the boulder; she saw Abraham, the son of Abraham, raise a hand above his head; she saw the torchlight play upon a knife; and then she turned away and hid her face in her hands.

3

The "Gunner"

DANNY "GUNNER" PATRICK stretched luxuriously in his deck chair. He was at peace with the world—temporarily, at least. In his clothes were 20 G. securely hidden. Beneath his left arm pit, also securely hidden, snuggled a .45 in a specially designed holster. "Gunner" Patrick did not expect to have to use it for a long, long time perhaps; but it was just as well to be prepared. "Gunner" hailed from Chicago where people in his circle of society believe in preparedness.

He had never been a Big Shot, and if he had been content to remain more or less obscure he might have gone along about his business for some time until there arrived the allotted moment when, like many of his late friends and acquaintances, he should be elected to stop his quota of machine gun bullets; but Danny Patrick was ambitious. For years he had been the right hand, and that means the pistol hand, of a Big Shot. He had seen his patron grow rich— "lousy rich," according to Danny's notion—and he had become envious.

So Danny double-crossed the Big Shot, went over to the other side, which, incidentally, boasted a bigger and better Big Shot, and was a party to the hijacking of several truck loads of booze belonging to his former employer.

Unfortunately, on the occasion of the hijacking of the last truck, one of his former pals in the service of the double-crossee recognized him; and Danny, knowing that he had been recognized, sought, quite pardonably, to eliminate this damaging evidence; but his unwilling target eluded him and before he could rectify his ballistic errors the police came.

It is true that they obligingly formed an escort to convoy the truck safely to the warehouse of the bigger and better Big Shot, but the witness to Danny's perfidy escaped.

Now Danny "Gunner" Patrick knew the temper of his erstwhile patron—and who better? Many of the Big Shot's enemies, and several of his friends, had Danny taken for a ride. He knew the power of the Big Shot, and he feared him. Danny did not want to go for a ride himself, but he knew that if he remained in dear old Chi he would go the way of all good gunmen much too soon to suit his plans.

And so, with the 20 G. that had been the price of his perfidy, he had slipped quietly out of town; and, being wise in his day and generation, he had also slipped quietly out of the country, another thread to be woven into Fate's tapestry.

He knew that the Big Shot was slipping (that was one reason he had deserted him); and he also knew that, sooner or later, the Big Shot would have a grand funeral with truck loads of flowers and, at least, a ten thousand dollar casket. So Danny would dally in foreign climes until after the funeral.

Just where he would dally he did not know, for Danny was shy of geographic lore; but he knew he was going at least as far as England, which he also knew to be somewhere in London.

So now he lolled in the sun, at peace with the world that immediately surrounded him; or almost at peace, for there rankled in his youthful breast various snubs that had been aimed in his direction by the few fellow passengers he had accosted. Danny was at a loss to understand why he was *persona non grata*. He was good looking. His clothes had been designed by one of Chicago's most exclusive tailors— they were quiet and in good taste. These things Danny knew, and he also knew that no one aboard ship had any inkling of his profession. Why then, after a few minutes conversation, did they invariably lose interest in him and thereafter look through him as though he did not exist? The "Gunner" was both puzzled and peeved.

It was the third day out, and Danny was already fed up on ocean travel. He almost wished that he were back in Chicago where he knew he could find congenial spirits with whom to foregather, but not quite. Better a temporary isolation above ground than a permanent one below.

A young man whom he had not before noticed among the passengers came and sat down in the chair next to his. He looked over at Danny and smiled. "Good morning," he said. "Lovely weather we're having."

Danny's cold, blue eyes surveyed the stranger. "Are we?" he replied in a tone as cold as his gaze; then he resumed his previous occupation of staring out across the rail at the illimitable expanse of rolling sea.

Lafayette Smith smiled, opened a book, settled himself more comfortably in his chair and proceeded to forget all about his discourteous neighbor.

Later that day Danny saw the young man at the swimming pool and was impressed by one of the few things that Danny could really understand—proficiency in a physical sport. The young man far outshone the other passengers both in swimming and diving, and his sun bronzed body evidenced long hours in a bathing suit.

The following morning when Danny came on deck he found that the young man had preceded him. "Good morning," said Danny pleasantly as he dropped into his chair. "Nice morning."

The young man looked up from his book. "Is it?" he asked and let his eyes fall again to the printed page.

Danny laughed. "Right back at me, eh?" he exclaimed. "You see I thought youse was one of them high hat guys. Then I seen you in the tank. You sure can dive, buddy."

Lafayette Smith, A.M., Ph.D., Sc.D., let his book drop slowly to his lap as he turned to survey his neighbor. Presently a smile stole across his face—a good natured, friendly smile. "Thanks," he said. "You see it is because I like it so well. A fellow who's spent as much time at it as I have ever since I was a little shaver would have to be an awful dub not to be fairly proficient."

"Yeah," agreed Danny. "It's your racket, I suppose."

Lafayette Smith looked about the deck around his chair. He thought, at first, that Danny was referring to a tennis racquet, as that would be the thing that the word would connote to the mind of so ardent a tennis enthusiast as he. Then he caught the intended meaning and smiled. "I am not a professional swimmer, if that is what you mean," he said.

"Pleasure trip?" inquired Danny.

"Well, I hope it will be," replied the other, "but it is largely what might be called a business trip, too. Scientific investigation. I am a geologist."

"Yeah? I never heard of that racket before."

"It is not exactly a racket," said Smith. "There is not enough money in it to raise it to the importance and dignity of a racket."

"Oh, well, I know a lot of little rackets that pay good— especially if a fellow goes it alone and doesn't have to split with a mob. Going to England?"

"I shall be in London a couple of days only," replied Smith.

"I thought maybe you was goin' to England."

Lafayette Smith looked puzzled. "I am," he said.

"Oh, you're goin' there from London?"

Was the young man trying to kid him? Very good! "Yes," he said, "if I can get permission from King George to do so I shall visit England while I am in London."

"Say, does that guy live in England? He's the fellow Big Bill was goin' to punch in the snoot. Geeze, but there is one big bag of hot wind."

"Who, King George?"

"No, I don't know him—I mean Thompson."

"I don't know either of them," admitted Smith; "but I've heard of King George."

"You ain't never heard of Big Bill Thompson, mayor of Chicago?"

"Oh, yes; but there are so many Thompson's—I didn't know to which one you referred."

"Do you have to get next to King George to get to England?" demanded Danny, and something in the earnestness of his tone assured Smith that the young man had not been kidding him.

"No," he replied. "You see London is the capital of England. When you are in London you are, of course, in England."

"Geeze!" exclaimed Danny. "I sure was all wet, wasn't I; but you see," he added confidentially, "I ain't never been out of America before."

"Are you making a protracted stay in England?"

"A what?"

"Are you going to remain in England for some time?"

"I'll see how I like it," replied Danny.

"I think you'll like London," Smith told him.

"I don't have to stay there," Danny confided; "I can go where I please. Where are you goin'?"

"To Africa."

"What sort of a burgh is it? I don't think I'd like bein' bossed by a lot of savages, though a lot of 'em is regular, at that. I knew some negro cops in Chi that never looked to frame a guy."

"You wouldn't be bothered by any policeman where I'm going," Smith assured him; "there are none."

"Geeze! you don't say? But get me right, mister, I ain't worried about no cops—they ain't got nothin' on me. Though I sure would like to go somewhere where I wouldn't never see none of their ugly mugs. You know, mister," he added confidentially, "I just can't like a cop."

This young man puzzled Lafayette Smith the while he amused him. Being a scholar, and having pursued scholarly ways in a quiet university town, Smith was only aware of the strange underworld of America's great cities to such a sketchy extent as might result from a cursory and disinterested perusal of the daily press. He could not catalog his new acquaintance by any first hand knowledge. He had never talked with exactly such a type before. Outwardly, the young man might be the undergraduate son of a cultured family, but when he spoke one had to revise this first impression.

"Say," exclaimed Danny, after a short silence; "I know about this here Africa, now. I seen a moving pitcher once— lions and elephants and a lot of foolish lookin' deer with funny monickers. So that's where you're goin'? Huntin', I suppose?"

"Not for animals, but for rocks," explained Smith.

"Geeze! Who ain't huntin' for rocks?" demanded Danny. "I know guys would croak their best friends for a rock."

"Not the sort I'm going to look for," Smith assured him.

"You don't mean diamonds then?"

"No, just rock formations that will teach me more about the structure of the earth."

"And you can't cash in on them after you find them?"

"No."

"Geeze, that's a funny racket. You know a lot about this here Africa, don't you?"

"Only what I've read in books," replied Smith.

"I had a book once," said Danny, with almost a verbal swagger.

"Yes?" said Smith politely. "Was it about Africa?"

"I don't know. I never read it. Say, I been thinkin'," he added. "Why don't I go to this here Africa? That pitcher I seen looked like they wasn't many people there, and I sure would like to get away from people for a while—I'm fed up on 'em. How big a place is Africa?"

"Almost four times as large as the United States."

"Geeze! An' no cops?"

"Not where I'm going, nor very many people. Perhaps I shall see no one but the members of my safari for weeks at a time."

"Safari?"

"My people—porters, soldiers, servants."

"Oh, your mob."

"It may be."

"What say I go with you, mister? I don't understand your racket and I don't want to, but I won't demand no cut-in whatever it is. Like the old dame that attended the funeral, I just want to go along for the ride—only I'll pay my way."

Lafayette Smith wondered. There was something about this young man he liked, and he certainly found him interesting as a type. Then, too, there was an indefinable something in his manner and in those cold, blue eyes that suggested he might be a good companion in an emergency. Furthermore, Lafayette Smith had recently been thinking that long weeks in the interior without the companionship of another white man might prove intolerable. Yet he hesitated. He knew nothing about the man. He might be a fugitive from justice. He might be anything. Well, what of it? He had about made up his mind.

"If it's expenses that's worrying you," said Danny, noting the other's hesitation, "forget 'em. I'll pay my share and then some, if you say so."

"I wasn't thinking of that, though the trip will be expensive—not much more for two, though, than for one."

"How much?"

"Frankly, I don't know, but I have been assuming that five thousand dollars should cover everything, though I may be wrong."

Danny Patrick reached into his trousers' pocket and brought forth a great roll of bills—50's and 100's. He counted out three thousand dollars. "Here's three G. to bind the bargain," he said, "and there's more where that came from. I ain't no piker. I'll pay my share and part of yours, too."

"No," said Smith, motioning the proffered bills aside. "It is not that. You see we don't know anything about each other. We might not get along together."

"You know as much about me as I do about you," replied Danny, "and I'm game to take a chance. Maybe the less we know the better. Anyhow, I'm goin' to this here Africa, and if you're goin' too, we might as well go together. It'll cut down expenses, and two white fellows is got a better chanct than one alone. Do we stick or do we split?"

Lafayette Smith laughed. Here, perhaps, was the making of an adventure, and in his scholarly heart he had long held the secret hope that some day he might go adventuring. "We stick," he said.

"Gimme five!" exclaimed "Gunner" Patrick, extending his hand.

"Five what?" asked Lafayette Smith, A.M., Ph.D., Sc.D.

4
Gathering the Strands

WEEKS rolled by. Trains rattled and chugged. Steamships plowed. Black feet padded well worn trails. Three safaris, headed by white men from far separated parts of the earth, moved slowly along different trails that led toward the wild fastnesses of the Ghenzis. None knew of the presence of the others, nor were their missions in any way related.

From the West came Lafayette Smith and "Gunner" Patrick; from the South, an English big game hunter, Lord Passmore; from the East, Leon Stabutch.

The Russian had been having trouble with his men. They had enlisted with enthusiasm, but their eagerness to proceed had waned as they penetrated more deeply into strange and unknown country. Recently they had talked with men of a village beside which they had camped, and these men had told them terrifying tales of the great band of *shiftas*, led by a white man, that was terrorizing the country toward which they were marching, killing and raping as they collected slaves to be sold in the north.

Stabutch had halted for the noonday rest upon the southern slopes of the foothills of the Ghenzis. To the north rose the lofty peaks of the main range; to the south, below them, they could see forest and jungle stretching away into the distance; about them were rolling hills, sparsely timbered, and between the hills and the forest an open, grassy plain where herds of antelope and zebra could be seen grazing.

The Russian called his headman to him. "What's the matter with those fellows?" he asked, nodding toward the porters, who were gathered, squatting, in a circle, jabbering in low voices.

"They are afraid, Bwana," replied the black.

"Afraid of what?" demanded Stabutch, though he well knew.

"Afraid of the *shiftas*, Bwana. Three more deserted last night."

"We didn't need them anyway," snapped Stabutch; "the loads are getting lighter."

"More will run away," said the headman. "They are all afraid."

"They had better be afraid of me," blustered Stabutch. "If any more men desert I'll—I'll——"

"They are not afraid of you, Bwana," the headman told him, candidly. "They are afraid of the *shiftas* and the white man who is their chief. They do not want to be sold into slavery, far from their own country."

"Don't tell me you believe in that cock-and-bull story, you black rascal," snapped Stabutch. "It's just an excuse to turn back. They want to get home so they can loaf, the lazy dogs. And I guess you're as bad as the rest of them. Who said you were a headman, anyway? If you were worth a kopeck you'd straighten those fellows out in no time; and we wouldn't have any more talk about turning back, nor any more desertions, either."

"Yes, Bwana," replied the black; but what he thought was his own business.

"Now, listen to me," growled Stabutch, but that to which he would have had the headman listen was never voiced. The interruption came from one of the porters, who leaped suddenly to his feet, voicing a low cry of warning pregnant with terror. "Look!" he cried, pointing toward the west. "The *shiftas!*"

Silhouetted against the sky, a group of mounted men had reined in their horses upon the summit of a low hill a mile away. The distance was too great to permit the excited watchers in the Russian's camp to distinguish details, but the very presence of a body of horsemen was all the assurance that the blacks needed to convince them that it was composed of members of the *shifta* band of which they had heard terrifying rumors that had filled their simple breasts with steadily increasing dread during the past several days. The white robes fluttering in the breeze at the summit of the distant hill, the barrels of rifles and the shafts of spears that, even at a distance, were sufficiently suggestive of their true nature to permit of no doubt, but served to definitely crystallize the conjectures of the members of Stabutch's safari and augment their panic.

They were standing now, every eye turned toward the menace of that bristling hill top. Suddenly one of the men ran toward the loads that had been discarded during the noonday halt, calling something back over his shoulder to his fellows. Instantly there was a break for the loads.

"What are they doing?" cried Stabutch. "Stop them!"

The headman and the askaris ran quickly toward the porters, many of whom already had shouldered their loads and were starting on the back trail. The headman sought to stop them, but one, a great, burly fellow, felled him with a single blow. Then another, glancing back toward the west, voiced a shrill cry of terror. "Look!" he cried. "They come!"

Those who heard him turned to see the horsemen, their robes fluttering backward in the breeze, reining down the hillside toward them at a gallop.

It was enough. As one man, porters, askaris, and the headman, they turned and fled. Those who had shouldered loads threw them to the ground lest their weight retard the runner's speed.

Stabutch was alone. For an instant he hesitated on the verge of flight, but almost immediately he realized the futility of attempted escape.

With loud yells the horsemen were bearing down upon his camp; and presently, seeing him standing there alone, they drew rein before him. Hard faced, villainous appearing, they presented such an appearance of evil as might have caused the stoutest heart to quail.

Their leader was addressing Stabutch in a strange tongue, but his attitude was so definitely menacing that the Russian had little need of knowledge of the other's language to interpret the threat reflected in the speaker's tones and scowling face; but he dissembled his fears and met the men with a cool equanimity that impressed them with the thought that the stranger must be sure of his power. Perhaps he was but the advance guard of a larger body of white men!

The *shiftas* looked about them uneasily as this thought was voiced by one of their number, for they well knew the temper and the arms of white men and feared both. Yet, notwithstanding their doubts, they could still appreciate the booty of the camp, as they cast covetous and appraising eyes upon the abandoned loads of the departed porters, most of whom were still in view as they scurried toward the jungle.

Failing to make himself understood by the white man, the leader of the *shiftas* fell into a heated argument with several of his henchmen and when one, sitting, stirrup to stirrup, beside him, raised his rifle and aimed it at Stabutch the leader struck the weapon up and berated his fellow angrily. Then he issued several orders, with the result that, while two of the band remained to guard Stabutch, the others dismounted and loaded the packs on several of the horses.

A half hour later the *shiftas* rode back in the direction from which they had come, taking with them all of the Russian's belongings and him, also, disarmed and a prisoner.

And, as they rode away, keen grey eyes watched them from the concealing verdure of the jungle—eyes that had been watching every turn of events in the camp of the Russian since Stabutch had called the halt for the disastrous noonday rest.

Though the distance from the jungle to the camp was considerable, nothing had escaped the keen eyes of the watcher reclining at ease in the fork of a great tree just at the edge of the plain. What his mental reactions to the happenings he had witnessed none might have guessed by any changing expression upon his stern, emotionless countenance.

He watched the retreating figures of the *shiftas* until they had disappeared from view, and then he sprang lightly to his feet and swung off through the jungle in the opposite direction —in the direction taken by the fleeing members of Stabutch's safari.

Goloba, the headman, trod fearfully the gloomy trails of the jungle; and with him were a considerable number of the other members of Stabutch's safari, all equally fearful lest the *shiftas* pursue them.

The first panic of their terror had abated; and as the minutes sped, with no sign of pursuit, they took greater heart, though there grew in the breast of Goloba another fear to replace that which was fading—it was the fear of the trusted lieutenant who has deserted his bwana. It was something that Goloba would have to explain one day, and even now he was formulating his excuse.

"They rode upon us, firing their rifles," he said. "There were many of them—at least a hundred." No one disputed him. "We fought bravely in defense of the Bwana, but we were few and could not repulse them." He paused and looked at those walking near him. He saw that they nodded their heads in assent. "And then I saw the Bwana fall and so, to escape being taken and sold into slavery, we ran away."

"Yes," said one walking at his side, "it is all as Goloba has said. I myself—" but he got no further. The figure of a bronzed white man, naked but for a loin cloth, dropped from the foliage of the trees into the trail a dozen paces ahead of them. As one man they halted, surprise and fear writ large upon their faces.

"Which is the headman?" demanded the stranger in their own dialect, and every eye turned upon Goloba.

"I am," replied the black leader.

"Why did you desert your bwana?"

Goloba was about to reply when the thought occurred to him that here was only a single, primitively armed white without companions, without a safari—a poor creature, indeed, in the jungle—lower than the meanest black.

"Who are you, to question Goloba, the headman?" he demanded, sneeringly. "Get out of my way," and he started forward along the trail toward the stranger.

But the white man did not move. He merely spoke, in low, even tones. "Goloba should know better," he said, "than to speak thus to any white man."

The black hesitated. He was not quite sure of himself, but yet he ventured to hold his ground. "Great bwanas do not go naked and alone through the forests, like the low Bagesu. Where is your safari?"

"Tarzan of the Apes needs no safari," replied the white man.

Goloba was stunned. He had never seen Tarzan of the Apes, for he came from a country far from Tarzan's stamping ground, but he had heard tales of the great bwana—tales that had lost nothing in the telling.

"You are Tarzan?" he asked.

The white man nodded, and Goloba sank, fearfully, to his knees. "Have mercy, great bwana!" he begged. "Goloba did not know."

"Now, answer my question," said Tarzan. "Why did you desert your bwana?"

"We were attacked by a band of *shiftas*," replied Goloba. "They rode upon us, firing their rifles. There were at least a hundred of them. We fought bravely——"

"Stop!" commanded Tarzan. "I saw all that transpired. No shots were fired. You ran away before you knew whether the horsemen were enemies or friends. Speak now, but speak true words."

"We knew that they were enemies," said Goloba, "for we had been warned by villagers, near whom we had camped, that these *shiftas* would attack us and sell into slavery all whom they captured."

"What more did the villagers tell you?" asked the ape-man.

"That the *shiftas* are led by a white man."

"That is what I wished to know," said Tarzan.

"And now may Goloba and his people go?" asked the black. "We fear that the *shiftas* may be pursuing us."

"They are not," Tarzan assured him. "I saw them ride away toward the west, taking your bwana with them. It is of him I would know more. Who is he? What does he here?"

"He is from a country far in the north," replied Goloba. "He called it Russa."

"Yes," said Tarzan. "I know the country. Why did he come here?"

"I do not know," replied Goloba. "It was not to hunt. He did not hunt, except for food."

"Did he speak ever of Tarzan?" demanded the ape-man.

"Yes," replied Goloba. "Often he asked about Tarzan. At every village he asked when they had seen Tarzan and where he was; but none knew."

"That is all," said the ape-man. "You may go."

5
When the Lion Charged

LORD Passmore was camped in a natural clearing on the bank of a small river a few miles south of the jungle's northern fringe. His stalwart porters and askaris squatted over their cooking fires laughing and joking among themselves. It was two hours past sunset; and Lord Passmore, faultlessly attired in dinner clothes, was dining, his native boy, standing behind his chair, ready to anticipate his every need. A tall, well built Negro approached the fly beneath which Lord Passmore's camp table had been placed. "You sent for me, bwana?" he asked.

Lord Passmore glanced up into the intelligent eyes of the handsome black. There was just the faintest shadow of a smile lurking about the corners of the patrician mouth of the white man. "Have you anything to report?" he asked.

"No, bwana," replied the black. "Neither to the east nor to the west were there signs of game. Perhaps the bwana had better luck."

"Yes," replied Passmore, "I was more fortunate. To the north I saw signs of game. Tomorrow, perhaps, we shall have better hunting. Tomorrow I shall—" He broke off abruptly. Both men were suddenly alert, straining their ears to a faint sound that rose above the nocturnal voices of the jungle for a few brief seconds.

The black looked questioningly at his master. "You heard it, bwana?" he asked. The white nodded. "What was it, bwana?"

"It sounded deucedly like a machine gun," replied Passmore. "It came from south of us; but who the devil would be firing a machine gun here? and why at night?"

"I do not know, bwana," replied the headman. "Shall I go and find out?"

"No," said the Englishman. "Perhaps tomorrow. We shall see. Go now, and get your sleep."

"Yes, bwana; good night."

"Good night—and warn the askari on sentry duty to be watchful."

"Yes, bwana." The black bowed very low and backed from beneath the fly. Then he moved silently away, the flickering flames of the cook fires reflecting golden high lights from his smooth brown skin, beneath which played the mighty muscles of a giant.

* * *

"This," remarked "Gunner" Patrick, "is the life. I ain't seen a çop for weeks."

Lafayette Smith smiled. "If cops are the only things you fear, Danny, your mind and your nerves can be at rest for several weeks more."

"What give you the idea I was afraid of cops?" demanded Danny. "I ain't never seen the cop I was afraid of. They're a bunch of punks. Anyhow, they ain't got nothin' on me. What a guy's got to look out for though is they might frame a guy. But, geeze, out here a guy don't have to worry about nothin'.'" He settled back easily in his camp chair and exhaled a slowly spiraling column of cigarette smoke that rose lazily in the soft night air of the jungle. "Geeze," he remarked after a brief silence, "I didn't know a guy could feel so peaceful. Say, do you know this is the first time in years I ain't packed a rod?"

"A what?"

"A rod, iron, a gat—you know—a gun."

"Why didn't you say so in the first place?" laughed Smith. "Why don't you try talking English once in a while?"

"Geeze!" exclaimed Danny. "You're a great guy to talk about a guy talkin' English. What's that you pulled on me the other day when we was crossin' that open rollin' country? I learned that by heart—'a country of low relief in an advanced stage of mature dissection'—an' you talk about me talkin' English! You and your thrust faults and escarpments, your calderas and solfataras—geeze!"

"Well, you're learning, Danny."

"Learnin' what? Every racket has its own lingo. What good is your line to me? But every guy wants to know what a rod is—if he knows what's good for his health."

"From what Ogonyo tells me it may be just as well to continue 'packing your rod,'" said Smith.

"How come?"

"He says we're getting into lion country. We may even find them near here. They don't often frequent jungles, but we're only about a day's march to more open terrain."

"Whatever that is. Talk English. Geeze! What was that?" A series of coughing grunts rose from somewhere in the solid black wall of jungle that surrounded the camp, to be followed by a thunderous roar that shook the earth.

"Simba!" cried one of the blacks, and immediately a half dozen men hastened to add fuel to the fires.

"Gunner" Patrick leaped to his feet and ran into the tent, emerging a moment later with a Thompson submachine gun. "T'ell with a rod," he said. "When I get that baby on the spot I want a typewriter."

"Are you going to take him for a ride?" inquired Lafayette Smith, whose education had progressed noticeably in the weeks he had spent in the society of Danny "Gunner" Patrick.

"No," admitted Danny, "unless he tries to muscle in on my racket."

Once again the rumbling roar of the lion shattered the quiet of the outer darkness. This time it sounded so close that both men started nervously.

"He appears to be harboring the thought," commented Smith.

"What thought?" demanded the "Gunner."

"About muscling in."

"The smokes got the same hunch," said Danny. "Look at 'em."

The porters were palpably terrified and were huddled close to the fires, the askaris fingering the triggers of their rifles. The "Gunner" walked over to where they stood straining their eyes out into the impenetrable darkness.

"Where is he?" he asked Ogonyo, the headman. "Have you seen him?"

"Over there," said Ogonyo. "It looks like something moving over there, bwana."

Danny peered into the darkness. He could see nothing, but now he thought he heard a rustling of foliage beyond the fires. He dropped to one knee and aimed the machine gun in the direction of the sound. There was a burst of flame and the sudden rat-a-tat-tat of the weapon as he squeezed the trigger. For a moment the ringing ears of the watchers heard nothing, and then, as their auditory nerves returned to normal, to the keenest ears among them came the sound of crashing among the bushes, diminishing in the distance.

"I guess I nicked him," said Danny to Smith, who had walked over and was standing behind him.

"You didn't kill him," said Smith. "You must have wounded him."

"Simba is not wounded, bwana," said Ogonyo.

"How do you know?" demanded Danny. "You can't see nothin' out there."

"If you had wounded him he would have charged," explained the headman. "He ran away. It was the noise that frightened him."

"Do you think he will come back?" asked Smith.

"I do not know, bwana," replied the negro. "No one knows what Simba will do."

"Of course he won't come back," said Danny. "The old typewriter scared him stiff. I'm goin' to turn in."

Numa, the lion, was old and hungry. He had been hunting in the open country; but his muscles, while still mighty, were not what they had been in his prime. When he reared to seize Pacco, the zebra, or Wappi, the antelope, he was always just a trifle slower than he had been in the past; and his prey eluded him. So Numa, the lion, had wandered into the jungle where the scent of man had attracted him to the camp. The beast fires of the blacks blinded him; but, beyond them, his still keen scent told him there was flesh and blood, and Numa, the lion, was ravenous.

Slowly his hunger was overcoming his inherent urge to avoid the man-things; little by little it drew him closer to the hated fires. Crouched almost upon his belly he moved forward a few inches at a time. In another moment he would charge—and then came the sudden burst of flame, the shattering crash of the machine gun, the shriek of bullets above his head.

The startling suddenness with which this unexpected tumult broke the fear laden silence of the camp and the jungle snapped the taut nerves of the great cat, and his reaction was quite as natural as it was involuntary. Wheeling in his tracks, he bounded away into the forest.

The ears of Numa, the lion, were not the only jungle ears upon which the discord of "Gunner" Patrick's typewriter impinged, for that seeming solitude of impenetrable darkness harbored a myriad life. For an instant it was motionless, startled into immobility; and then it moved on again upon the multitudinous concerns of its varied existence. Some, concerned by the strangeness of the noise, moved farther from the vicinity of the camp of the man-things; but there was at least one that curiosity attracted to closer investigation.

Gradually the camp was settling down for the night. The two bwanas had retired to the seclusion of their tent. The porters had partially overcome their nervousness, and most of them had lain down to sleep. A few watched the beast fires near which two askaris stood on guard, one on either side of the camp.

Numa stood with low hung head out there, somewhere, in the night. The tattoo of the machine gun had not appeased his appetite, but it had added to his nervous irritability—and to his caution. No longer did he rumble forth his coughing protests against the emptiness of his belly as he watched the flames of the beast fires that now fed the flood of his anger until it submerged his fears.

And as the camp drifted gradually into sleep the tawny body of the carnivore slunk slowly closer to the dancing circle of the beast fires' light. The yellow-green eyes stared in savage fixity at an unsuspecting askari leaning sleepily upon his rifle.

The man yawned and shifted his position. He noted the condition of the fire. It needed new fuel, and the man turned to the pile of branches and dead wood behind him. As he stooped to gather what he required, his back toward the jungle, Numa charged.

The great lion wished to strike swiftly and silently; but something within him, the mark of the ages of charging forebears that had preceded him, raised a low, ominous growl in his throat.

The victim heard and so did "Gunner" Patrick, lying sleepless on his cot. As the askari wheeled to the menace of that awesome warning, the "Gunner" leaped to his feet, seizing the Thompson as he sprang into the open just as Numa rose, towering, above the black. A scream of terror burst from the lips of the doomed man in the instant that the lion's talons buried themselves in his shoulders. Then the giant jaws closed upon his face.

The scream, fraught with the terror of utter hopelessness, awakened the camp. Men, startled into terrified consciousness, sprang to their feet, most of them in time to see Numa, half carrying, half dragging his victim, bounding off into the darkness.

The "Gunner" was the first to see all this and the only one to act. Without waiting to kneel he raised the machine gun to his shoulder. That his bullets must indubitably find the man if they found the lion was of no moment to Danny Patrick, intimate of sudden and violent death. He might have argued that the man was already dead, but he did not waste a thought upon a possibility which was, in any event, of no consequence, so do environment and habitude warp or dull the sensibilities of man.

The lion was still discernible in the darkness when Danny squeezed the trigger of his beloved typewriter, and this time he did not miss—perhaps unfortunately, for a wounded lion is as dangerous an engine of destruction as an all wise Providence can create.

Aroused by the deafening noise of the weapon, enraged by the wound inflicted by the single slug that entered his body, apprehending that he was to be robbed of his prey, and bent upon swift and savage reprisal, Numa dropped the askari, wheeled about, and charged straight for Danny Patrick.

The "Gunner" was kneeling, now, to take better aim. Lafayette Smith stood just behind him, armed only with a nickel plated .32 caliber revolver that some friend had given him years before. A great tree spread above the two men —a sanctuary that Lafayette Smith, at least, should have sought, but his mind was not upon flight, for, in truth, Lafayette was assailed by no fear for his own welfare or that of his companion. He was excited, but not afraid, since he could conceive of no disaster, in the form of man or beast, overwhelming one under the protection of Danny Patrick and his submachine gun. And even in the remote contingency that they should fail, was not he, himself, adequately armed? He grasped the grip of his shiny toy more tightly and with a renewed sensation of security.

The porters, huddled in small groups, stood wide eyed awaiting the outcome of the event, which was accomplished in a few brief seconds from the instant that one of Danny's slugs struck the fleeing carnivore.

And now as the lion came toward him, not in bounds, but rather in a low gliding rush of incredible speed, several things, surprising things, occurred almost simultaneously. And if there was the element of surprise, there was also, for Danny, at least one cause for embarrassment.

As the lion had wheeled Danny had again squeezed the trigger. The mechanism of the piece was set for a continuous discharge of bullets as long as Danny continued to squeeze and the remainder of the one hundred rounds in the drum lasted; but there was only a brief spurt of fire, and then the gun jammed.

How may one record in slow moving words the thoughts and happenings of a second and impart to the narration any suggestion of the speed and action of the instant?

Did the "Gunner" seek, frantically, to remove the empty cartridge that had caused the jam? Did terror enter his heart, causing his fingers to tremble and bungle? What did Lafayette Smith do? Or rather, what did he contemplate doing? since he had no opportunity to do aught but stand there, a silent observer of events. I do not know.

Before either could formulate a plan wherewith to meet the emergency, a bronzed white man, naked but for a G string, dropped from the branches of the tree above them directly into the path of the charging lion. In the man's hand was a heavy spear, and as he alighted silently upon the soft mold he was already braced to receive the shock of the lion's charge upon the point of his weapon.

The impact of Numa's heavy body would have hurled a lesser man to earth; but this one kept his feet, and the well placed thrust drove into the carnivore's chest a full two feet, while in the same instant the man stepped aside. Numa, intercepted before the completion of his charge, had not yet reared to seize his intended victim. Now, surprised and thwarted by this new enemy, while the other was almost within his grasp, he was momentarily confused; and in that brief moment the strange man-thing leaped upon his back. A giant arm encircled his throat, legs of steel locked around his shrunken waist, and a stout blade was driven into his side.

Spellbound, Smith and Patrick and their men stood staring incredulously at the sight before them. They saw Numa turn quickly to seize his tormentor. They saw him leap and bound and throw himself to the ground in an effort to dislodge his opponent. They saw the free hand of the man repeatedly drive home the point of his knife in the tawny side of the raging lion.

From the tangled mass of man and lion there issued frightful snarls and growls, the most terrifying element of which came to the two travellers with the discovery that these bestial sounds issued not alone from the savage throat of the lion but from that of the man as well.

The battle was brief, for the already sorely wounded animal had received the spear thrust directly through its heart, only its remarkable tenacity of life having permitted it to live for the few seconds that intervened between the death blow and the collapse.

As Numa slumped suddenly to his side, the man leaped clear. For a moment he stood looking down upon the death throes of his vanquished foe, while Smith and Patrick remained in awestruck contemplation of the savage, primordial scene; and then he stepped closer; and, placing one foot upon the carcass of his kill, he raised his face to the heavens and gave tongue to a cry so hideous that the negroes dropped to the ground in terror while the two whites felt the hair rise upon their scalps.

Once again upon the jungle fell the silence and the paralysis of momentary terror. Then faintly, from the far distance, came an answering challenge. Somewhere out there in the black void of night a bull ape, awakened, had answered the victory cry of his fellow. More faintly, and from a greater distance, came the rumbling roar of a lion.

The stranger stooped and seized the haft of his spear. He placed a foot against Numa's shoulder and withdrew the weapon from the carcass. Then he turned toward the two white men. It was the first intimation he had given that he had been aware of their presence.

"Geeze!" exclaimed "Gunner" Patrick, beyond which his vocabulary failed to meet the situation.

The stranger surveyed them coolly. "Who are you?" he asked. "What are you doing here?"

That he spoke English was both a surprise and a relief to Lafayette Smith. Suddenly he seemed less terrifying. "I am a geologist," he explained. "My name is Smith—Lafayette Smith—and my companion is Mr. Patrick. I am here to conduct some field research work—purely a scientific expedition."

The stranger pointed to the machine gun. "Is that part of the regular field equipment of a geologist?" he asked.

"No," replied Smith, "and I'm sure I don't know why Mr. Patrick insisted on bringing it along."

"I wasn't takin' no chances in a country full of strange characters," said the "Gunner." "Say, a broad I meets on the boat tells me some of these guys eats people."

"It would come in handy, perhaps, for hunting," suggested the stranger. "A herd of antelope would make an excellent target for a weapon of that sort."

"Geeze!" exclaimed the "Gunner," "wot do you think I am, Mister, a butcher? I packs this for insurance only. It sure wasn't worth the premium this time though," he added disgustedly; "jammed on me right when I needed it the most. But say, you were there all right. I gotta hand it to you. You're regular, Mister, and if I can ever return the favor—" He made an expansive gesture that completed the sentence and promised all that the most exacting might demand of a reciprocatory nature.

The giant nodded. "Don't use it for hunting," he said, and then, turning to Smith, "Where are you going to conduct your research?"

Suddenly a comprehending light shone in the eyes of the "Gunner," and a pained expression settled definitely upon his face. "Geeze!" he exclaimed disgustedly to Smith. "I might have known it was too good to be true."

"What?" asked Lafayette.

"What I said about there not bein' no cops here."

"Where are you going?" asked the stranger, again.

"We are going to the Ghenzi Mountains now," replied Smith.

"Say, who the hell are you, anyhow?" demanded the "Gunner," "and what business is it of yours where we go?"

The stranger ignored him and turned again toward Smith. "Be very careful in the Ghenzi country," he said. "There is a band of slave raiders working there at present, I understand. If your men learn of it they may desert you."

"Thanks," replied Smith. "It is very kind of you to warn us. I should like to know to whom we are indebted," but the stranger was gone.

As mysteriously and silently as he had appeared, he swung again into the tree above and disappeared. The two whites looked at one another in amazement.

"Geeze," said Danny.

"I fully indorse your statement," said Smith.

"Say, Ogonyo," demanded the "Gunner," "who was that bozo? You or any of your men know?"

"Yes, bwana," replied the headman, "that was Tarzan of the Apes."

6
The Waters of Chinnereth

LADY Barbara Collis walked slowly along the dusty path leading from the Midian village down to the lake that lay in the bottom of the ancient crater which formed the valley of the Land of Midian. At her right walked Abraham, the son of Abraham, and at her left the golden haired Jezebel. Behind them came the apostles, surrounding a young girl whose sullen countenance was enlivened occasionally by the fearful glances she cast upon the old men who formed her escort or her guard. Following the apostles marched the remainder of the villagers, headed by the elders. Other than these general divisions of the cortege, loosely observed, there was no attempt to maintain a semblance of orderly formation. They moved like sheep, now huddled together, now spewing beyond the limits of the narrow path to spread out on either side, some forging ahead for a few yards only to drop back again.

Lady Barbara was apprehensive. She had learned many things in the long weeks of her virtual captivity among this strange religious sect. Among other things she had learned their language, and the mastery of it had opened to her inquiring mind many avenues of information previously closed. And now she was learning, or she believed she was, that Abraham, the son of Abraham, was nursing in his bosom a growing skepticism of her divinity.

Her first night in Midian had witnessed her introduction to the cruel customs and rites of this degenerate descendant of the earliest Christian Church, and as she acquired a working knowledge of the language of the land and gained an appreciation of the exalted origin the leaders of the people attributed to her, and her position of spokesman for their god, she had used her influence to discourage, and even to prohibit, the more terrible and degrading practices of their religion.

While recollection of the supernatural aspects of her descent from the clouds remained clear in the weak mind of Abraham, the son of Abraham, Lady Barbara had been successful in her campaign against brutality; but daily association with this celestial visitor had tended to dissipate the awe that had at first overwhelmed the prophet of Paul, the son of Jehovah. The interdictions of his heavenly guest were all contrary to the desires of Abraham, the son of Abraham, and to the word of Jehovah as it had been interpreted by the prophets beyond the memory of man. Such were the foundations of the prophet's increasing skepticism, nor was the changing attitude of the old man toward her unrecognized by the English girl.

Today he had ignored her and was even forcing her to accompany them and witness the proof of his apostasy. What would come next? She had had not only ocular proof of the fanatical blood frenzy of the terrible old man, but she had listened for hours to detailed descriptions of orgies of frightfulness from the lips of Jezebel. Yes, Lady Barbara Collis was apprehensive, and not without reason; but she determined to make a last effort to reassert her waning authority.

"Think well Abraham, the son of Abraham," she said to the man walking at her side, "of the wrath of Jehovah when he sees that you have disobeyed him."

"I walk in the path of the prophets," replied the old man. "Always we have punished those who defied the laws of Jehovah, and Jehovah has rewarded us. Why should he be wroth now? The girl must pay the price of her iniquity."

"But she only smiled," argued Lady Barbara.

"A sin in the eyes of Jehovah," replied Abraham, the son of Abraham. "Laughter is carnal, and smiles lead to laughter, which gives pleasure; and all pleasures are the lures of the devil. They are wicked."

"Do not say any more," said Jezebel, in English. "You will only anger him, and when he is angry he is terrible."

"What sayest thou, woman?" demanded Abraham, the son of Abraham.

"I was praying to Jehovah in the language of Heaven," replied the girl.

The Prophet let his scowling gaze rest upon her. "Thou doest well to pray, woman. Jehovah looks not with pleasure upon thee."

"Then I shall continue praying," replied the girl meekly, and to Lady Barbara, in English; "The old devil is already planning my punishment. He has always hated me, just as they always hate us poor creatures who are not created in the same image as they."

The remarkable difference in physical appearance and mentality that set Jezebel apart from the other Midians was an inexplicable phenomenon that had constantly puzzled Lady Barbara and would continue to puzzle her, since she could not know of the little fair haired slave girl whose virile personality still sought to express itself beyond a grave nineteen centuries old. How greatly Jezebel's mentality surpassed that of her imbecilic fellows had been demonstrated to Lady Barbara by the surprising facility with which the girl had learned to speak English while she was teaching Lady Barbara the language of the Midians. How often and how sincerely had she thanked a kindly Providence for Jezebel!

The procession had now arrived at the shore of the lake, which legend asserted to be bottomless, and had halted where a few flat lava rocks of great size overhung the waters. The apostles took their places with Abraham, the son of Abraham, upon one of the rocks, the girl in their midst; and then a half dozen younger men came forward at a signal from Jobab. One of their number carried a fibre net, and two others brought a heavy piece of lava. Quickly they threw the net over the now terrified and screaming girl and secured the lava rock to it.

Abraham, the son of Abraham, raised his hands above his head, and at the signal all knelt. He commenced to pray in that now familiar gibberish that was not Midian, nor, according to Jezebel, any language whatsoever, for she insisted that the Prophet and the Apostles, to whose sole use it was restricted, could not understand it themselves. The girl, kneeling, was weeping softly now, sometimes choking down a muffled sob, while the young men held the net securely.

Suddenly Abraham, the son of Abraham, abandoned the ecclesiastical tongue and spoke in the language of his people. "For as she has sinned so shall she suffer," he cried. "It is the will of Jehovah, in his infinite mercy, that she shall not be consumed by fire, but that she shall be immersed three times in the waters of Chinnereth that her sins may be washed from her. Let us pray that they may be not too grievous, since otherwise she shall not survive." He nodded to the six young men, who seemed well schooled in their parts.

Four of them seized the net and raised it between them, while the remaining two held the ends of long fibre ropes

that were attached to it. As the four commenced to swing
the body of the girl pendulum like between them, her screams
and pleas for mercy rose above the silent waters of Chinnereth in a diapason of horror, mingled with which were the
shrieks and groans of those who, excited beyond the capacity
of their nervous systems, were falling to the ground in the
throes of epileptic seizures.

To and fro, with increasing rapidity, the young men swung
their terror crazed burden. Suddenly one of them collapsed
to sink, writhing and foaming, to the surface of the great
block of lava upon which they stood, dropping the soft
body of the girl heavily to the hard rocks. As Jobab signaled
to another young man to take the place of him who had
fallen, an apostle screamed and dropped in his tracks.

But no one gave heed to those who had succumbed, and
a moment later the girl was swinging to and fro out over
the waters of Chinnereth, back over the hard face of the lava.

"In the name of Jehovah! In the name of Jehovah!" chanted
Abraham, the son of Abraham, to the cadence of the swinging sack. "In the name of Jehovah! In the name of his
son—" there was a pause, and as the body of the girl swung
again out over the water—"Paul!"

It was the signal. The four young men released their holds
upon the net, and the body of the girl shot downward toward the dark waters of the lake. There was a splash.
The screaming ceased. The waters closed in above the victim
of cruel fanaticism, leaving only a widening circle of retreating wavelets and two fibre ropes extending upward to
the altar of castigation.

For a few seconds there was silence and immobility, except for the groans and contortions of the now greatly
increased numbers of the victims of the Nemesis of the
Midians. Then Abraham, the son of Abraham, spoke again
to the six executioners, who immediately laid hold of the
two ropes and hauled the girl upward until she swung, dripping and choking, just above the surface of the water.

For a brief interval they held her there; and then, at a
word from the Prophet, they dropped her again beneath the
waters.

"You murderer!" cried Lady Barbara, no longer able to
control her anger. "Order that poor creature drawn ashore
before she is drowned."

Abraham, the son of Abraham, turned eyes upon the English girl that almost froze her with horror—the wild, staring
eyes of a maniac; piercing pupils rimmed round with white.
"Silence, blasphemer!" screamed the man. "Last night I

walked with Jehovah, and He told me that you would be next."

"Oh, please," whispered Jezebel, tugging at Lady Barbara's sleeve. "Do not anger him more or you are lost."

The Prophet turned again to the six young men, and again, at his command, the victim was drawn above the surface of the lake. Fascinated by the horror of the situation, Lady Barbara had stepped to the edge of the rock, and, looking down, saw the poor creature limp but still gasping in an effort to regain her breath. She was not dead, but another immersion must surely prove fatal.

"Oh, please," she begged, turning to the Prophet, "in the name of merciful God, do not let them lower her again!"

Without a word of reply Abraham, the son of Abraham, gave the signal; and for the third time the now unconscious girl was dropped into the lake. The English girl sank to her knees in an attitude of prayer, and raising her eyes to heaven plead fervently to her Maker to move the heart of Abraham, the son of Abraham, to compassion, or out of the fulness of His own love to save the victim of these misguided creatures from what seemed now certain death. For a full minute she had prayed, and still the girl was left beneath the waters. Then the Prophet commanded that she be raised.

"If she is now pure in the eyes of Jehovah," he cried, "she will emerge alive. If she be dead, it is the will of Jehovah. I have but walked in the paths of the Prophets."

The six young men raised the sagging net to the surface of the rocks where they rolled the limp form of the girl from it close to where Lady Barbara kneeled in prayer. And now the Prophet appeared to notice the attitude and the pleading voice of the English girl for the first time.

"What doest thou?" he demanded.

"I pray to a God whose power and mercy are beyond your understanding," she replied. "I pray for the life of this poor child."

"There is the answer to your prayer," sneered the Prophet contemptuously, indicating the still body of the girl. "She is dead, and Jehovah has revealed to all who may have doubted that Abraham, the son of Abraham, is His prophet and that thou art an impostor."

"We are lost," whispered Jezebel.

Lady Barbara thought as much herself; but she thought quickly, for the emergency was critical. Rising, she faced the Prophet. "Yes, she is dead," she replied, "but Jehovah can resurrect her."

"He can, but He will not," said Abraham, the son of Abraham.

"Not for you, for He is angry with him who dares to call himself His prophet and yet disobeys His commands." She stepped quickly to the side of the lifeless body. "But for me He will resurrect her. Come Jezebel and help me!"

Now Lady Barbara, in common with most modern, athletically inclined young women, was familiar with the ordinary methods for resuscitating the drowned; and she fell to work upon the victim of the Prophet's homicidal mania with a will born not only of compassion, but of vital necessity. She issued curt orders to Jezebel from time to time, orders which broke but did not terminate a constant flow of words which she voiced in chant-like measures. She started with The Charge of the Light Brigade, but after two stanzas her memory failed and she had recourse to Mother Goose, snatches from the verse in Alice in Wonderland, Kipling, Omar Khayyam; and, as the girl after ten minutes of heartbreaking effort commenced to show signs of life, Lady Barbara closed with excerpts from Lincoln's Gettysburg Address.

Crowded about them were the Prophet, the Apostles, the Elders, and the six executioners, while beyond these the villagers pressed as close as they dared to witness the miracle if such it were to be.

" 'And that government of the people, by the people, and for the people shall not perish from the earth,' " chanted Lady Barbara, rising to her feet. "Lay the child in the net," she commanded, turning to the wide eyed young men who had cast her into the lake, "and carry her tenderly back to the cave of her parents. Come Jezebel!" To Abraham, the son of Abraham, she vouchsafed not even a glance.

That night the two girls sat at the entrance of their cave looking out across the uncharted valley of Midian. A full moon silvered the crest of the lofty escarpment of the crater's northern rim. In the middle distance the silent waters of Chinnereth lay like a burnished shield.

"It is beautiful," sighed Jezebel.

"But, oh, how horrible, because of man," replied Lady Barbara, with a shudder.

"At night, when I am alone, and can see only the beautiful things, I try to forget man," said the golden one. "Is there so much cruelty and wickedness in the land from which you come, Barbara?"

"There are cruelty and wickedness everywhere where men are, but in my land it is not so bad as here where the church rules and cruelty is the sole business of the church."

"They say the men over there are very cruel," said Jezebel, pointing across the valley; "but they are beautiful—not like our people."

"You have seen them?"

"Yes. Sometimes they come searching for their strayed goats, but not often. Then they chase us into our caves, and we roll rocks down on them to keep them from coming up and killing us. They steal our goats at such times; and if they catch any of our men they kill them, too. If I were alone I would let them catch me for they are very beautiful, and I do not think they would kill me. I think they would like me."

"I don't doubt it," agreed Lady Barbara, "but if I were you I would not let them catch me."

"Why not? What have I to hope for here? Perhaps some day I shall be caught smiling or singing; and then I shall be killed, and you have not seen all of the ways in which the Prophet can destroy sinners. If I am not killed I shall certainly be taken to his cave by some horrible old man; and there, all my life, I shall be a slave to him and his other women; and the old women are more cruel to such as I than even the men. No, if I were not afraid of what lies between I should run away and go to the land of the North Midians."

"Perhaps your life will be happier and safer here with me since we showed Abraham, the son of Abrahm, that we are more powerful than he; and when the time comes that my people find me, or I discover an avenue of escape, you shall come away with me, Jezebel; though I don't know that you will be much safer in England than you are here."

"Why?" demanded the girl.

"You are too beautiful ever to have perfect safety or perfect happiness."

"You think I am beautiful? I always thought so, too. I saw myself when I looked into the lake or into a vessel of water; and I thought that I was beautiful, although I did not look like the other girls of the land of Midian. Yet you are beautiful and I do not look like you. Have you never been safe or happy, Barbara?"

The English girl laughed. "I am not *too* beautiful, Jezebel," she explained.

A footfall on the steep pathway leading to the cave caught their attention. "Someone comes," said Jezebel.

"It is late," said Lady Barbara. "No one should be coming now to our cave."

"Perhaps it is a man from North Midian," suggested Jezebel. "Is my hair arranged prettily?"

"We had better be rolling a rock into position than thinking about our hair," said Lady Barbara, with a short laugh.

"Ah, but they are such beautiful men!" sighed Jezebel.

Lady Barbara drew a small knife from one of her pockets and opened the blade. "I do not like 'beautiful' men," she said.

The approaching footfalls were coming slowly nearer; but the two young women, sitting just within the entrance to their cave, could not see the steep pathway along which the nocturnal visitor was approaching. Presently a shadow fell across their threshold and an instant later a tall old man stepped into view. It was Abraham, the son of Abraham.

Lady Barbara rose to her feet and faced the Prophet. "What brings you to my cave at this time of night?" she demanded. "What is it, of such importance, that could not wait until morning? Why do you disturb me now?"

For a long moment the old man stood glaring at her. "I have walked with Jehovah in the moonlight," he said, presently; "and Jehovah hath spoken in the ear of Abraham, the son of Abraham, Prophet of Paul, the son of Jehovah."

"And you have come to make your peace with me as Jehovah directed?"

"Such are not the commands of Jehovah," replied the Prophet. "Rather He is wroth with thee who didst seek to deceive the Prophet of His son."

"You must have been walking with someone else," snapped Lady Barbara.

"Nay. I walked with Jehovah," insisted Abraham, the son of Abraham. "Thou hast deceived me. With trickery, perhaps even with sorcery, thou didst bring to life her who was dead by the will of Jehovah; and Jehovah is wroth."

"You heard my prayers, and you witnessed the miracle of the resurrection," Lady Barbara reminded him. "Thinkest thou that I am more powerful than Jehovah? It was Jehovah who raised the dead child."

"Thou speakest even as Jehovah prophesied," said the Prophet. "And He spoke in my ear and commanded that I should prove thee false, that all men might see thy iniquity."

"Interesting, if true," commented Lady Barbara; "but not true."

"Thou darest question the word of the Prophet?" cried the man angrily. "But tomorrow thou shalt have the oppor-

tunity to prove thy boasts. Tomorrow Jehovah shall judge
thee. Tomorrow thou shalt be cast into the waters of
Chinnereth in a weighted net, nor will there be cords attached whereby it may be drawn above the surface."

7

The Slave Raider

L EON STABUTCH, mounted behind one of his captors, riding to an unknown fate, was warrantably perturbed. He
had been close to death at the hands of one of the band
already, and from their appearance and their attitude toward
him it was not difficult for him to imagine that they would
require but the slightest pretext to destroy him.

What their intentions might be was highly problematical,
though he could conceive of but one motive which might
inspire such as they to preserve him. But if ransom were
their aim he could not conjecture any method by which
these semi-savages might contact with his friends or su-
periors in Russia. He was forced to admit that his prospects
appeared most discouraging.

The *shiftas* were forced to move slowly because of the
packs some of their horses were carrying since the looting
of the Russian's camp. Nor could they have ridden much
more rapidly, under any circumstances, on the trail that they
entered shortly following their capture of Stabutch.

Entering a narrow, rocky canyon the trail wound steeply
upward to debouch at last upon a small, level mesa, at the
upper end of which Stabutch saw what, at a distance, appeared to be a palisaded village nestling close beneath a
rocky cliff that bounded the mesa in that direction.

This evidently was the destination of his captors, who
were doubtless members of the very band the mere rumor
of which had filled his men with terror. Stabutch was only
sorry that the balance of the story, postulating the existence
of a white leader, was evidently erroneous, since he would
have anticipated less difficulty in arranging the terms and
collection of a ransom with a European than with these ignorant savages.

As they neared the village Stabutch discovered that their
approach had been made beneath the scrutiny of lookouts
posted behind the palisade, whose heads and shoulders were

now plainly visible above the crude though substantial rampart.

And presently these sentries were shouting greetings and queries to the members of the returning band as the village gate swung slowly open and the savage horsemen entered the enclosure with their captive, who was soon the center of a throng of men, women, and children, curious and questioning—a savage throng of surly blacks.

Although there was nothing actively menacing in the attitude of the savages there was a definite unfriendliness in their demeanor that cast a further gloom of apprehension upon the already depressed spirits of the Russian; and as the cavalcade entered the central compound, about which the huts were grouped, he experienced a sensation of utter hopelessness.

It was at this moment that he saw a short, bearded white man emerge from one of the squalid dwellings; and instantly the depression that had seized him was, partially at least, relieved.

The *shiftas* were dismounting, and now he was roughly dragged from the animal which had borne him from his camp and pushed unceremoniously toward the white man, who stood before the doorway from whence he had appeared surveying the prisoner sullenly, while he listened to the report of the leader of the returning band.

There was no smile upon the face of the bearded man as he addressed Stabutch after the black *shifta* had completed his report. The Russian recognized that the language employed by the stranger was Italian, a tongue which he could neither speak nor understand, and this he explained in Russian; but the bearded one only shrugged and shook his head. Then Stabutch tried English.

"That is better," said the other brokenly. "I understand English a little. Who are you? What was the language you first spoke to me? From what country do you come?"

"I am a scientist," replied Stabutch. "I spoke to you in Russian."

"Is Russia your country?"

"Yes."

The man eyed him intently for some time, as though attempting to read the innermost secrets of his mind, before he spoke again. Stabutch noted the squat, powerful build of the stranger, the cruel lips, only partially concealed by the heavy, black beard, and the hard, crafty eyes, and guessed that he might have fared as well at the hands of the blacks.

"You say you are a Russian," said the man. "Red or white?"

Stabutch wished that he might know how to answer this question. He was aware that the Red Russians were not well beloved by all peoples; and that the majority of Italians were trained to hate them, and yet there was something in the personality of this stranger that suggested that he might be more favorably inclined to a Red than to a White Russian. Furthermore, to admit that he was a Red might assure the other that a ransom could be obtained more surely than from a White, whose organization was admittedly weak and poverty stricken. For these reasons Stabutch decided to tell the truth.

"I am a Red," he said.

The other considered him intently and in silence for a moment; then he made a gesture that would have passed unnoticed by any but a Red Communist. Leon Stabutch breathed an inaudible sigh of relief, but his facial expression gave no indication of recognition of this secret sign as he answered it in accordance with the ritual of his organization, while the other watched him closely.

"Your name, comrade?" inquired the bearded one in an altered tone.

"Leon Stabutch," replied the Russian; "and yours, comrade?"

"Dominic Capietro. Come, we will talk inside. I have a bottle there wherewith we may toast the cause and become better acquainted."

"Lead on, comrade," said Stabutch; "I feel the need of something to quiet my nerves. I have had a bad few hours."

"I apologize for the inconvenience to which my men have put you," replied Capietro, leading the way into the hut; "but all shall be made right again. Be seated. As you see, I lead the simple life; but what imperial throne may compare in grandeur with the bosom of Mother Earth!"

"None, comrade," agreed Stabutch, noting the entire absence of chairs, or even stools, that the other's speech had already suggested and condoned. "Especially," he added, "when enjoyed beneath a friendly roof."

Capietro rummaged in an old duffle bag and at last withdrew a bottle which he uncorked and handed to Stabutch. "Golden goblets are for royal tyrants, Comrade Stabutch," he declaimed, "but not for such as we, eh?"

Stabutch raised the bottle to his lips and took a draught of the fiery liquid, and as it burned its way to his stomach and the fumes rose to his head the last of his fears and doubts vanished. "Tell me now," he said, as he passed the bottle back to his host, "why I was seized, who you are, and what is to become of me?"

"My headman told me that he found you alone, deserted by your safari, and not knowing whether you were friend or enemy he brought you here to me. You are lucky, comrade, that Dongo chanced to be in charge of the scouting party today. Another might have killed you first and inquired later. They are a pack of murderers and thieves, these good men of mine. They have been oppressed by cruel masters, they have felt the heel of the tyrant upon their necks, and their hands are against all men. You cannot blame them.

"But they are good men. They serve me well. They are the man power, I am the brains; and we divide the profits of our operations equally—half to the man power, half to the brains," and Capietro grinned.

"And your operations?" asked Stabutch.

Capietro scowled; then his face cleared. "You are a comrade, but let me tell you that it is not always safe to be inquisitive."

Stabutch shrugged. "Tell me nothing," he said. "I do not care. It is none of my business."

"Good," exclaimed the Italian, "and why you are here in Africa is none of my business, unless you care to tell me. Let us drink again."

While the conversation that ensued, punctuated by numerous drinks, carefully eschewed personalities, the question of the other's occupation was uppermost in the mind of each; and as the natural effects of the liquor tended to disarm their suspicions and urge confidence it also stimulated the curiosity of the two, each of whom was now mellow and genial in his cups.

It was Capietro who broke first beneath the strain of an overpowering curiosity. They were sitting side by side upon a disreputably filthy rug, two empty bottles and a newly opened one before them. "Comrade," he cried, throwing an arm about the shoulders of the Russian affectionately, "I like you. Dominic Capietro does not like many men. This is his motto: Like few men and love all women," whereat he laughed loudly.

"Let's drink to that," suggested Stabutch, joining in the laughter. " 'Like few men and love all women.' That is the idea!"

"I knew the minute I saw you that you were a man after my own heart, comrade," continued Capietro, "and why should there be secrets between comrades?"

"Certainly, why?" agreed Stabutch.

"So I shall tell you why I am here with this filthy band of thieving cutthroats. I was a soldier in the Italian army. My regiment was stationed in Eritrea. I was fomenting discord and mutiny, as a good Communist should, when some dog of a Fascist reported me to the commanding officer. I was arrested. Doubtless, I should have been shot, but I escaped and made my way to Abyssinia, where Italians are none too well liked; but when it was known that I was a deserter I was treated well.

"After a while I obtained employment with a powerful ras to train his soldiers along European lines. There I became proficient in Amharic, the official language of the country, and also learned to speak that of the Gallas, who constituted the bulk of the population of the principality of the ras for whom I worked. Naturally, being averse to any form of monarchistic government, I commenced at once to instill the glorious ideals of Communism into the breasts of the retainers of the old ras; but once again I was frustrated by an informer, and only by chance did I escape with my life.

"This time, however, I succeeded in enticing a number of men to accompany me. We stole horses and weapons from the ras and rode south where we joined a band of *shiftas,* or rather, I should say, absorbed them.

"This organized body of raiders and thieves made an excellent force with which to levy tribute upon chance travellers and caravans, but the returns were small and so we drifted down into this remote country of the Ghenzi where we can ply a lucrative trade in black ivory."

"Black ivory? I never knew there was such a thing."

Capietro laughed. "Two legged ivory," he explained.

Stabutch whistled. "Oh," he said, "I think I understand. You are a slave raider; but where is there any market for slaves, other than the wage slaves of capitalistic countries?"

"You would be surprised, comrade. There are still many markets, including the mandates and protectorates of several highly civilized signatories to world court conventions aimed at the abolition of human slavery. Yes, I am a slave raider —rather a remarkable vocation for a university graduate and the former editor of a successful newspaper."

"And you prefer this?"

"I have no alternative, and I must live. At least I think I must live—a most common form of rationalization. You see, my newspaper was anti-Fascist. And now, comrade, about yourself—what 'scientific' research is the Soviet government undertaking in Africa?"

"Let us call it anthropology," replied Stabutch. "I am looking for a man."

"There are many men in Africa and much nearer the coast than the Ghenzi country. You have travelled far inland looking for a man."

"The man I look for I expected to find somewhere south of the Ghenzies," replied Stabutch.

"Perhaps I can aid you. I know many men, at least by name and reputation, in this part of the world," suggested the Italian.

Stabutch, had he been entirely sober, would have hesitated to give this information to a total stranger, but alcohol induces thoughtless confidences. "I search for an Englishman known as Tarzan of the Apes," he explained.

Capietro's eyes narrowed. "A friend of yours?" he asked.

"I know of no one I would rather see," replied Stabutch.

"You say he is here in the Ghenzi country?"

"I do not know. None of the natives I have questioned knew his whereabouts."

"His country is far south of the Ghenzies," said Capietro.

"Ah, you know of him, then?"

"Yes. Who does not? But what business have you with Tarzan of the Apes?"

"I have come from Moscow to kill him," blurted Stabutch, and in the same instant regretted his rash admission.

Capietro relaxed. "I am relieved," he said.

"Why?" demanded the Russian.

"I feared he was a friend of yours," explained the Italian. "In which case we could not be friends; but if you have come to kill him you shall have nothing but my best wishes and heartiest support."

Stabutch's relief was almost a thing of substance, so considerable and genuine was it. "You, too, have a grievance against him?" he asked.

"He is a constant threat against my little operations in black ivory," replied Capietro. "I should feel much safer if he were out of the way."

"Then perhaps you will help me, comrade?" inquired Stabutch eagerly.

"I have lost no ape-man," replied Capietro, "and if he leaves me alone I shall never look for him. That adventure, comrade, you will not have to share with me."

"But you have taken away my means of carrying out my plans. I cannot seek Tarzan without a safari," complained Stabutch.

"That is right," admitted the raider; "but perhaps the mistake of my men may be rectified. Your equipment and goods are safe. They will be returned to you, and, as for men, who better could find them for you than Dominic Capietro, who deals in men?"

The safari of Lord Passmore moved northward, skirting the western foothills of the Ghenzi Mountains. His stalwart porters marched almost with the precision of trained soldiers, at least in that proper distances were maintained and there were no stragglers. A hundred yards in advance were three askaris and behind these came Lord Passmore, his gun bearer, and his headman. At the head and rear of the column of porters was a detachment of askaris—well armed, efficient appearing men. The whole entourage suggested intelligent organization and experienced supervision. Evidence of willingly observed discipline was apparent, a discipline that seemed to be respected by all with the possible exception of Isaza, Lord Passmore's "boy," who was also his cook.

Isaza marched where his fancy dictated, laughing and joking with first one and then another of the members of the safari—the personification of good nature that pervaded the whole party and that was constantly manifested by the laughter and singing of the men. It was evident that Lord Passmore was an experienced African traveller and that he knew what treatment to accord his followers.

How different, indeed, this well ordered safari, from another that struggled up the steep slopes of the Ghenzies a few miles to the east. Here the column was strung out for fully a mile, the askaris straggling along among the porters, while the two white men whom they accompanied forged far ahead with a single boy and a gun bearer.

"Geeze," remarked the "Gunner," "you sure picked on a lousy racket! I could of stayed home and climbed up the front of the Sherman Hotel, if I had of wanted to climb, and always been within a spit of eats and drinks."

"Oh, no you couldn't," said Lafayette Smith.

"Why not? Who'd a stopped me?"

"Your friends, the cops."

"That's right; but don't call 'em my friends—the lousy bums. But wherinel do you think you're going?"

"I think I perceive in this mountain range evidences of upthrust by horizontal compression," replied Lafayette Smith, "and I wish to examine the surface indications more closely than it is possible to do from a distance. Therefore, we must go to the mountains, since they will not come to us."

"And what does it get you?" demanded "Gunner" Patrick. "Not a buck. It's a bum racket."

Lafayette Smith laughed good naturedly. They were crossing a meadowland through which a mountain stream wound. Surrounding it was a forest. "This would make a good camp," he said, "from which to work for a few days. You can hunt, and I'll have a look at the formations in the vicinity. Then we'll move on."

"It's jake with me," replied the "Gunner." "I'm fed up on climbing."

"Suppose you remain with the safari and get camp made," suggested Smith. "I'll go on up a little farther with my boy and see what I can see. It's early yet."

"Oke," assented the "Gunner." "I'll park the mob up near them trees. Don't get lost, and, say, you better take my protection guy with you," he added, nodding in the direction of his gun bearer.

"I'm not going to hunt," replied Smith. "I won't need him."

"Then take my rod here." The "Gunner" started to unbuckle his pistol belt. "You might need it."

"Thanks, I have one," replied Smith, tapping his .32.

"Geeze, you don't call that thing a rod, do you?" demanded the "Gunner," contemptuously.

"It's all I need. I'm looking for rocks, not trouble. Come on Obambi," and he motioned his boy to follow him as he started up the slope toward the higher mountains.

"Geeze," muttered the "Gunner," "I seen pipies what ain't as much of a nut as that guy; but," he added, "he's a regular guy at that. You can't help likin' him." Then he turned his attention to the selection of a campsite.

Lafayette Smith entered the forest beyond the meadowland; and here the going became more difficult, for the ground rose rapidly; and the underbrush was thick. He fought his way upward, Obambi at his heels; and at last he reached a higher elevation, where the forest growth was much thinner because of the rocky nature of the ground and the absence of top soil. Here he paused to examine the formation, but only to move on again, this time at right angles to his original direction.

Thus, stopping occasionally to investigate, he moved erratically upward until he achieved the summit of a ridge from which he had a view of miles of rugged mountains in the distance. The canyon that lay before him, separating him from the next ridge, aroused his interest. The formation of the opposite wall, he decided, would bear closer investigation.

Obambi had flung himself to the ground when Smith

halted. Obambi appeared exhausted. He was not. He was merely disgusted. To him the bwana was mad, quite mad. Upon no other premises could Obambi explain the senseless climbing, with an occasional pause to examine rocks. Obambi was positive that they might have discovered plenty of rocks at the foot of the mountains had they but searched for them. And then, too, this bwana did not hunt. He supposed all bwanas came to Africa to hunt. This one, being so different, must be mad.

Smith glanced at his boy. It was too bad, he thought, to make Obambi do all this climbing unnecessarily. Certainly there was no way in which the boy might assist him, while seeing him in a constant state of exhaustion reacted unfavorably on Smith. Better by far be alone. He turned to the boy. "Go back to camp, Obambi," he said. "I do not need you here."

Obambi looked at him in surprise. Now he knew the bwana was very mad. However, it would be much more pleasant in camp than climbing about in these mountains. He rose to his feet. "The bwana does not need me?" he asked. "Perhaps he will need me." Obambi's conscience was already troubling him. He knew that he should not leave his bwana alone.

"No, I shan't need you, Obambi," Smith assured him. "You run along back to camp. I'll come in pretty soon."

"Yes, bwana," and Obambi turned back down the mountain side.

Lafayette Smith clambered down into the canyon, which was deeper than he had supposed, and then worked his way up the opposite side that proved to be even more precipitous than it had appeared from the summit of the ridge. However, he found so much to interest him that he considered it well worth the effort, and so deeply absorbed was he that he gave no heed to the passage of time.

It was not until he reached the top of the far side of the canyon that he noted the diminishing light that presaged the approach of night. Even then he was not greatly concerned; but he realized that it would be quite dark before he could hope to recross the canyon, and it occurred to him that by following up the ridge on which he stood he could reach the head of the canyon where it joined the ridge from which he had descended into it, thus saving him a long, arduous climb and shortening the time, if not the distance, back to camp.

As he trudged upward along the ridge, night fell; but

still he kept on, though now he could only grope his way slowly, nor did it occur to him for several hours that he was hopelessly lost.

8

The Baboons

A NEW day had dawned, and Africa greeted the age old miracle of Kudu emerging from his lair behind the eastern hills and smiled. With the exception of a few stragglers the creatures of the night had vanished, surrendering the world to their diurnal fellows.

Tongani, the baboon, perched upon his sentinel rock, surveyed the scene and, perhaps, not without appreciation of the beauties; for who are we to say that God touched so many countless of his works with beauty yet gave to but one of these the power of appreciation?

Below the sentinel fed the tribe of Zugash, the king; fierce tongani shes with their balus clinging to their backs, if very young, while others played about, imitating their elders in their constant search for food; surly, vicious bulls; old Zugash himself, the surliest and most vicious.

The keen, close-set eyes of the sentinel, constantly upon the alert down wind, perceived something moving among the little hills below. It was the top of a man's head. Presently the whole head came into view; and the sentinel saw that it belonged to a tarmangani; but as yet he sounded no alarm, for the tarmangani was still a long way off and might not be coming in the direction of the tribe. The sentinel would watch yet a little longer and make sure, for it was senseless to interrupt the feeding of the tribe if no danger threatened.

Now the tarmangani was in full view. Tongani wished that he might have the evidence of his keen nose as well as his eyes; then there would be no doubt, for, like many animals, the tonganis preferred to submit all evidence to their sensitive nostrils before accepting the verdict of their eyes; but the wind was in the wrong direction.

Perhaps, too, Tongani was puzzled, for this was such a tarmangani as he had never before seen—a tarmangani who walked almost as naked as Tongani himself. But for the white skin he might have thought him a gomangani. This being a tarmangani, the sentinel looked for the feared thunder stick; and because he saw none he waited before giving the alarm. But presently he saw that the creature was coming directly toward the tribe.

The tarmangani had long been aware of the presence of the baboons, being down wind from them where their strong scent was borne to his keen nostrils. Also, he had seen the sentinel at almost the same instant that the sentinel had seen him; yet he continued upward, swinging along in easy strides that suggested the power and savage independence of Numa, the lion.

Suddenly Tongani, the baboon, sprang to his feet, uttering a sharp bark, and instantly the tribe awoke to action, swarming up the low cliffs at the foot of which they had been feeding. Here they turned and faced the intruder, barking their defiance as they ran excitedly to and fro.

When they saw that the creature was alone and bore no thunder stick they were more angry than frightened, and they scolded noisily at this interruption of their feeding. Zugash and several of the other larger bulls even clambered part way down the cliff to frighten him away; but in this they only succeeded in increasing their own anger, for the tarmangani continued upward toward them.

Zugash, the king, was now beside himself with rage. He stormed and threatened. "Go away!" he barked. "I am Zugash. I kill!"

And now the stranger halted at the foot of the cliff and surveyed him. "I am Tarzan of the Apes," he said. "Tarzan does not come to the stamping grounds of the tongani to kill. He comes as a friend."

Silence fell upon the tribe of Zugash; the silence of stunning surprise. Never before had they heard either tarmangani or gomangani speak the language of the ape-people. They had never heard of Tarzan of the Apes, whose country was far to the south; but nevertheless they were impressed by his ability to understand them and speak to them. However, he was a stranger, and so Zugash ordered him away again.

"Tarzan does not wish to remain with the tongani," replied the ape-man; "he desires only to pass them in peace."

"Go away!" growled Zugash. "I kill. I am Zugash."

Tarzan swung up the cliff quite as easily as had the baboons. It was his answer to Zugash, the king. None was there who better knew the strength, the courage, the ferocity of the tongani than he, yet he knew, too, that he might be in this country for some time and that, if he were to survive, he must establish himself definitely in the minds of all lesser creatures as one who walked without fear and whom it was well to let alone.

Barking furiously, the baboons retreated; and Tarzan gained the summit of the cliff, where he saw that the shes and balus had scattered, many of them going farther up into the hills, while the adult bulls remained to contest the way.

As Tarzan paused, just beyond the summit of the cliff, he found himself the center of a circle of snarling bulls against the combined strength and ferocity of which he would be helpless. To another than himself his position might have appeared precarious almost to the point of hopelessness; but Tarzan knew the wild peoples of his savage world too well to expect an unprovoked attack, or a killing for the love of killing such as only man, among all the creatures of the world, habitually commits. Neither was he unaware of the danger of his position should a bull, more nervous or suspicious than his fellows, mistake Tarzan's intentions or misinterpret some trivial act or gesture as a threat against the safety of the tribe.

But he knew that only an accident might precipitate a charge and that if he gave them no cause to attack him they would gladly let him proceed upon his way unmolested. However, he had hoped to achieve friendly relations with the tongani, whose knowledge of the country and its inhabitants might prove of inestimable value to him. Better, too, that the tribe of Zugash be allies than enemies. And so he assayed once more to win their confidence.

"Tell me, Zugash," he said, addressing the bristling king baboon, "if there be many tarmangani in your country. Tarzan hunts for a bad tarmangani who has many gomangani with him. They are bad men. They kill. With thunder sticks they kill. They will kill the tongani. Tarzan has come to drive them from your country."

But Zugash only growled and placed the back of his head against the ground in challenge. The other males moved restlessly sideways, their shoulders high, their tails bent in crooked curves. Now some of the younger bulls rested the backs of their heads upon the ground, imitating the challenge of their king.

Zugash, grimacing at Tarzan, raised and lowered his brows rapidly, exposing the white skin about his eyes. Thus did the savage old king seek to turn the heart of his antagonist to water by the frightfulness of his mien; but Tarzan only shrugged indifferently and moved on again as though convinced that the baboons would not accept his overtures of friendship.

Straight toward the challenging bulls that stood in his path he walked, without haste and apparently without concern; but his eyes were narrowed and watchful, his every sense on the alert. One bull, stiff legged and arrogant, moved grudgingly aside; but another stood his ground. Here, the ape-man knew the real test would come that should decide the issue.

The two were close now, face to face, when suddenly there burst from the lips of the man-beast a savage growl, and simultaneously he charged. With an answering growl and a catlike leap the baboon bounded aside; and Tarzan passed beyond the rim of the circle, victor in the game of bluff which is played by every order of living thing sufficiently advanced in the scale of intelligence to possess an imagination.

Seeing that the man-thing did not follow upward after the shes and balus, the bulls contented themselves with barking insults after him and aiming uncomplimentary gestures at his retreating figure; but such were not the acts that menaced safety, and the ape-man ignored them.

Purposely he had turned away from the shes and their young, with the intention of passing around them, rather than precipitate a genuine attack by seeming to threaten them. And thus his way took him to the edge of a shallow ravine into which, unknown either to Tarzan or the tongani, a young mother had fled with her tiny balu.

Tarzan was still in full view of the tribe of Zugash, though he alone could see into the ravine, when suddenly three things occurred that shattered the peace that seemed again descending upon the scene. A vagrant air current wafted upward from the thick verdure below him the scent of Sheeta, the panther; a baboon voiced a scream of terror; and, looking down, the ape-man saw the young she, her balu clinging to her back, fleeing upward toward him with savage Sheeta in pursuit.

As Tarzan, reacting instantly to the necessity of the moment, leaped downward with back thrown spear hand, the bulls of Zugash raced forward in answer to the note of terror in the voice of the young mother.

From his position above the actors in this sudden tragedy of the wilds the ape-man could see the panther over the head of the baboon and realizing that the beast must reach his victim before succor could arrive he hurled his spear in the forlorn hope of stopping the carnivore, if only for a moment.

The cast was one that only a practiced hand might have dared attempt, for the danger to the baboon was almost as great as that which threatened the panther should the aim of the ape-man not be perfect.

Zugash and his bulls, bounding forward at an awkward gallop, reached the edge of the ravine just in time to see the heavy spear hurtle past the head of the she by a margin of inches only and bury itself in the breast of Sheeta. Then they were down the slope, a snarling, snapping pack, and with them went an English viscount, to fall upon a surprised, pain-maddened panther.

The baboons leaped in to snap at their hereditary foe and leaped out again, and the man-beast, as quick and agile as they, leaped and struck with his hunting knife, while the frenzied cat lunged this way and that, first at one tormentor and then at another.

Twice those powerful, raking talons reached their mark and two bulls sprawled, torn and bloody, upon the ground; but the bronzed hide of the ape-man ever eluded the rage of the wounded cat.

Short was the furious battle, ferocious the growls and snarls of the combatants, prodigious the leaps and bounds of the excited shes hovering in the background; and then Sheeta, rearing high upon his hind feet, struck savagely at Tarzan and, in the same instant, plunged to earth dead, slain by the spear point puncturing his heart.

Instantly the great tarmangani, who had once been king of the great apes, leaped close and placed a foot upon the carcass of his kill. He raised his face toward Kudu, the sun; and from his lips broke the horrid challenge of the bull ape that has killed.

For a moment silence fell upon the forest, the mountain, and the jungle. Awed, the baboons ceased their restless movement and their din. Tarzan stooped and drew the spear from the quivering body of Sheeta, while the tongani watched him with a new interest.

Then Zugash approached. This time he did not rest the back of his head against the ground in challenge. "The bulls of the tribe of Zugash are the friends of Tarzan of the Apes," he said.

"Tarzan is the friend of the bulls of the tribe of Zugash," responded the ape-man.

"We have seen a tarmangani," said Zugash. "He has many gomangani. There are many thunder sticks among them. They are bad. Perhaps it is they whom Tarzan seeks."

"Perhaps," admitted the slayer of Sheeta. "Where are they?"

"They were camped where the rocks sit upon the mountain side, as here." He nodded toward the cliff.

"Where?" asked Tarzan again, and this time Zugash motioned along the foothills toward the south.

9

The Great Fissure

THE morning sun shone upon the bosom of Chinnereth, glancing from the breeze born ripples that moved across its surface like vast companies of soldiers passing in review with their countless spears gleaming in the sunlight—a dazzling aspect of beauty.

But to Lady Barbara Collis it connoted something quite different—a shallow splendor concealing cruel and treacherous depths, the real Chinnereth. She shuddered as she approached its shore surrounded by the apostles, preceded by Abraham, the son of Abraham, and followed by the elders and the villagers. Among them, somewhere, she knew were the six with their great net and their fibre ropes.

How alike were they all to Chinnereth, hiding their cruelty and their treachery beneath a thin veneer of godliness! But there the parallel terminated, for Chinnereth was beautiful. She glanced at the faces of the men nearest her, and again she shuddered. " 'So God created man in his own image,' " she mused. "Who, then, created these?"

During the long weeks that fate had held her in this land of Midian she had often sought an explanation of the origin of this strange race, and the deductions of her active mind had not deviated greatly from the truth. Noting the exaggerated racial characteristics of face and form that distinguished them from other peoples she had seen, recalling their common tendency to epilepsy, she had concluded that they were the inbred descendants of a common ancestor, himself a defective and an epileptic.

This theory explained much; but it failed to explain Jezebel, who insisted that she was the child of two of these creatures and that, insofar as she knew, no new strain of blood had ever been injected into the veins of the Midian by intermating with other peoples. Yet, somehow, Lady Barbara knew that such a strain must have been introduced, though she could not guess the truth nor the antiquity of the fact that lay buried in the grave of a little slave girl.

And their religion! Again she shuddered. What a hideous travesty of the teachings of Christ! It was a confused jumble of ancient Christianity and still more ancient Judaism, handed down by word of mouth through a half imbecile people who had no written language; a people who had confused Paul the Apostle with Christ the Master and lost entirely the essence of the Master's teachings, while interpolating hideous barbarisms of their own invention. Sometimes she thought she saw in this exaggerated deviation a suggestion of parallel to other so-called Christian sects of the civilized outer world.

But now her train of thoughts was interrupted by the near approach of the procession to the shore of the lake. Here was the flat-topped lava rock of grim suggestiveness and hideous memory. How long it seemed since she had watched the six hurl their screaming victim from its well worn surface, and yet it had been but yesterday. Now it was her turn. The Prophet and the Apostles were intoning their senseless gibberish, meant to impress the villagers with their erudition and cloak the real vacuity of their minds, a practice not unknown to more civilized sects.

She was halted now upon the smooth surface of the lava, polished by soft sandals and naked feet through the countless years that these cruel rites had been enacted beside the waters of Chinnereth. Again she heard the screams of yesterday's victim. But Lady Barbara Collis had not screamed, nor would she. She would rob them of that satisfaction at least.

Abraham, the son of Abraham, motioned the six to the fore; and they came, bearing their net and their cords. At their feet lay the lava fragment that would weight the net and its contents. The Prophet raised his hands above his head and the people kneeled. In the forefront of their ranks Lady Barbara saw the golden haired Jezebel; and her heart was touched, for there were anguish in the beautiful face and tears in the lovely eyes. Here was one, at least, who could harbor love and compassion.

"I have walked with Jehovah," cried Abraham, the son of Abraham, and Lady Barbara wondered that he did not have blisters on his feet, so often he walked with Jehovah. The levity of the conceit brought an involuntary smile to her lips, a smile that the Prophet noticed. "You smile," he said, angrily. "You smile when you should scream and beg for mercy as the others do. Why do you smile?"

"Because I am not afraid," replied Lady Barbara, though she was very much afraid.

"Why art thou not afraid, woman?" demanded the old man.

"I, too, have walked with Jehovah," she replied, "and He told me to fear not, because you are a false prophet, and——"

"Silence!" thundered Abraham, the son of Abraham. "Blaspheme no more. Jehovah shall judge you in a moment." He turned to the six. "Into the net with her!"

Quickly they did his bidding; and as they commenced to swing her body to and fro, to gain momentum against the moment that they would release their holds and cast her into the deep lake, she heard The Prophet reciting her iniquities that Jehovah was about to judge in his own peculiar way. His speech was punctuated by the screams and groans of those of the company who were seized in the grip of the now familiar attacks to which Lady Barbara had become so accustomed as to be almost as callous to as the Midians themselves.

From her pocket the girl extracted the little pen knife that was her only weapon and held it firmly in one hand, the blade open and ready for the work she intended it to do. And what work was that? Surely, she could not hope to inflict instant death upon herself with that inadequate weapon! Yet, in the last stages of fear induced by utter helplessness and hopelessness one may attempt anything, even the impossible.

Now they were swinging her far out over Chinnereth. The Apostles and the elders were intoning their weird chant in voices excited to frenzy by the imminence of death, those who were not writhing upon the rocky face of the altar in the throes of seizures.

Suddenly came the word from Abraham, the son of Abraham. Lady Barbara caught her breath in a last frightened gasp. The six released their holds. A loud scream arose from the huddled villagers—the scream of a woman—and as she plunged toward the dark waters Lady Barbara knew that it was the voice of Jezebel crying out in the anguish of sorrow. Then mysterious Chinnereth closed above her head.

At that very moment Lafayette Smith, A.M., Ph.D., Sc.D., was stumbling along a rocky mountain side that walled the great crater where lay the land of Midian and Chinnereth. He was no less aware of the tragedy being enacted upon the opposite side of that stupendous wall than of the fact that he was moving directly away from the camp he was seeking.

Had there been anyone there to tell him, and had they told him, that he was hopelessly lost he would have been inclined to dispute the statement, so positive was he that he was taking a short cut to camp, which he imagined was but a little distance ahead.

Although he had been without supper and breakfast, hunger had not as yet caused him any annoyance, partially because of the fact that he had had some chocolate with him, which had materially assisted in allaying its pangs, and partially through his interest in the geologic formations that held the attention of his scholarly mind to the exclusion of such material considerations as hunger, thirst, and bodily comfort. Even the question of personal safety was relegated to the oblivion that usually engulfed all practical issues when Lafayette Smith was immersed in the pleasant waters of research.

Consequently he was unaware of the proximity of a tawny body, nor did the fixed and penetrating gaze of a pair of cruel, yellow-green eyes penetrate the armor of his preoccupation to disturb that sixth sense that is popularly supposed to warn us of unseen danger. Yet even had any premonition of threat to his life or safety disturbed him he doubtless would have ignored it, safe in the consciousness that he was adequately protected by the possession of his .32 caliber, nickel plated pistol.

Moving northward along the lower slopes of a conical mountain, the mind of the geologist became more and more deeply engrossed in the rocky story that Nature had written upon the landscape, a story so thrilling that even the thoughts of camp were forgotten; and as he made his way farther and farther from camp a great lion stalked in his wake.

What hidden urge prompted Numa thus to follow the man-thing perhaps the great cat, himself, could not have guessed. He was not hungry, for he had but recently finished a kill, nor was he a man-eater, though a properly balanced combination of circumstances might easily find the scales tipped in that direction by hunger, inevitable and oft recurring. It may have been only curiosity, or, again, some motive akin to that playfulness which is inherent in all cats.

For an hour Numa followed the man—an hour of intense interest for both of them—an hour that would have been replete with far greater interest for the man, if less pleasurable, had he shared with Numa the knowledge of their propinquity. Then the man halted before a narrow vertical cleft in the rocky escarpment towering above him. Here was an interesting entry in the book of Nature! What titanic force had thus rent the solid rock of this mighty mountain? It had its own peculiar significance, but what was it? Perhaps elsewhere on the face of the mountain, that here became precipitous, there would be other evidence to point the way to a solution. Lafayette Smith looked up at the face of the cliff towering above him, he looked ahead in the direction he had been going; and then he looked back in the direction from which he had come—and saw the lion.

For a long moment the two stared at one another. Surprise and interest were the most definitely registered of the emotions that the discovery engendered in the mind of the man. Suspicion and irritability were aroused in Numa.

"Most interesting," thought Lafayette Smith. "A splendid specimen;" but his interest in lions was purely academic, and his thoughts quickly reverted to the more important phenomenon of the crack in the mountain, which now, again, claimed his undivided attention. From which it may be inferred that Lafayette Smith was either an inordinately courageous man or a fool. Neither assumption, however, would be wholly correct, especially the latter. The truth of the matter is that Lafayette Smith suffered from inexperience and impracticality. While he knew that a lion was, *per se*, a threat to longevity he saw no reason why this lion should attack him. He, Lafayette Smith, had done nothing to offend this, or any other, lion; he was attending to his own affairs and, like the gentleman he was, expected others, including lions, to be equally considerate. Furthermore, he had a childlike faith in the infallibility of his nickel plated .32 should worse develop into worst. Therefore he ignored Numa and returned to contemplation of the intriguing crack.

It was several feet wide and was apparent as far up the face of the cliff as he could see. Also there was every indication that it continued far below the present surface of the ground, but had been filled by débris brought down by erosion from above. How far into the mountain it extended he could not guess; but he hoped that it ran back, and was open, for a great distance, in which event it would offer a most unique means for studying the origin of this mountain massif.

Therefore, with this thought uppermost in his mind, and the lion already crowded into the dim background of his consciousness, he entered the narrow opening of the intriguing fissure. Here he discovered that the cleft curved gradually to the left and that it extended upward to the surface, where it was considerably wider than at the bottom, thus affording both light and air for the interior.

Thrilled with excitement and glowing with pride in his discovery, Lafayette clambered inward over the fallen rocks that littered the floor of the fissure, intent now on exploring the opening to its full extent and then working back slowly to the entrance in a more leisurely manner, at which time he would make a minute examination of whatever geological record Nature had imprinted upon the walls of this majestic corridor. Hunger, thirst, camp, and the lion were forgotten.

Numa, however, was no geologist. The great cleft aroused no palpitant enthusiasm within his broad breast. It did not cause him to forget anything, and it intrigued his interest only to the extent of causing him to speculate on why the man-thing had entered it. Having noted the indifferent attitude of the man, his lack of haste, Numa could not attribute his disappearance within the maw of the fissure to flight, of which it bore not a single earmark; and it may be recorded here that Numa was an expert on flight. All of his life things had been fleeing from him.

It had always seemed to Numa an unfair provision of Nature that things should so almost inevitably seek to escape him, especially those things he most coveted. There were, for example, Pacco, the zebra, and Wappi, the antelope, the tenderest and most delicious of his particular weaknesses, and, at the same time, the fleetest. It would have been much simpler all around had Kota the tortoise been endowed with the speed of Pacco and Pacco with the torpidity of Kota.

But in this instance there was nothing to indicate that the man-thing was fleeing him. Perhaps, then, there was treachery afoot. Numa bristled. Very cautiously he approached the fissure into which his quarry had disappeared. Numa was beginning to think of Lafayette Smith in terms of food, now, since his long stalking had commenced to arouse within his belly the first, faint suggestions of hunger. He approached the cleft and looked in. The tarmangani was not in sight. Numa was not pleased, and he evidenced his displeasure by an angry growl.

A hundred yards within the fissure Lafayette Smith heard the growl and halted abruptly. "That damn lion!" he ejaculated. "I had forgotten all about him." It now occurred to him that this might be the beast's lair—a most unhappy contretemps, if true. A realization of his predicament at last supplanted the geologic reveries that had filled his mind. But what to do? Suddenly his faith in his trusty .32 faltered. As he recalled the appearance of the great beast the weapon seemed less infallible, yet it still gave him a certain sense of assurance as his fingers caressed its grip.

He determined that it would not be wise to retrace his steps toward the entrance at this time. Of course the lion might not have entered the fissure, might not even be harboring any intention of so doing. On the other hand, he might, in which event a return toward the opening could prove embarrassing, if not disastrous. Perhaps, if he waited a while, the lion would go away; and in the meantime, he decided, it would be discreet to go still farther along the cleft, as the lion, if it entered at all, might conceivably not proceed to the uttermost depths of the corridor. Further, there was the chance that he would find some sort of sanctuary farther in—a cave, a ledge to which he could climb, a miracle. Lafayette Smith was open to anything by this time.

And so he scrambled on, tearing his clothes and his flesh as well on sharp fragments of tumbled rock, going deeper into this remarkable corridor that seemed endless. In view of what might be behind him he hoped that it was endless. He had shuddered regularly to the oft recurring expectation of running into a blank wall just beyond that portion of the gently curving fissure that lay within his view ahead. He pictured the event. With his back to the rocky end of the cul-de-sac he would face back down the corridor, his pistol ready in his hand. Presently the lion would appear and discover him.

At this point he had some difficulty in constructing the scene, because he did not know just what the lion would do. Perhaps, seeing a man, cowed by the superior gaze of the human eye, he would turn in hasty retreat. And then again, perhaps not. Lafayette Smith was inclined to the conclusion that he would not. But then, of course, he had not had sufficient experience of wild animals to permit him to pose as an authority on the subject. To be sure, upon another occasion, while engaged in field work, he had been chased by a cow. Yet even this experience had not been conclusive—it had not served to definitely demonstrate the cow's ultimate intent—for the very excellent reason that Lafayette had attained a fence two jumps ahead of her.

Confused as the issue now seemed to be by his total ignorance of leonine psychology, he was convinced that he must attempt to visualize the expectant scene that he might be prepared for the eventuality.

Forging grimly ahead over the roughly tumbled fragments, casting an occasional glance backward, he again pictured his last stand with his back against the corridor's rocky end. The lion was creeping slowly toward him, but Lafayette was waiting until there should be no chance of a miss. He was very cool. His hand was steady as he took careful aim.

Here regrets interrupted the even tenor of his musing—regrets that he had not practiced more assiduously with his revolver. The fact that he had never discharged it troubled him, though only vaguely, since he harbored the popular subconscious conviction that if a firearm is pointed in the general direction of an animate object it becomes a deadly weapon.

However, in this mental picture he took careful aim—the fact that he was utilizing the front sight only giving him no concern. He pulled the trigger. The lion staggered and almost fell. It required a second shot to finish him, and as he sank to the ground Lafayette Smith breathed a genuine sigh of relief. He felt himself trembling slightly to the reaction of the nervous strain he had been undergoing. He stopped, and, withdrawing a handkerchief from his pocket, mopped the perspiration from his forehead, smiling a little as he realized the pitch of excitement to which he had aroused himself. Doubtless the lion had already forgotten him and had gone on about his business, he soliloquized.

He was facing back in the direction from which he had come as this satisfying conclusion passed through his mind; and then, a hundred feet away, where the corridor passed from view around a curve, the lion appeared.

10

In the Clutches of the Enemy

THE "Gunner" was perturbed. It was morning, and Lafayette Smith was still missing. They had searched for him until late the previous night, and now they were setting forth again. Ogonyo, the headman, acting under instructions from the "Gunner" had divided the party into pairs and, with the exception of four men left to guard the camp, these were to search in different directions combing the country carefully for trace of the missing man.

Danny had selected Obambi as his companion, a fact which irked the black boy considerably as he had been the target for a great deal of angry vituperation ever since Danny had discovered, the afternoon before, that he had left Smith alone in the mountains.

"It don't make no difference what he told you, you punk," the "Gunner" assured him, "you didn't have no business leavin' him out there alone. Now I'm goin' to take you for a walk, and if we don't find Lafayette you ain't never comin' back."

"Yes, bwana," replied Obambi, who had not even a crude idea of what the white man was talking about. One thing, however, pleased him immensely and that was that the bwana insisted on carrying his own gun, leaving nothing for Obambi to carry but a light lunch and two fifty-round drums of ammunition. Not that the nine pounds and thirteen ounces of a Thompson submachine gun would have been an exceptionally heavy burden, but that Obambi was always glad to be relieved of any burden. He would have been mildly grateful for a load reduction of even thirteen ounces.

The "Gunner," in attempting to determine the probable route that Smith would have followed in his search for the camp, reasoned in accordance with what he assumed he would have done under like circumstances; and, knowing that Smith had been last seen well above the camp and a little to the north of it, he decided to search in a northerly direction along the foothills, it being obvious that a man would come down hill rather than go farther up in such an emergency.

The day was hot and by noon the "Gunner" was tired, sweating, and disgusted. He was particularly disgusted with Africa, which, he informed Obambi, was "a hell of a burgh."

"Geeze," he grumbled; "I've walked my lousy legs off, and I ain't been no further than from The Loop to Cicero. I been six hours, and I could of done it in twenty minutes in a taxi. Of course they ain't got no cops in Africa, but they ain't got no taxis either."

"Yes, bwana," agreed Obambi.

"Shut up!" growled the "Gunner."

They were sitting beneath the shade of a tree on a hillside, resting and eating their lunch. A short distance below them the hillside dropped sheer in a fifty foot cliff, a fact that was not apparent from where they sat, any more than was the palisaded village at the cliff's base. Nor did they see the man squatting by a bush at the very brink of the cliff. His back was toward them, as, from the concealment of the bush, he gazed down upon the village below.

Here, the watcher believed, was the man he sought; but he wished to make sure, which might require days of watching. Time, however, meant little or nothing to Tarzan—no more than it did to any other jungle beast. He would come back often to this vantage spot and watch. Sooner or later he would discover the truth or falsity of his suspicion that one of the white men he saw in the village below was the slave raider for whom he had come north. And so, like a great lion, the ape-man crouched, watching his quarry.

Below him Dominic Capietro and Leon Stabutch lolled in the shade of a tree outside the hut of the raider, while a half dozen slave girls waited upon them as they leisurely ate their belated breakfast.

A couple of fiery liquid bracers had stimulated their jaded spirits, which had been at low ebb after their awakening following their debauch of the previous day, though, even so, neither could have been correctly described as being in fine fettle.

Capietro, who was even more surly and quarrelsome than usual, vented his spleen upon the hapless slaves, while Stabutch ate in morose silence, which he finally broke to revert to the subject of his mission.

"I ought to get started toward the south," he said. "From all I can learn there's nothing to be gained looking for the ape-man in this part of the country."

"What you in such a hurry to find him for?" demanded Capietro. "Ain't my company good enough for you?"

" 'Business before pleasure,' you know, comrade," Stabutch reminded the Italian in a conciliatory tone.

"I suppose so," grunted Capietro.

"I should like to visit you again after I have come back from the south," suggested Stabutch.

"You may not come back."

"I shall. Peter Zveri must be avenged. The obstacle in the path of communism must be removed."

"The monkey-man killed Zveri?"

"No, a woman killed him," replied the Russian, "but the monkey-man, as you call him, was directly responsible for the failure of all Zveri's plans and thus indirectly responsible for his death."

"You expect to fare better than Zveri, then? Good luck to you, but I don't envy you your mission. This Tarzan is like a lion with the brain of a man. He is savage. He is terrible. In his own country he is also very powerful."

"I shall get him, nevertheless," said Stabutch, confidently. "If possible I shall kill him the moment I first see him, before he has an opportunity to become suspicious; or, if I cannot do that, I shall win his confidence and his friendship and then destroy him when he least suspects his danger."

Voices carry upward to a great distance, and so, though Stabutch spoke only in normal tones, the watcher, squatting at the cliff top, smiled—just the faintest suggestion of a grim smile.

So that was why the man from "Russa," of whom Goloba the headman had told him, was inquiring as to his whereabouts? Perhaps Tarzan had suspected as much, but he was glad to have definite proof.

"I shall be glad if you do kill him," said Capietro. "He would drive me out of business if he ever learned about me. He is a scoundrel who would prevent a man from earning an honest dollar."

"You may put him from your mind, comrade," Stabutch assured the raider. "He is already as good as dead. Furnish me with men, and I shall soon be on my way toward the south."

"My villains are already saddling to go forth and find men for your safari," said Capietro, with a wave of his hand in the direction of the central compound, where a score of cutthroats were saddling their horses in preparation for a foray against a distant Galla village.

"May luck go with them," said Stabutch. "I hope— What was that?" he demanded, leaping to his feet as a sudden crash of falling rock and earth came from behind them.

Capietro was also upon his feet. "A landslide," he exclaimed. "A portion of the cliff has fallen. Look! What is that?" he pointed at an object half way up the cliff—the figure of a naked white man clinging to a tree that had found lodgment for its roots in the rocky face of the cliff. The tree, a small one, was bending beneath the weight of the man. Slowly it gave way, there was the sound of rending wood, and then the figure hurtled downward into the village where it was hidden from the sight of the two white watchers by an intervening hut.

But Stabutch had seen the giant figure of the almost naked white long enough to compare it with the description he had had of the man for whom he had come all the long way from Moscow. There could not be two such, of that he was certain. "It is the ape-man!" he cried. "Come, Capietro, he is ours!"

Instantly the Italian ordered several *shiftas* to advance and seize the ape-man.

Fortune is never necessarily with either the brave or the virtuous. She is, unfortunately, quite as likely to perch upon the banner of the poltroon or the blackguard. Today she deserted Tarzan completely. As he squatted upon the edge of the cliff, looking down upon the village of Dominic Capietro, he suddenly felt the earth giving beneath him. Cat-like, he leaped to his feet, throwing his hands above his head, as one does, mechanically, to preserve his balance or seek support, but too late. With a small avalanche of earth and rock he slid over the edge of the cliff. The tree, growing part way down the face of the escarpment, broke his fall and, for a moment, gave him hope that he might escape the greater danger of the final plunge into the village, where, if the fall did not kill him it was quite evident that his enemies would. But only for a moment were his hopes aroused. With the breaking of the bending stem hope vanished as he plunged on downward.

Danny "Gunner" Patrick, having finished his lunch, lighted a cigarette and let his gaze wander out over the landscape that unfolded in a lovely panorama before him. City bred, he saw only a part of what there was to be seen and under-stood but little of that. What impressed him most was the loneliness of the prospect. "Geeze," he soliloquized, "what a hideout! No one wouldn't ever find a guy here." His eyes suddenly focused upon an object in the foreground. "Hey, feller," he whispered to Obambi, "what's that?" He pointed in the direction of the thing that had aroused his curiosity.

Obambi looked and, when they found it, his keen eyes recognized it for what it was. "It is a man, bwana," he said. "It is the man who killed Simba in our camp that night. It is Tarzan of the Apes."

"How t'ell do you know?" demanded the "Gunner."

"There is only one Tarzan," replied the black. "It could be no other, as no other white man in all the jungle coun-try or the mountain country or the plains country goes thus naked."

The "Gunner" rose to his feet. He was going down to have a talk with the ape-man, who, perhaps, could help him in his search for Lafayette Smith; but as he arose he saw the man below him leap to his feet and throw his arms above his head. Then he disappeared as though swallowed up by the earth. The "Gunner" knitted his brows.

"Geeze," he remarked to Obambi, "he sure screwed, didn't he?"

"What, bwana?" asked Obambi.

"Shut up," snapped the "Gunner." "That was funny," he muttered. "Wonder what became of him. Guess I'll give him a tail. Come on," he concluded aloud to Obambi.

Having learned through experience (wholly the experience of others who had failed to do so, that attention to details is essential to the continued pursuit of life, liberty, and happiness, the "Gunner" looked carefully to his Thompson as he walked rapidly but cautiously toward the spot where Tarzan had disappeared. He saw that there was a cartridge in the chamber, that the magazine drum was properly attached and that the fire control lever was set for full automatic fire.

In the village, which he could not yet see and of the presence of which he did not dream, the *shiftas* were running toward the place where they knew the body of the fallen man must lie; and in the van were Stabutch and Capietro, when suddenly there stepped from the interior of the last hut the man they sought. They did not know that he had alighted on the thatched roof of the hut from which he had just emerged, nor that, though he had broken through it to the floor below, it had so broken his fall that he had suffered no disabling injury.

To them it seemed a miracle; and to see him thus, apparently uninjured, took the two white men so by surprise that they halted in their tracks while their followers, imitating their example, clustered about them.

Stabutch was the first to regain his presence of mind. Whipping a revolver from its holster he was about to fire point blank at the ape-man, when Capietro struck his hand up. "Wait," growled the Italian. "Do not be too fast. I am in command here."

"But it is the ape-man," cried Stabutch.

"I know that," replied Capietro, "and for that very reason I wish to take him alive. He is rich. He will bring a great ransom."

"Damn the ransom," ejaculated Stabutch. "It is his life I want."

"Wait until I have the ransom," said Capietro, "and then you can go after him."

In the meantime Tarzan stood watching the two. He saw that his situation was fraught with exceptional danger. It was to the interest of either one of these men to kill him; and while the ransom of which one spoke might deter him temporarily he knew that but little provocation would be required to induce this one to kill him rather than to take the chance that he might escape, while it was evident that the Russian already considered that he had sufficient provocation, and Tarzan did not doubt but that he would find the means to accomplish his design even in the face of the Italian's objections.

If he could but get among them, where they could not use

firearms against him, because of the danger that they might kill members of their own party, he felt that, by virtue of his superior strength, speed and agility, he might fight his way to one of the palisaded walls of the village where he would have a fair chance to escape. Once there he could scale the palisade with the speed of Manu, the monkey, and with little danger other than from the revolvers of the two whites, since he held the marksmanship of the *shiftas* in contempt.

He heard Capietro call to his men to take him alive; and then, waiting not upon them, he charged straight for the two whites, while from his throat burst the savage growl of a wild beast that had, upon more than a single occasion in the past, wrought havoc with the nerves of human antagonists.

Nor did it fail in its purpose now. Shocked and unnerved for the instant, Stabutch fell back while Capietro, who had no desire to kill the ape-man unless it became necessary, leaped to one side and urged his followers to seize him.

For a moment bedlam reigned in the village of the white raider. Yelling, cursing men milled about a white giant who fought with his bare hands, seizing an antagonist and hurling him in the faces of others, or, using the body of another like a flail, sought to mow down those who opposed him.

Among the close massed fighters, excited curs ran yelping and barking, while children and women upon the outskirts of the mêlée shrieked encouragement to the men.

Slowly Tarzan was gaining ground toward one of the coveted walls of the village where, as he stepped quickly backward to avoid a blow, he stumbled over a yapping cur and went down beneath a dozen men.

From the top of the cliff "Gunner" Patrick looked down upon this scene. "That mob has sure got him on the spot," he said aloud. "He's a regular guy, too. I guess here's where I step for him."

"Yes, bwana," agreed the willing Obambi.

"Shut up," said the "Gunner," and then he raised the butt of the Thompson to his shoulder and squeezed the trigger.

Mingled with the rapid reports of the machine gun were the screams and curses of wounded and frightened men and the shrieks of terrified women and children. Like snow before a spring shower, the pack that had surrounded Tarzan melted away as men ran for the shelter of their huts or for their saddled ponies.

Capietro and Stabutch were among the latter, and even before Tarzan could realize what had happened he saw the two racing through the open gates of the village.

The "Gunner," noting the satisfactory effect of his fire,

had ceased, though he stood ready again to rain a hail of death down upon the village should necessity require. He had aimed only at the outskirts of the crowd surrounding the ape-man, for fear that a bullet might strike the man he was endeavoring to succor; but he was ready to risk finer shooting should any press the naked giant too closely.

He saw Tarzan standing alone in the village street like a lion at bay, and then he saw his eyes ranging about for an explanation of the burst of fire that had liberated him.

"Up here, feller!" shouted the "Gunner."

The ape-man raised his eyes and located Danny instantly. "Wait," he called; "I'll be up there in a moment."

11

The Crucifixion

AS THE waters of Chinnereth closed over the head of Lady Barbara, the golden haired Jezebel sprang to her feet and ran swiftly forward among the men congregated upon the great flat lava rock from which the victim of their cruel fanaticism had been hurled to her doom. She pushed apostles roughly aside as she made her way toward the brink, tears streaming from her eyes and sobs choking her throat.

Abraham, the son of Abraham, standing directly in her path, was the first to guess her purpose to throw herself into the lake and share the fate of her loved mistress. Impelled by no humanitarian urge, but rather by a selfish determination to save the girl for another fate which he already had chosen for her, the Prophet seized her as she was about to leap into the water.

Turning upon the old man like a tigress, Jezebel scratched, bit, and kicked in an effort to free herself, which she would have succeeded in doing had not the Prophet called the six executioners to his aid. Two of them seized her; and, seeing that her efforts were futile, the girl desisted; but now she turned the flood gates of her wrath upon Abraham, the son of Abraham.

"Murderer!" she cried. "Son of Satan! May Jehovah strike thee dead for this. Curses be upon thy head and upon those of all thy kin. Damned be they and thee for the foul crime thou hast committed here this day."

"Silence, blasphemer!" screamed Abraham, the son of Abraham. "Make thy peace with Jehovah, for tonight thou shalt be judged by fire. Take her back to the village," he directed the two who held her, "and make her secure in a cave. Seest thou, too, that she escapeth not."

"Fire or water, it be all the same to me," cried the girl as they dragged her away, "just so it takes me away forever from this accursed land of Midian and the mad beast who poseth as the prophet of Jehovah."

As Jezebel moved off toward the village between her two guards the villagers fell in behind them, the women calling her foul names and otherwise reviling her, and in the rear of all came the Prophet and the Apostles, leaving a score of their fellows still lying upon the ground, where they writhed, unnoticed, in the throes of epilepsy.

The impact with the surface of the water had almost stunned Lady Barbara, but she had managed to retain her senses and control of her mental and physical powers, so that, although dazed, she was able to put into effect the plan that she had nursed from the moment that she was aware of the fate to which the Prophet had condemned her.

Being an excellent swimmer and diver the thought of being immersed below the surface of Chinnereth for a few minutes had not, in itself, caused her any great mental perturbation. Her one fear had lain in the very considerable possibility that she might be so badly injured by the impact with the water, or stunned, as to be helpless to effect her own release from the net. Her relief was great, therefore, when she discovered that she was far from helpless, nor did she delay an instant in bringing her small pocket knife to play upon the fibre strands of the net that enmeshed her.

Slashing rapidly, but yet, at the same time, in accordance with a practical plan, she severed strand after strand in a straight line, as the rock dragged her downward toward the bottom. Constantly through her mind ran a single admonition—"Keep cool! Keep cool!" Should she permit herself to give away to hysteria, even for an instant, she knew that she must be lost. The lake seemed bottomless, the strands innumerable, while the knife grew constantly duller, and her strength appeared to be rapidly ebbing.

"Keep cool! Keep cool!" Her lungs were bursting. "Just a moment more! Keep cool!" She felt unconsciousness creeping upon her. She struggled to drag herself through the opening she had made in the net—her senses reeled dizzily—she was almost unconscious as she shot rapidly toward the surface.

As her head rose above the surface those standing upon

the rock above her had their attention riveted upon Jezebel who was engaged at that moment in kicking the prophet of Paul, the son of Jehovah, on the shins. Lady Barbara was ignorant of all this; but it was fortunate for her, perhaps, because it prevented any of the Midians from noticing her resurrection from the deep and permitted her to swim, unseen, beneath the shelter of the overhanging rock from which she had been precipitated into the lake.

She was very weak, and it was with a prayer of thanksgiving that she discovered a narrow ledge of beach at the water's edge beneath the great lava block that loomed above her. As she dragged herself wearily out upon it she heard the voices of those upon the rock overhead—the voice of Jezebel cursing the Prophet and the old man's threat against the girl.

A thrill of pride in the courage of Jezebel warmed the heart of Lady Barbara, as did the knowledge that she had won a friend so loyal and devoted that she would put her own life in jeopardy merely for the sake of openly accusing the murderer of her friend. How magnificent she was in the primitive savagery of her denunciation! Lady Barbara could almost see her standing there defying the greatest power that her world knew, her golden hair framing her oval face, her eyes flashing, her lips curling in scorn, her lithe young body tense with emotion.

And what she had heard, and the thought of the helplessness of the young girl against the power of the vile old man, changed Lady Barbara's plans completely. She had thought to remain in hiding until night and then seek to escape this hideous valley and its mad denizens. There would be no pursuit, for they would think her dead at the bottom of Chinnereth; and thus she might seek to find her way to the outer world with no danger of interference by the people of the land of Midian.

She and Jezebel had often speculated upon the likelihood of the existence of a possible avenue of ascent of the crater wall; and from the entrance of their cave they had chosen a spot about midway of the western face of the crater, where the rim had fallen inward, as offering the best chance of escape. Tumbled masses of rock rose here from the bottom of the valley almost to the summit of the crater, and here Lady Barbara had decided to make her first bid for freedom.

But now all was changed. She could not desert Jezebel, whose life was now definitely jeopardized because of her friendship and loyalty. But what was she to do? How could she be of assistance to the girl? She did not know. Of only one thing was she certain—she must try.

She had witnessed enough horrors in the village of the South Midians to know that whatever Abraham, the son of Abraham, planned for Jezebel would doubtless be consummated after dark, the time he chose, by preference, for all the more horrible of his so-called religious rites. Only those which took them to a distance from the village, such as immersions in the waters of Chinnereth, were performed by daylight.

With these facts in mind, Lady Barbara decided that she might, with safety, wait until after dark before approaching the village. To do so earlier might only result in her own recapture, an event that would render her helpless in effecting the succor of Jezebel, while giving the Prophet two victims instead of one.

The sound of voices above her had ceased. She had heard the vituperations of the women diminishing in the distance, and by this she had known that the party had returned to the village. It was cold beneath the shadow of the rock, with her wet clothing clinging to her tired body; and so she slipped back into the water and swam along the shore a few yards until she found a spot where she could crawl out and lie in the pleasant warmth of the sun.

Here she rested again for a few minutes, and then she cautiously ascended the bank until her eyes were on a level with the ground. At a little distance she saw a woman, lying prone, who was trying to raise herself to a sitting position. She was evidently weak and dazed, and Lady Barbara realized that she was recovering from one of those horrid seizures to which nearly all the inhabitants of the village were subject. Near her were others, some lying quietly, some struggling; and in the direction of the village she saw several who had recovered sufficiently to attempt the homeward journey.

Lying very still, her forehead concealed behind a low shrub, Lady Barbara watched and waited for half an hour, until the last of the unfortunate band had regained consciousness and self control sufficiently to permit them to depart in the direction of their squalid habitations.

She was alone now with little or no likelihood of discovery. Her clothes were still wet and exceedingly uncomfortable; so she quickly removed them and spread them in the hot sun to dry, while she luxuriated in the soothing comfort of a sun bath, alternated with an occasional dip in the waters of the lake.

Before the sun dropped to the western rim of the crater her clothing had dried; and now she sat, fully dressed again, waiting for darkness to fall. Below her lay the waters of the lake and beyond its farther shore she could dimly see the outlines of the village of the North Midians, where dwelt the mysterious "beautiful men" of Jezebel's day dreams.

Doubtless, thought Lady Barbara, the prince charming of the golden one's imagination would prove to be a whiskered Adonis with a knotted club; but, even so, it were difficult to imagine more degraded or repulsive males than those of her own village. Almost anything—even a gorilla—might seem preferable to them.

As night approached, the girl saw little lights commence to twinkle in the northern village—the cooking fires, doubt-less—and then she rose and turned her face toward the vil-lage of Abraham, the son of Abraham, of Jobab and Timo-thy and Jezebel, toward certain danger and possible death.

As she walked along the now familiar path toward the village, the mind of Lady Barbara Collis was vexed by the seemingly hopeless problem that confronted her, while hover-ing upon the verge of her consciousness was that fear of the loneliness and the darkness of an unfamiliar and inhospitable country that is inherent in most of us. Jezebel had told her that dangerous beasts were almost unknown in the land of Midian, yet her imagination conjured slinking forms in the darkness and the sound of padded feet upon the trail be-hind her and the breathing of savage lungs. Yet ahead of her lay a real menace more terrible, perhaps, than swiftly striking talons and powerful jaws.

She recalled that she had heard that men who had been mauled by lions, and lived to narrate their experiences, had all testified uniformly to the fact that there had been no pain and little terror during the swift moments of the experience; and she knew that there was a theory propounded by certain students of animal life that the killing of the carnivores was always swift, painless, and merciful. Why was it, she won-dered, that of all created things only man was wantonly cruel and only man, and the beasts that were trained by man, killed for pleasure?

But now she was nearing the village and passing from the possibility of attack by merciful beasts to the assurance of attack by merciless men, should she be apprehended by them. To reduce this risk she skirted the village at a little distance and came to the foot of the cliff where the caves were located and where she hoped to find Jezebel and, perhaps, discover a means of liberating her.

She glanced up the face of the cliff, which seemed to be deserted, most of the villagers being congregated about a group of small cooking fires near the few huts at the foot of the cliff. They often cooked thus together gossiping and praying and narrating experiences and revelations—they all received revelations from Jehovah when they "walked" with Him, which was their explanation of their epileptic seizures.

The more imaginative members of the community were the recipients of the most remarkable revelations; but, as all of them were stupid, Jehovah had not, at least during Lady Barbara's sojourn among them, revealed anything of a particularly remarkable or inspiring nature. Their gossip, like their "experiences," was mean and narrow and sordid. Each sought constantly to discover or invent some scandal or heresy in the lives of his fellows, and if the finger pointed at one not in the good graces of the Prophet or the Apostles the victim was quite likely to make a Roman holiday.

Seeing the villagers congregated about their fires, Lady Barbara commenced the ascent of the steep path that zigzagged up the face of the cliff. She moved slowly and cautiously, stopping often to look about her, both above and below; but, notwithstanding her fears and doubts she finally reached the mouth of the cave that she and Jezebel had occupied. If she hoped to find the golden one there she was disappointed; but at least, if Jezebel were not there, it was a relief to find that no one else was; and with a sense of greater security than she had felt since the dawn of this eventful day she crawled into the interior and threw herself down upon the straw pallet that the girls had shared.

Home! This rough lair, no better than that which housed the beasts of the wilds, was home now to Lady Barbara Collis whose life had been spent within the marble halls of the Earl of Whimsey. Permeating it were memories of the strange friendship and affection that had gradually united these two girls whose origins and backgrounds could scarcely have been more dissimilar. Here each had learned the language of the other, here they had laughed and sung together, here they had exchanged confidences, and here they had planned together a future in which they would not be separated. The cold walls seemed warmer because of the love and loyalty to which they had been silent witnesses.

But now Lady Barbara was here alone. Where was Jezebel? It was the answer to that question that the English girl must find. She recalled the Prophet's threat—"for tonight thou shalt be judged by fire." She must hasten, then, if she were to save Jezebel. But how was she to accomplish it in the face of all the seemingly insurmountable obstacles which confronted her?—her ignorance of where Jezebel was being held, the numbers of her enemies, her lack of knowledge of the country through which they would be forced to flee should she be so fortunate as to effect the girl's escape from the village.

She roused herself. Lying here upon her pallet would accomplish nothing. She rose and looked down toward the village; and instantly she was all alertness again, for there was Jezebel. She was standing between two guards, surrounded by many villagers who maintained an open space about her. Presently the spectators separated and men appeared carrying a burden. What was it? They laid it in the center of the open space, in front of Jezebel; and then Lady Barbara saw what it was—a large wooden cross.

A man was digging a hole at the center of the circular space that had been left around the prisoner; others were bringing brush and fagots. Now the men who guarded Jezebel seized her and bore her to the ground. They laid her upon the cross and stretched her arms out upon the wooden cross arm.

Lady Barbara was horror stricken. Were they going to perpetrate the horrible atrocity of nailing her to the cross? Abraham, the son of Abraham, stood at the head of the cross, his hands in the attitude of prayer, a personification of pious hypocrisy. The girl knew that no cruelty, however atrocious, was beyond him. She knew, too, that she was powerless to prevent the consummation of this foul deed, yet she cast discretion and self interest to the winds, as, with a warning cry that shattered the silence of the night, she sped swiftly down the steep pathway toward the village—a self-sacrifice offered willingly upon the altar of friendship.

Startled by her scream, every eye was turned upward toward her. In the darkness they did not recognize her, but their stupid minds were filled with questioning and with terror as they saw something speeding down the cliff face toward them. Even before she reached the circle of firelight where they stood many had collapsed in paroxysms of epilepsy induced by the nervous shock of this unexpected visitation.

When she came closer, and was recognized, others succumbed, for now indeed it appeared that a miracle had been worked and that the dead had been raised again, even as they had seen the dead girl resurrected the previous day.

Pushing aside those who did not quickly enough make way for her, Lady Barbara hastened to the center of the circle. As his eyes fell upon her, Abraham, the son of Abraham, paled and stepped back. For a moment he seemed upon the verge of a stroke.

"Who are you?" he cried. "What are you doing here?"

"You know who I am," replied Lady Barbara. "Why do you tremble if you do not know that I am the messenger of Jehovah whom you reviled and sought to destroy? I am here to save the girl Jezebel from death. Later Jehovah will send His wrath upon Abraham, the son of Abraham, and upon all the people of the land of Midian for their cruelties and their sins."

"I did not know," cried the Prophet. "Tell Jehovah that I did not know. Intercede for me, that Jehovah may forgive me; and anything within my power to grant shall be yours."

So great was her surprise at the turn events had taken that Lady Barbara, who had expected only opposition and attack, was stunned for the moment. Here was an outcome so foreign to any that she had imagined that she had no response ready. She almost laughed aloud as she recalled the fears that had constantly harassed her since she had determined to attempt Jezebel's escape. And now it was all so easy.

"Liberate the girl, Jezebel," she commanded, "and then make food ready for her and for me."

"Quick!" cried the Prophet. "Raise the girl and set her free."

"Wait!" exclaimed a thin, querulous voice behind him. "I have walked with Jehovah." All turned in the direction of the speaker. He was Jobab the apostle.

"Quick! Release her!" demanded Lady Barbara, who, in this interruption and in the manner and voice of the speaker, whom she knew as one of the most fanatically intolerant of the religious bigots of Midian, saw the first spark that might grow into a flame of resistance to the will of the Prophet; for she knew these people well enough to be sure that they would grasp at any excuse to thwart the abandonment of their cruel pleasure.

"Wait!" shrieked Jobab. "I have walked with Jehovah, and He hath spoken unto me, saying: 'Behold, Jobab the Apostle, a seeming miracle shall be wrought out of Chinnereth; but be not deceived, for I say unto ye that it shall be the work of Satan; and whosoever believeth in it shall perish.'"

"Hallelujah!" shrieked a woman, and the cry was taken up by the others. To right and left the excited villagers were being stricken by their Nemesis. A score of writhing bodies jerked and struggled upon the ground in the throes of convulsions, the horrible choking, the frothing at the mouth, adding to the horror of the scene.

For a moment, Abraham, the son of Abraham, stood silent in thought. A cunning light flickered suddenly in his crafty eyes, and then he spoke. "Amen!" he said. "Let the will of Jehovah be done as revealed to the Apostle Jobab. Let Jobab speak the word of Jehovah, and upon Jobab's head be the reward."

"Another cross," screamed Jobab; "bring another cross. Let two beacon fires light the path of Jehovah in the heavens, and if either of these be His children He will not let them be consumed," and so, as Abraham, the son of Abraham, had passed the buck to Jobab, Jobab passed it along to Jehovah, who has been the recipient of more than His share through the ages.

Futile were the threats and arguments of Lady Barbara against the blood lust of the Midians. A second cross was brought, a second hole dug, and presently both she and Jezebel were lashed to the symbols of love and raised to an upright position. The bottoms of the crosses were sunk in the holes prepared for them and earth tamped around them to hold them upright. Then willing hands brought faggots and brushwood and piled them about the bases of the two pyres.

Lady Barbara watched these preparations in silence. She looked upon the weak, degenerate faces of this degraded people; and she could not, even in the extremity of her danger, find it in her heart to condemn them too severely for doing what supposedly far more enlightened people had done, within the memory of man, in the name of religion.

She glanced at Jezebel and found the girl's eyes upon her. "You should not have come back," said the girl. "You might have escaped." Lady Barbara shook her head. "You did it for me," continued Jezebel. "May Jehovah reward you, for I may only thank you."

"You would have done the same for me at Chinnereth," replied Lady Barbara. "I heard you defy the Prophet there."

Jezebel smiled. "You are the only creature I have ever loved," she said; "the only one who I ever thought loved me. Of course I would die for you."

Abraham, the son of Abraham, was praying. Young men stood ready with flaming torches, the flickering light from which danced grotesquely upon the hideous features of the audience, upon the two great crosses, and upon the beautiful faces of the victims.

"Good bye, Jezebel," whispered Lady Barbara.

"Good bye," replied the golden one.

NOTWITHSTANDING the fact that Lafayette Smith had so recently visualized this very emergency and had, as it were, rehearsed his part in it, now that he stood face to face with the lion he did none of the things exactly as he had pictured. He was not at all cool when he saw the carnivore appear at the turn in the fissure; he did not face him calmly, draw a deadly bead, and fire. Nothing was in the least as he had imagined it would be. In the first place the distance between them seemed entirely inadequate and the lion much larger than he had supposed any lion could be, while his revolver seemed to shrink to proportions that represented utter futility.

All this, however, was encompassed in a single, instantaneous and overwhelming conception. No appreciable time elapsed, therefore, between the instant that he perceived the lion and that at which he commenced to jerk the trigger of his pistol, which he accomplished, without aiming, while in the act of turning to flee.

Running headlong over the jumbled rocks Lafayette Smith fled precipitately into the unknown depths of the ancient rift, at his elbow the ghastly fear that beyond each successive turn would loom the rocky terminus of his flight, while just behind him he pictured the ravenous carnivore thirsting for his blood. The fall of swiftly moving padded feet close behind him urged him to greater speed, the hot breath of the lion surged from the savage lungs to pound upon his ears like surf upon an ocean beach.

Such is the power of imagination. It is true that Numa was bounding along the bottom of the rift, but in the opposite direction to that in which Lafayette Smith bounded. Fortunately, for Lafayette, none of his wild shots had struck the lion; but the booming reverberation of the explosions in the narrow fissure had so surprised and unnerved him that he had wheeled and fled even as the man had.

Had the pursuit been as real as Lafayette imagined it, it could have urged him to no greater speed, nor could the consequent terror have nerved him to greater endurance; but physical powers have their limits, and presently the realization that his had about reached theirs forced itself upon Lafayette's consciousness and with it realization of the futility of further flight.

It was then that he turned to make his stand. He was trembling, but with fatigue rather than fear; and inwardly he was cool as he reloaded his revolver. He was surprised to discover that the lion was not on top of him, but he expected momentarily to see him appear where the fissure turned from his sight. Seating himself on a flat rock he waited the coming of the carnivore while he rested, and as the minutes passed and no lion came his wonderment increased.

Presently his scientific eye commenced to note the structure of the fissure's walls about him, and as his interest grew in the geologic facts revealed or suggested his interest in the lion waned, until, once again, the carnivore was relegated to the background of his consciousness, while in its place returned the momentarily forgotten plan to explore the rift to its farthest extent.

Recovered from the excessive fatigue of his strenuous exertion he undertook once more the exploration so rudely interrupted. Regained was the keen pleasure of discovery; forgotten, hunger, fatigue, and personal safety as he advanced along this mysterious path of adventure.

Presently the floor of the rift dropped rapidly until it was inclined at an angle that made progress difficult; and at the same time it narrowed, giving evidence that it might be rapidly pinching out. There was now barely width for him to squeeze forward between the walls when the fissure ahead of him became suddenly shrouded in gloom. Glancing up in search of an explanation of this new phenomenon Lafayette discovered that the walls far above were converging, until directly above him there was only a small streak of sky visible while ahead the rift was evidently closed entirely at the top.

As he pushed on, the going, while still difficult because of the steepness of the floor of the fissure, was improved to some extent by the absence of jumbled rocks underfoot, the closed ceiling of the corridor having offered no crumbling rim to the raging elements of the ages; but presently another handicap made itself evident—darkness, increasing steadily with each few yards until the man was groping his way blindly, though none the less determinedly, toward the unknown that lay ahead.

That an abyss might yawn beyond his next step may have occurred to him, but so impractical was he in all worldly matters while his scientific entity was in the ascendancy that he ignored the simplest considerations of safety. However, no abyss yawned; and presently, at a turning, daylight showed ahead. It was only a small patch of daylight; and when he reached the opening through which it shone it appeared, at first, that he had achieved the end of his quest—that he could proceed no farther.

Dropping to his hands and knees he essayed the feat of worming his way through the aperture, which he then discovered was amply large to accommodate his body; and a moment later he stood erect in astonished contemplation of the scene before him.

He found himself standing near the base of a lofty escarpment overlooking a valley that his practised eye recognized immediately as the crater of a long extinct volcano. Below him spread a panorama of rolling, tree-dotted landscape, broken by occasional huge outcroppings of weathered lava rock; and in the center a blue lake danced in the rays of an afternoon sun.

Thrilling to an identical reaction such as doubtless dominated Balboa as he stood upon the heights of Darien overlooking the broad Pacific, Lafayette Smith experienced that spiritual elation that is, perhaps, the greatest reward of the explorer. Forgotten, for the moment, was the scientific interest of the geologist, submerged by intriguing speculation upon the history of this lost valley, upon which, perhaps, the eyes of no other white man had ever gazed.

Unfortunately for the permanency of this beatific state of mind two other thoughts rudely obtruded themselves, as thoughts will. One appertained to the camp, for which he was supposed to be searching, while the other involved the lion, which was supposedly searching for him. The latter reminded him that he was standing directly in front of the mouth of the fissure, at the very spot where the lion would emerge were he following; and this suggested the impracticability of the fissure as an avenue of return to the opposite side of the crater wall.

A hundred yards away Smith espied a tree, and toward this he walked as offering the nearest sanctuary in the event the lion should reappear. Here, too, he might rest while considering plans for the future; and, that he might enjoy uninterrupted peace of mind while so engaged, he climbed up into the tree, where, straddling a limb, he leaned his back against the bole.

It was a tree of meager foliage, thus affording him an almost unobstructed view of the scene before him, and as his eyes wandered across the landscape they were arrested by

something at the foot of the southern wall of the crater—
something that did not perfectly harmonize with its natural
surroundings. Here his gaze remained fixed as he sought to
identify the thing that had attracted his attention. What it
looked like he was positive that it could not be, so definitely
had his preconception of the inaccessibility of the valley to
man impressed itself upon his mind; yet the longer he looked
the more convinced he became that what he saw was a small
village of thatched huts.

And what thoughts did this recognition inspire? What
noble and aesthetic emotions were aroused within his breast
by the sight of this lonely village in the depths of the great
crater which should, by all the proofs that he had seen,
have been inaccessible to man?

No, you are wrong again. What it suggested was food.
For the first time since he had become lost Lafayette Smith
was acutely conscious of hunger, and when he recalled that
it had been more than twenty-four hours since he had eaten
anything more substantial than a few chocolates his appetite
waxed ravenous. Furthermore, he suddenly realized that he
was actually suffering from thirst.

At a little distance lay the lake. Glancing back toward
the entrance to the fissure he discovered no lion; and so he
dropped to the ground and set off in the direction of the water,
laying his course so that at no time was he at any great
distance from a tree.

The water was cool and refreshing; and when he had
drunk his fill he became acutely conscious, for the first time
during the day, of an overpowering weariness. The water
had temporarily relieved the pangs of hunger, and he determined to rest a few minutes before continuing on toward
the distant village. Once again he assured himself that there
was no pursuing lion in evidence; and then he stretched himself at full length in the deep grass that grew near the edge
of the lake, and with a low tree as protection from the hot
sun relaxed his tired muscles in much needed rest.

He had not intended to sleep; but his fatigue was greater
than he had supposed, so that, with relaxation, unconsciousness crept upon him unawares. Insects buzzed lazily about
him, a bird alighted in the tree beneath which he lay and
surveyed him critically, the sun dropped lower toward the
western rim, and Lafayette Smith slept on.

He dreamed that a lion was creeping toward him through
high grass. He tried to rise, but he was powerless. The horror
of the situation was intolerable. He tried to cry out and
frighten the lion away, but no sound issued from his throat.

Then he made a final supreme effort, and the shriek that resulted awakened him. He sat up, dripping with perspiration, and looked quickly and fearfully about him. There was no lion. "Whew!" he exclaimed. "What a relief."

Then he glanced at the sun and realized that he had slept away the greater part of the afternoon. Now his hunger returned and with it recollection of the distant village. Rising, he drank again at the lake, and then started on his journey toward the base of the southern rim, where he hoped he would find friendly natives and food.

The way led for the greater part around the edge of the lake; and as dusk settled and then darkness it became more and more difficult to move except at a slow and cautious pace, since the ground was often strewn with fragments of lava that were not visible in the darkness.

Night brought the cheering sight of fires in the village; and these, seeming nearer than they really were, buoyed his spirits by the assurance that his journey was nearing completion. Yet, as he stumbled onward, the conviction arose that he was pursuing a will-o'-the-wisp, as the firelight appeared to retreat as rapidly as he advanced.

At last, however, the outlines of mean huts, illumined by the fires, became distinguishable and then the figures of people clustered about them. It was not until he was almost within the village that he saw with astonishment that the people were white, and then he saw something else that brought him to a sudden halt. Upon two crosses, raised above the heads of the villagers, were two girls. The firelight played upon their faces, and he saw that both were beautiful.

What weird, unholy rite was this? What strange race inhabited this lost valley? Who were the girls? That they were not of the same race as the villagers was apparent at the first casual glance at the degraded features of the latter.

Lafayette Smith hesitated. It was evident that he was witnessing some sort of religious rite or pageant; and he assumed that to interrupt it would prove far from a satisfactory introduction to these people, whose faces, which had already repelled him, impressed him so unfavorably that he questioned the friendliness of his reception even under the most favorable auspices.

And then a movement of the crowd opened for a moment an avenue to the center of the circle where the crosses stood; and the man was horrified by what was revealed for an instant to his amazed eyes, for he saw the dry brush and the faggots piled about the bottoms of the crosses and the young men with the flaming torches ready to ignite the inflammable piles.

An old man was intoning a prayer. Here and there villagers writhed upon the ground in what Smith thought were evidences of religious ecstacy. And then the old man gave a signal, and the torch bearers applied the flames to the dry brush.

Lafayette Smith waited to see no more. Leaping forward he thrust surprised villagers from his path and sprang into the circle before the crosses. With a booted foot he kicked the already burning brush aside; and then, with his little .32 shining in his hand, he turned and faced the astonished and angry crowd.

For a moment Abraham, the son of Abraham, was paralyzed by surprise. Here was a creature beyond his experience or his ken. It might be a celestial messenger; but the old man had gone so far now, and his crazed mind was so thoroughly imbued with the lust for torture, that he might even have defied Jehovah Himself rather than forego the pleasures of the spectacle he had arranged.

At last he found his voice. "What blasphemy is this?" he screamed. "Set upon this infidel, and tear him limb from limb."

"You will have to shoot, now," said an English voice at Smith's back, "for if you don't they will kill you."

He realized that it was one of the girls upon the crosses—another astonishing mystery in this village of mysteries, that cool English voice. Then one of the torch bearers rushed him with a maniacal shriek, and Smith fired. With a scream the fellow clutched his chest and sprawled at the American's feet; and at the report of the pistol and the sudden collapse of their fellow the others, who had been moving forward upon the intruder, fell back, while upon all sides the over-excited creatures succumbed to the curse that had descended to them from Angustus the Ephesian, until the ground was strewn with contorted forms.

Realizing that the villagers were, for the moment at least, too disconcerted and overawed by the death of their fellow to press their attack, Smith turned his attention at once to the two girls. Replacing his pistol in its holster, he cut their bonds with his pocket knife before Abraham, the son of Abraham, could collect his scattered wits and attempt to urge his followers to a renewed attack.

It was more than the work of a moment to liberate the two captives as, after he had cut the bonds that held their feet Smith had been compelled to partially support each with one arm as he severed the fibres that secured their wrists to the cross arms, lest a bone be broken or a muscle wrenched as the full weight of the victim was thrown suddenly upon one wrist.

He had cut Lady Barbara down first; and she was assisting him with Jezebel, who, having been crucified for a longer time, was unable to stand alone, when Abraham, the son of Abraham, regained sufficient composure to permit him to think and act.

Both Lady Barbara and Smith were supporting Jezebel into whose numbed feet the blood was again beginning to circulate. Their backs were toward the Prophet; and, taking advantage of their preoccupation, the old man was creeping stealthily upon them from the rear. In his hand was a crude knife, but none the less formidable for its crudeness. It was the blood stained sacrificial knife of this terrible old high priest of the Midians, more terrible now because of the rage and hatred that animated the cruel, defective mind that directed the claw-like hand that wielded it.

All of his rage, all of his hatred were directed against the person of Lady Barbara, in whom he saw the author of his humiliation and his thwarted desires. Stealthily he crept upon her from behind while his followers, frozen to silence by his terrible glances, watched in breathless anticipation.

Occupied with the half-fainting Jezebel none of the three at the crosses saw the repulsive figure of the avenger as he towered suddenly behind the English girl, his right hand raised high to drive the blade deeply into her back; but they heard his sudden, choking, gasping scream and turned in time to see the knife fall from his nerveless fingers as they clutched at his throat, and to witness his collapse.

Angustus the Ephesian had reached out of a grave digged two thousand years before, to save the life of Lady Barbara Collis—though doubtless he would have turned over in that same grave had he realized the fact.

13

The "Gunner" Walks

LIKE a great cat, Tarzan of the Apes scaled the palisade of the raiders' village, dropped lightly to the ground upon the opposite side and ascended the cliffs a little to the south of the village where they were less precipitous. He might have taken advantage of the open gate; but the direction he chose was the shorter way; and a palisade constituted no obstacle to the foster son of Kala, the she-ape.

The "Gunner" was waiting for him upon the summit of the cliff directly behind the village, and for the second time these strangely dissimilar men met—dissimilar, and yet, in some respects, alike. Each was ordinarily quiet to taciturnity, each was self-reliant, each was a law unto himself in his own environment; but there the similarity ceased for the extremes of environment had produced psychological extremes as remotely separated as the poles.

The ape-man had been reared amidst scenes of eternal beauty and grandeur, his associates the beasts of the jungle, savage perhaps, but devoid of avarice, petty jealousy, treachery, meanness, and intentional cruelty; while the "Gunner" had known naught but the squalid aspects of scenery defiled by man, of horizons grotesque with screaming atrocities of architecture, of an earth hidden by concrete and asphaltum and littered with tin cans and garbage, his associates, in all walks of life, activated by grand and petty meannesses unknown to any but mankind.

"A machine gun has its possibilities," said the ape-man, with the flicker of a smile.

"They had you in a bad spot, mister," remarked the "Gunner."

"I think I should have gotten out all right," replied Tarzan, "but I thank you none the less. How did you happen to be here?"

"I been looking for my side-kick, and I happened to see you go over the edge here. Obambi here, tipped me off that you was the guy saved me from the lion,—so I was glad to step for you."

"You are looking for whom?"

"My side-kick, Smith."

"Where is he?"

"I wouldn't be lookin' for him if I knew. He's went and lost himself. Been gone since yesterday afternoon."

"Tell me the circumstances," said Tarzan, "perhaps I can help you."

"That's what I was goin' to ask you," said the "Gunner." "I know my way around south of Madison Street, but out here I'm just a punk. I aint got no idea where to look for him. Geeze, take a slant at them mountains. You might as well try to meet a guy at the corner of Oak and Polk as hunt for him there. I'll tell you how it happened," and then he briefly narrated all that was known of the disappearance of Lafayette Smith.

"Was he armed?" asked the ape-man.

"He thought he was."

"What do you mean?"

"He packed a shiny toy pistol, what if anybody ever shot me with it, and I found it out, I'd turn him over my knee and spank him."

"It might serve him in getting food," said Tarzan, "and that will be of more importance to him than anything else. He's not in much danger, except from men and starvation. Where's your camp?"

Danny nodded toward the south. "Back there about a thousand miles," he said.

"You'd better go to it and remain there where he can find you if he can make his way back to it, and where I can find you if I locate him."

"I want to help you hunt for him. He's a good guy, even if he is legitimate."

"I can move faster alone," replied the ape-man. "If you start out looking for him I'll probably have to find you, too."

The "Gunner" grinned. "I guess you aint so far off, at that," he replied. "All right, I'll beat it for camp and wait there for you. You know where our camp is at?"

"I'll find out," replied Tarzan and turned to Obambi to whom he put a few questions in the native Bantu dialect of the black. Then he turned again to the "Gunner." "I know where your camp is now. Watch out for these fellows from that village, and don't let your men wander very far from the protection of your machine gun."

"Why," demanded Danny, "what are them guys?"

"They are robbers, murderers, and slave raiders," replied Tarzan.

"Geeze," exclaimed the "Gunner," "they's rackets even in Africa, aint they?"

"I do not know what a racket is," replied the ape-man, "but there is crime wherever there are men, and nowhere else." He turned then, without word of parting, and started upward toward the mountains.

"Geeze!" muttered the "Gunner." "That guy aint so crazy about men."

"What, bwana?" asked Obambi.

"Shut up," admonished Danny.

The afternoon was almost spent when the "Gunner" and Obambi approached camp. Tired and footsore as he was the white man had, none the less, pushed rapidly along the backtrail lest night descend upon them before they reached their destination, for Danny, in common with most city-bred humans, had discovered something peculiarly depressing and awe-inspiring in the mysterious sounds and silences of the nocturnal wilds. He wished the fires and companionship of men after the sun had set. And so the two covered the distance on the return in much less time than had been consumed in traversing it originally.

As he came in sight of the camp the brief twilight of the tropics had already fallen, the cooking fires were burning, and to a trained eye a change would have been apparent from the appearance of the camp when he had left it early that morning; but Danny's eyes were trained in matters of broads, bulls, and beer trucks and not in the concerns of camps and safaris; so, in the failing light of dusk, he did not notice that there were more men in camp than when he had left, nor that toward the rear of it there were horses tethered where no horses had been before.

The first intimation he had of anything unusual came from Obambi. "White men are in the camp, bwana," said the black—"and many horses. Perhaps they found the mad bwana and brought him back."

"Where do you see any white men?" demanded the "Gunner."

"By the big fire in the center of camp, bwana," replied Obambi.

"Geeze, yes, I see 'em now," admitted Danny. "They must have found old Smithy all right; but I don't see him, do you?"

"No, bwana, but perhaps he is in his tent."

The appearance of Patrick and Obambi caused a commotion in the camp that was wholly out of proportion to its true significance. The white men leaped to their feet and drew their revolvers while strange blacks, in response to the commands of one of these, seized rifles and stood nervously alert.

"You don't have to throw no fit," called Danny, "it's only me and Obambi."

The white men were advancing to meet him now, and the two parties halted face to face near one of the fires. It was then that the eyes of one of the two strange white men alighted on the Thompson submachine gun. Raising his revolver he covered Danny.

"Put up your hands!" he commanded sharply.

"Wotell?" demanded the "Gunner," but he put them up as every sensible man does when thus invited at the business end of a pistol.

"Where is the ape-man?" asked the stranger.

"What ape-man? What you talkin' about? What's your racket?"

"You know who I mean—Tarzan," snapped the other. The "Gunner" glanced quickly about the camp. He saw his own men herded under guard of villainous looking blacks in long robes that had once been white; he saw the horses tethered just beyond them; he saw nothing of Lafayette Smith. The training and the ethics of gangland controlled him on the instant. "Don't know the guy," he replied sullenly.

"You were with him today," snarled the bearded white. "You fired on my village."

"Who, me?" inquired the "Gunner" innocently. "You got me wrong, mister. I been hunting all day. I aint seen no one. I aint fired at nothing. Now it's my turn. What are you guys doin' here with this bunch of Ku Klux Klanners? If it's a stick up, hop to it; and get on your way. You got the drop on us, and they aint no one to stop you. Get it over with. I'm hungry and want to feed."

"Take the gun away from him," said Capietro, in Galla, to one of his men, "also his pistol," and there was nothing for Danny "Gunner" Patrick, with his hands above his head, to do but submit. Then they sent Obambi, under escort, to be herded with the other black prisoners and ordered the "Gunner" to accompany them to the large fire that blazed in front of Smith's tent and his own.

"Where is your companion?" demanded Capietro.

"What companion?" inquired Danny.

"The man you have been travelling with," snapped the Italian. "Who else would I mean?"

"Search me," replied the "Gunner."

"What you mean by that? You got something concealed upon your person?"

"If you mean money, I aint got none."

"You did not answer my question," continued Capietro.

"What question?"

"Where is your companion?"

"I aint got none."

"Your headman told us there were two of you. What is your name?"

"Bloom," replied Danny.

Capietro looked puzzled. "The headman said one of you was Smith and the other Patrick."

"Never heard of 'em," insisted Danny. "The guy must of been stringin' you. I'm here alone, hunting, and my name's Bloom."

"And you didn't see Tarzan of the Apes today?"

"Never even heard of a guy with that monacker."

"Either he's lying to us," said Stabutch, "or it was the other one who fired on the village."

"Sure, it must of been two other fellows," Danny assured them. "Say, when do I eat?"

"When you tell us where Tarzan is," replied Stabutch.

"Then I guess I don't eat," remarked Danny. "Geeze, didn't I tell you I never heard of the guy? Do you think I know every monkey in Africa by his first name? Come on now, what's your racket? If we got anything you want, take it and screw. I'm sick lookin' at your mugs."

"I do not understand English so well," whispered Capietro to Stabutch. "I do not always know what he says."

"Neither do I," replied the Russian; "but I think he is lying to us. Perhaps he is trying to gain time until his companion and Tarzan arrive."

"That is possible," replied Capietro in his normal voice.

"Let's kill him and get out of here," suggested Stabutch. "We can take the prisoners and as much of the equipment as you want and be a long way from here in the morning."

"Geeze," exclaimed Danny, "this reminds me of Chi. It makes me homesick."

"How much money you pay if we don't kill you?" asked Capietro. "How much your friends pay?"

The "Gunner" laughed. "Say, mister, you're giving yourself a bum steer." He was thinking how much more one might collect for killing him, if one could make connections with certain parties on the North Side of Chicago, than for sparing his life. But here was an opportunity, perhaps, to gain time. The "Gunner" did not wish to be killed, and so he altered his technique. "My friends ain't rich," he said, "but they might come across with a few grand. How much do you want?"

Capietro considered. This must be a rich American, for only rich men could afford these African big game expeditions. "One hundred thousand should not be excessive for a rich man like you," he said.

"Quit your kidding," said the "Gunner." "I ain't rich."

"What could you raise?" asked Capietro, who saw by the prisoner's expression of astonishment that the original bid was evidently out of the question.

"I might scrape up twenty grand," suggested Danny.

"What are grand?" demanded the Italian.

"Thousand—twenty thousand," explained the "Gunner."

"Poof!" cried Capietro. "That would not pay me for the trouble of keeping you until the money could be forwarded from America. Make it fifty thousand lire and it's a bargain."

"Fifty thousand lire? What's them?"

"A lire is an Italian coin worth about twenty cents in American money," explained Stabutch.

Danny achieved some rapid mental calculations before he replied; and when he had digested the result he had difficulty in repressing a smile, for he discovered that his offer of twenty thousand grand was actually twice what the Italian was now demanding. Yet he hesitated to agree too willingly. "That's ten thousand iron men," he said. "That's a lot of jack."

"Iron men? Jack? I do not understand," said Capietro.

"Smackers," explained Danny lucidly.

"Smackers? Is there such a coin in America?" asked Capietro, turning to Stabutch.

"Doubtless a vernacularism," said the Russian.

"Geeze, you guys is dumb," growled the "Gunner." "A smacker's a buck. Every one knows that."

"Perhaps if you would tell him in dollars it would be easier," suggested Stabutch. "We all understand the value of an American dollar."

"That's a lot more than some Americans understand," Danny assured him; "but it's just what I been saying right along—ten thousand dollars—and it's too damn much."

"That is for you to decide," said Capietro. "I am tired of bargaining—nobody but an American would bargain over a human life."

"What you been doing?" demanded the "Gunner." "You're the guy that started it."

Capietro shrugged. "It is not my life," he said. "You will pay me ten thousand American dollars, or you will die. Take your choice."

"Oke," said Danny. "I'll pay. Now do I eat? If you don't feed me I won't be worth nothing."

"Tie his hands," Capietro ordered one of the *shiftas*, then he fell to discussing plans with Stabutch. The Russian finally agreed with Capietro that the palisaded village of the raider would be the best place to defend themselves in the event that Tarzan enlisted aid and attacked them in force. One of their men had seen Lord Passmore's safari; and, even if their prisoner was lying to them, there was at least another white, probably well armed, who might be considered a definite menace. Ogonyo had told them that this man was alone and probably lost, but they did not know whether or not to believe the headman. If Tarzan commandeered these forces, which Capietro knew he had the influence to do, they might expect an attack upon their village.

By the light of several fires the blacks of the captured safari were compelled to break camp and, when the loads were packed, to carry them on the difficult night march toward Capietro's village. With mounted *shiftas* in advance, upon the flanks, and bringing up the rear there was no lagging and no chance to escape.

The "Gunner," plodding along at the head of his own porters, viewed the prospect of that night march with unmitigated disgust. He had traversed the route twice already since sunrise; and the thought of doing it again, in the dark, with his hands tied behind him was far from cheering. To add to his discomfort he was weak from hunger and fatigue, and now the pangs of thirst were assailing him.

"Geeze," he soliloquized, "this aint no way to treat a regular guy. When I took 'em for a ride I never made no guy walk, not even a rat. I'll get these lousy bums yet—a thinkin' they can put Danny Patrick on the spot, an' make him walk all the way!"

14
Flight

As THE choking cry broke from the lips of Abraham, the son of Abraham, Lady Barbara and Smith wheeled to see him fall, the knife clattering to the ground from his nerveless fingers. Smith was horrified, and the girl blenched, as they realized how close death had been. She saw Jobab and the others standing there, their evil faces contorted with rage.

"We must get away from here," she said. "They will be upon us in a moment."

"I'm afraid you'll have to help me support your friend," said Smith. "She cannot walk alone."

"Put your left arm around her," directed Lady Barbara. "That will leave your right hand free for your pistol. I will support her on the other side."

"Leave me," begged Jezebel. "I will only keep you from escaping."

"Nonsense," said Smith. "Put your arm across my shoulders."

"You will soon be able to walk," Lady Barbara told her, "when the blood gets back into your feet. Come! Let's get away from here while we can."

Half carrying Jezebel, the two started to move toward the circle of menacing figures surrounding them. Jobab was the first to regain his wits since the Prophet had collapsed at the critical moment. "Stop them!" he cried, as he prepared to block their way, at the same time drawing a knife from the folds of his filthy garment.

"One side, fellow!" commanded Smith, menacing Jobab with his pistol.

"The wrath of Jehovah will be upon you," cried Lady Barbara in the Midian tongue, "as it has been upon the others who would have harmed us, if you fail to let us pass in peace."

"It is the work of Satan," shrilled Timothy. "Do not let them weaken your heart with lies, Jobab. Do not let them pass!" The elder was evidently under great mental and nervous strain. His voice shook as he spoke, and his muscles were trembling. Suddenly he, too, collapsed as had Abraham, the son of Abraham. But still Jobab stood his ground, his knife raised in a definite menace against them. All around them the circle was growing smaller and its circumference more solidly knit by the forward pressing bodies of the Midians.

"I hate to do it," said Smith, half aloud, as he raised his pistol and aimed it at Jobab. The Apostle was directly in front of Lafayette Smith and little more than a yard distant when the American, aiming point blank at his chest, jerked the trigger and fired.

An expression of surprise mingled with that of rage which had convulsed the unbecoming features of Jobab the Apostle. Lafayette Smith was also surprised and for the same reason —he had missed Jobab. It was incredible—there must be something wrong with the pistol!

But Jobab's surprise, while based upon the same miracle, was of a loftier and nobler aspect. It was clothed in the sanctity of divine revelation. It emanated from a suddenly acquired conviction that he was immune to the fire and thunder of this strange weapon that he had seen lay Lamech low but a few minutes earlier. Verily, Jehovah was his shield and his buckler!

For a moment, as the shot rang out, Jobab paused and then, clothed in the fancied immunity of this sudden revelation, he leaped upon Lafayette Smith. The sudden and unexpected impact of his body knocked the pistol from Smith's hand and simultaneously the villagers closed in upon him. A real menace now that they had witnessed the futility of the strange weapon.

Lafayette Smith was no weakling, and though his antagonist was inspired by a combination of maniacal fury and religious fanaticism the outcome of their struggle must have been a foregone conclusion had there been no outside influences to affect it. But there were. Beside the villagers, there was Lady Barbara Collis.

With consternation she had witnessed the futility of Smith's marksmanship; and when she saw him disarmed and in the grip of Jobab, with others of the villagers rushing to his undoing, she realized that now, indeed, the lives of all three of them were in direct jeopardy.

The pistol lay at her feet, but only for a second. Stooping, she seized it; and then, with the blind desperation of self-preservation, she shoved the muzzle against Jobab's side and pulled the trigger; and as he fell, a hideous shriek upon his lips, she turned the weapon upon the advancing villagers and fired again. It was enough. Screaming in terror, the Midians turned and fled. A wave of nausea swept over the girl; she swayed and might have fallen had not Smith supported her.

"I'll be all right in a moment," she said. "It was so horrible!"

"You were very brave," said Lafayette Smith.

"Not as brave as you," she replied with a weak little smile; "but a better shot."

"Oh," cried Jezebel, "I thought they would have us again. Now that they are frightened, let us go away. It will require only a word from one of the apostles to send them upon us again."

"You are right," agreed Smith. "Have you any belongings you wish to take with you?"

"Only what we wear," replied Lady Barbara.

"What is the easiest way out of the valley?" asked the man, on the chance that there might be another and nearer avenue of escape than the fissure through which he had come.

"We know of no way out," replied Jezebel.

"Then follow me," directed Smith. "I'll take you out the way I came in."

They made their way from the village and out onto the dark plain toward Chinnereth, nor did they speak again until they had gone some distance from the fires of the Midians and felt that they were safe from pursuit. It was then that Lafayette Smith asked a question prompted by natural curiosity.

"How can it be possible that you young ladies know of no

way out of this valley?" he asked. "Why can't you go out the way you came in?"

"I could scarcely do that," replied Jezebel; "I was born here."

"Born here?" exclaimed Smith. "Then your parents must live in the valley. We can go to their home. Where is it?"

"We just came from it," explained Lady Barbara. "Jezebel was born in the village from which we have just escaped."

"And those beasts killed her parents?" demanded Lafayette.

"You do not understand," said Lady Barbara. "Those people are her people."

Smith was dumbfounded. He almost ejaculated: "How horrible!" but stayed the impulse. "And you?" he asked presently. "Are they your people, too?" There was a note of horror in his voice.

"No," replied Lady Barbara. "I am English."

"And you don't know how you got into this valley?"

"Yes, I know—I came by parachute."

Smith halted and faced her. "You're Lady Barbara Collis!" he exclaimed.

"How did you know?" she asked. "Have you been searching for me?"

"No, but when I passed through London the papers were full of the story of your flight and your disappearance—pictures and things, you know."

"And you just stumbled onto me? What a coincidence! And how fortunate for me."

"To tell you the truth, I am lost myself," admitted Smith. "So possibly you are about as badly off as you were before."

"Scarcely," she said. "You have at least prevented my premature cremation."

"They were really going to burn you? It doesn't seem possible in this day and age of enlightenment and civilization."

"The Midians are two thousand years behind the times," she told him, "and in addition to that they are religious, as well as congenital, maniacs."

Smith glanced in the direction of Jezebel whom he could see plainly in the light of a full moon that had but just topped the eastern rim of the crater. Perhaps Lady Barbara sensed the unspoken question that disturbed him.

"Jezebel is different," she said. "I cannot explain why, but she is not at all like her people. She tells me that occasionally one such as she is born among them."

"But she speaks English," said Smith. "She cannot be of the same blood as the people I saw in the village, whose language is certainly not the same as hers, to say nothing of the dissimilarity of their physical appearance."

"I taught her English," explained Lady Barbara.

"She wants to go away and leave her parents and her people?" asked Smith.

"Of course I do," said Jezebel. "Why should I want to stay here and be murdered? My father, my mother, my brothers and sisters were in that crowd you saw about the crosses to-night. They hate me. They have hated me from the day I was born, because I am not like them. But then there is no love in the land of Midian—only religion, which preaches love and practices hate."

Smith fell silent as the three plodded on over the rough ground down toward the shore of Chinnereth. He was considering the responsibility that Fate had loaded upon his shoulders so unexpectedly and wondering if he were equal to the emergency, who, as he was becoming to realize, could scarcely be sure of his ability to insure his own existence in this savage and unfamiliar world.

Keenly the realization smote him that in almost thirty hours that he had been thrown exclusively upon his own resources he had discovered not a single opportunity to provide food for himself, the result of which was becoming increasingly apparent in a noticeable loss of strength and endurance. What then might he hope to accomplish with two additional mouths to feed?

And what if they encountered either savage beasts or unfriendly natives? Lafayette Smith shuddered. "I hope they can run fast," he murmured.

"Who?" asked Lady Barbara. "What do you mean?"

"Oh," stammered Lafayette. "I—I did not know that I spoke aloud." How could he tell her that he had lost confidence even in his .32? He could not. Never before in his life had he felt so utterly incompetent. His futility seemed to him to border on criminality. At any rate it was dishonorable, since it was deceiving these young women who had a right to expect guidance and protection from him.

He was very bitter toward himself; but that, perhaps, was due partly to the nervous reaction following the rather horrible experience at the village and physical weakness that was bordering on exhaustion. He was excoriating himself for having dismissed Obambi, which act, he realized, was at the bottom of all his troubles; and then he recalled that had it not been for that there would have been no one to save these two girls from the horrible fate from which he had preserved them. This thought somewhat restored his self-esteem, for he could not escape the fact that he had, after all, saved them.

Jezebel, the circulation restored to her feet, had been walking without assistance for some time. The three had lapsed into a long silence, each occupied with his own thoughts, as Smith led the way in search of the opening into the fissure.

A full African moon lighted their way, its friendly beams lessening the difficulties of the night march. Chinnereth lay upon their right, a vision of loveliness in the moonlight, while all about them the grim mass of the crater walls seemed to have closed in upon them and to hang menacingly above their heads, for night and moonlight play strange tricks with perspective.

It was shortly after midnight that Smith first stumbled and fell. He arose quickly, berating his awkwardness; but as he proceeded, Jezebel, who was directly behind him, noticed that he walked unsteadily, stumbling more and more often. Presently he fell again, and this time it was apparent to both girls that it was only with considerable effort that he arose. The third time he fell they both helped him to his feet.

"I'm terribly clumsy," he said. He was swaying slightly as he stood between them.

Lady Barbara observed him closely. "You are exhausted," she said.

"Oh, no," insisted Smith. "I'm all right."

"When did you eat last?" demandd thee girl.

"I had some chocolate with me," replied Smith. "I ate the last of it this afternoon sometime."

"When did you eat a meal, I mean?" persisted Lady Barbara.

"Well," he admitted, "I had a light lunch yesterday noon, or rather day before yesterday. It must be after midnight now."

"And you have been walking all the time since?"

"Oh, I ran part of the time," he replied, with a weak laugh. "That was when the lion chased me. And I slept in the afternoon before I came to the village."

"We are going to stop right here until you are rested," announced the English girl.

"Oh, no," he demurred, "we mustn't do that. I want to get you out of this valley before daylight, as they will probably pursue us as soon as the sun comes up."

"I don't think so," said Jezebel. "They are too much afraid of the North Midians to come this far from the village; and, anyway, we have such a start that we can reach the cliffs, where you say the fissure is, before they could overtake us."

"You must rest," insisted Lady Barbara.

Reluctantly Lafayette sat down. "I'm afraid I'm not going to be much help to you," he said. "You see I am not really familiar with Africa, and I fear that I am not adequately armed for your protection. I wish Danny were here."

"Who is Danny?" asked Lady Barbara.

"He's a friend who accompanied me on this trip."

"He's had African experience?"

"No," admitted Lafayette, "but one always feels safe with Danny about. He seems so familiar with firearms. You see he is a protection guy."

"What is a protection guy?" asked Lady Barbara.

"To be quite candid," replied Lafayette, "I am not at all sure that I know myself what it is. Danny is not exactly garrulous about his past; and I have hesitated to pry into his private affairs, but he did volunteer the information one day that he had been a protection guy for a big shot. It sounded reassuring."

"What is a big shot?" inquired Jezebel.

"Perhaps a big game hunter," suggested Lady Barbara.

"No," said Lafayette. "I gather from Danny's remarks that a big shot is a rich brewer or distiller who also assists in directing the affairs of a large city. It may be just another name for political boss."

"Of course," said Lady Barbara, "it would be nice if your friend were here; but he is not, so suppose you tell us something about yourself. Do you realize that we do not even know your name?"

Smith laughed. "That's about all there is to know about me," he said. "It's Lafayette Smith, and now will you introduce me to this other young lady? I already know who you are."

"Oh, this is Jezebel," said Lady Barbara.

There was a moment's silence. "Is that all?" asked Smith.

Lady Barbara laughed. "Just Jezebel," she said. "If we ever get out of here we'll have to find a surname for her. They don't use 'em in the land of Midian."

Smith lay on his back looking up at the moon. Already he was commencing to feel the beneficial effects of relaxation and rest. His thoughts were toying with the events of the past thirty hours. What an adventure for a prosaic professor of geology, he thought. He had never been particularly interested in girls, although he was far from being a misogynist, and to find himself thus thrown into the intimate relationship of protector to two beautiful young women was somewhat disconcerting. And the moon had revealed that they were beautiful. Perhaps the sun might have a different story to tell. He had heard of such things and he wondered. But sunlight could not alter the cool, crisp, well bred voice of Lady Barbara Collis. He liked to hear her talk. He had always enjoyed the accent and diction of cultured English folk.

He tried to think of something to ask her that he might listen to her voice again. That raised the question of just how he should address her. His contacts with nobility had been few—in fact almost restricted to a single Russian prince who had been a door man at a restaurant he sometimes patronized, and he had never heard him addressed otherwise than as Mike. He thought Lady Barbara would be the correct formula, though that smacked a little of familiarity. Lady Collis seemed, somehow, even less appropriate. He wished he were sure. Mike would never do. Jezebel. What an archaic name! And then he fell asleep.

Lady Barbara looked down at him and raised a warning finger to her lips lest Jezebel awaken him. Then she rose and walked away a short distance, beckoning the golden one to follow.

"He is about done up," she whispered, as they seated themselves again. "Poor chap, he has had a rough time of it. Imagine being chased by a lion with only that little popgun with which to defend oneself."

"Is he from your country?" asked Jezebel.

"No, he's an American. I can tell by his accent."

"He is very beautiful," said Jezebel, with a sigh.

"After looking at Abraham, the son of Abraham, and Jobab, for all these weeks I could agree with you if you insisted that St. Ghandi is an Adonis," replied Lady Barbara.

"I do not know what you mean," said Jezebel; "but do you not think him beautiful?"

"I am less interested in his pulchritude than in his marksmanship, and that is positively beastly. He's got sand though, my word! no end. He walked right into that village and took us out from under the noses of hundreds of people with nothing but his little peashooter for protection. That, Jezebel, was top hole."

The golden Jezebel sighed. "He is much more beautiful than the men of the land of North Midian," she said.

Lady Barbara looked at her companion for a long minute; then she sighed. "If I ever get you to civilization," she said, "I'm afraid you are going to prove something of a problem." Wherewith she stretched herself upon the ground and was soon asleep, for she, too, had had a strenuous day.

THE sun shining on his upturned face awakened Lafayette Smith. At first he had difficulty in collecting his thoughts. The events of the previous night appeared as a dream, but when he sat up and discovered the figures of the sleeping girls a short distance from him his mind was jerked rudely back into the world of realities. His heart sank. How was he to acquit himself creditably of such a responsibility? Frankly, he did not know.

He had no doubt but that he could find the fissure and lead his charges to the outer world, but how much better off would they be then? He had no idea now, and he realized that he never had, where his camp lay. Then there was the possibility of meeting the lion again in the fissure, and if they did not there was still the question of sustenance. What were they going to use for food, and how were they going to get it?

The thought of food awoke a gnawing hunger within him. He arose and walked to the shore of the lake where he lay on his belly and filled himself with water. When he stood up the girls were sitting up looking at him.

"Good morning," he greeted them. "I was just having breakfast. Will you join me?"

They returned his salutation as they arose and came toward him. Lady Barbara was smiling. "Thank the lord, you have a sense of humor," she said. "I think we are going to need a lot of it before we get out of this."

"I would much prefer ham and eggs," he replied ruefully.

"Now I know you're an American," she said.

"I suppose you are thinking of tea and marmalade," he rejoined.

"I am trying not to think of food at all," she replied.

"Have some lake," he suggested. "You have no idea how satisfying it is if you take enough of it."

After the girls had drunk the three set off again, led by Smith, in search of the opening to the fissure. "I know just where it is," he had assured them the night before, and even now he thought that he would have little difficulty in finding it, but when they approached the base of the cliff at the point where he had expected to find it it was not there.

Along the foot of the beetling escarpment he searched, almost frantically now, but there was no sign of the opening through which he had crawled into the valley of the land of Midian. Finally, crushed, he faced Lady Barbara. "I cannot find it," he admitted, and there was a quality of hopelessness in his voice that touched her.

"Never mind," she said. "It must be somewhere. We shall just have to keep searching until we find it."

"But it's so hard on you young ladies," he said. "It must be a bitter disappointment to you. You don't know how it makes me feel to realize that, with no one to depend on but me, I have failed you so miserably."

"Don't take it that way, please," she begged. "Anyone might have lost his bearings in this hole. These cliffs scarcely change their appearance in miles."

"It's kind of you to say that, but I cannot help but feel guilty. Yet I know the opening cannot be far from here. I came in on the west side of the valley, and that is where we are now. Yes, I am sure I must find it eventually; but there is no need for all of us to search. You and Jezebel sit down here and wait while I look for it."

"I think we should remain together," suggested Jezebel.

"By all means," agreed Lady Barbara.

"As you wish," said Smith. "We will search toward the north as far as it is possible that the opening can lie. If we don't find it we can come back here and search toward the south."

As they moved along the base of the cliff in a northerly direction Smith became more and more convinced that he was about to discover the entrance to the fissure. He thought that he discerned something familiar in the outlook across the valley from this location, but still no opening revealed itself after they had gone a considerable distance.

Presently, as they climbed the rise and gained the summit of one of the numerous low ridges that ran, buttress-like, from the face of the cliff down into the valley, he halted in discouragement.

"What is it?" asked Jezebel.

"That forest," he replied. "There was no forest in sight of the opening."

Before them spread an open forest of small trees that grew almost to the foot of the cliffs and stretched downward to the shore of the lake, forming a landscape of exceptional beauty in its park-like aspect. But Lafayette Smith saw no beauty there—he saw only another proof of his inefficiency and ignorance.

"You came through no forest on your way from the cliffs to the village?" demanded Lady Barbara.

He shook his head. "We've got to walk all the way back now," he said, "and search in the other direction. It is most disheartening. I wonder if you can forgive me."

"Don't be silly," said Lady Barbara. "One might think that you were a Cook's Tour courier who had got lost during a personally conducted tour of the art galleries of Paris and expected to lose his job in consequence."

"I feel worse than that," Smith admitted with a laugh, "and I imagine that's saying a lot."

"Look!" exclaimed Lady Barbara. "There are animals of some sort down there in the forest. Don't you see them?"

"Oh, yes," cried Jezebel, "I see them."

"What are they?" asked Smith. "They look like deer."

"They are goats," said Jezebel. "The North Midians have goats. They roam over this end of the valley."

"They look like something to eat, to me," said Lady Barbara. "Let's go down and get one of them."

"They will probably not let us catch them," suggested Lafayette.

"You've a pistol," the English girl reminded him.

"That's a fact," he agreed. "I can shoot one."

"Maybe," qualified Lady Barbara.

"I'd better go down alone," said Smith. "Three of us together might frighten them."

"You'll have to be mighty careful or you'll frighten them yourself," warned Lady Barbara. "Have you ever stalked game?"

"No," admitted the American, "I never have."

Lady Barbara moistened a finger and held it up. "The wind is right," she announced. "So all you have to do is keep out of sight and make no noise."

"How am I going to keep out of sight?" demanded Smith.

"You'll have to crawl down to them, taking advantage of trees, rocks and bushes—anything that will conceal you. Crawl forward a few feet and then stop, if they show any sign of nervousness, until they appear unconcerned again."

"That will take a long time," said Smith.

"It may be a long time before we find anything else to eat," she reminded him, "and nothing we do find is going to walk up to us and lie down and die at our feet."

"I suppose you are right," assented Smith. "Here goes! Pray for me." He dropped to his hands and knees and crawled slowly forward over the rough ground in the direction of the forest and the goats. After a few yards he turned and whispered: "This is going to be tough on the knees."

"Not half as hard as it's going to be on our stomachs if you don't succeed," replied Lady Barbara.

Smith made a wry face and resumed his crawling while the two girls, lying flat now to conceal themselves from the quarry, watched his progress.

"He's not doing half badly," commented Lady Barbara after several minutes of silent watching.

"How beautiful he is," sighed Jezebel.

"Just at present the most beautiful things in the landscape are those goats," said Lady Barbara. "If he gets close enough for a shot and misses I shall die—and I know he will miss."

"He didn't miss Lamech last night," Jezebel reminded her.

"He must have been aiming at someone else," commented Lady Barbara shortly.

Lafayette Smith crawled on apace. With numerous halts, as advised by Lady Barbara, he drew slowly nearer his unsuspecting quarry. The minutes seemed hours. Pounding constantly upon his brain was the consciousness that he must not fail, though not for the reason that one might naturally assume. The failure to procure food seemed a less dreadful consequence than the contempt of Lady Barbara Collis.

Now, at last, he was quite close to the nearest of the herd. Just a few more yards and he was positive that he could not miss. A low bush, growing just ahead of him, concealed his approach from the eyes of his victim. Lafayette Smith reached the bush and paused behind it. A little farther ahead he discovered another shrub still closer to the goat, a thin nanny with a large udder. She did not look very appetizing, but beneath that unprepossessing exterior Lafayette Smith knew there must be hidden juicy steaks and cutlets. He crawled on. His knees were raw and his neck ached from the unnatural position his unfamiliar method of locomotion had compelled it to assume.

He passed the bush behind which he had paused, failing to see the kid lying hidden upon its opposite side—hidden by a solicitous mamma while she fed. The kid saw Lafayette but it did not move. It would not move until its mother called it, unless actually touched by something, or terrified beyond the limit of its self control.

It watched Lafayette crawling toward the next bush upon his itinerary—the next and last. What it thought is unrecorded, but it is doubtful that it was impressed by Lafayette's beauty.

Now the man had reached the concealment of the last bush, unseen by any other eyes than those of the kid. He drew his pistol cautiously, lest the slightest noise alarm his potential dinner. Raising himself slightly until his eyes were above the level of the bush he took careful aim. The goat was so close that a miss appeared such a remote contingency as to be of negligible consideration.

Lafayette already felt the stirring warmth of pride with which he would toss the carcass of his kill at the feet of Lady Barbara and Jezebel. Then he jerked the trigger.

Nanny leaped straight up into the air, and when she hit the ground again she was already streaking north in company with the balance of the herd. Lafayette Smith had missed again.

He had scarcely time to realize the astounding and humiliating fact as he rose to his feet when something struck him suddenly and heavily from behind—a blow that bent his knees beneath him and brought him heavily to earth in a sitting posture. No, not to earth. He was sitting on something soft that wriggled and squirmed. His startled eyes, glancing down, saw the head of a kid protruding from between his legs—little Capra hircus had been terrified beyond the limit of his self-control.

"Missed!" cried Lady Barbara Collis. "How could he!" Tears of disappointment welled to her eyes.

Eshbaal, hunting his goats at the northern fringe of the forest cocked his ears and listened. That unfamiliar sound! And so near. From far across the valley, toward the village of the South Midians, Eshbaal had heard a similar sound, though faintly from afar, the night before. Four times it had broken the silence of the valley and no more. Eshbaal had heard it and so had his fellows in the village of Elija, the son of Noah.

Lafayette Smith seized the kid before it could wriggle free, and despite its struggles he slung it across his shoulder and started back toward the waiting girls.

"He didn't miss it!" exclaimed Jezebel. "I knew he wouldn't," and she went down to meet him, with Lady Barbara, perplexed, following in her wake.

"Splendid!" cried the English girl as they came closer. "You really did shoot one, didn't you? I was sure you missed."

"I did miss," admitted Lafayette ruefully.

"But how did you get it?"

"If I must admit it," explained the man, "I sat on it. As a matter of fact it got me."

"Well, anyway, you have it," she said.

"And it will be a whole lot better eating than the one I missed," he assured them. "That one was terribly thin and very old."

"How cute it is," said Jezebel.

"Don't," cried Lady Barbara. "We mustn't think of that. Just remember that we are starving."

"Where shall we eat it?" asked Smith.

"Right here," replied the English girl. "There is plenty of deadwood around these trees. Have you matches?"

"Yes. Now you two look the other way while I do my duty. I wish I'd hit the old one now. This is like murdering a baby."

Upon the opposite side of the forest Eshbaal was once again experiencing surprise, for suddenly the goats for which he had been searching came stampeding toward him.

"The strange noise frightened them," soliloquized Eshbaal. "Perhaps it is a miracle. The goats for which I have searched all day have been made to return unto me."

As they dashed past, the trained eye of the shepherd took note of them. There were not many goats in the bunch that had strayed, so he had no difficulty in counting them. A kid was missing. Being a shepherd there was nothing for Eshbaal to do but set forth in search of the missing one. He advanced cautiously, alert because of the noise he had heard.

Eshbaal was a short, stocky man with blue eyes and a wealth of blond hair and beard. His features were regular and handsome in a primitive, savage way. His single garment, fashioned from a goat skin, left his right arm entirely free, nor did it impede his legs, since it fell not to his knees. He carried a club and a rude knife.

Lady Barbara took charge of the culinary activities after Lafayette had butchered the kid and admitted that, beyond hard boiling eggs, his knowledge of cooking was too sketchy to warrant serious mention. "And anyway," he said, "we haven't any eggs."

Following the directions of the English girl, Smith cut a number of chops from the carcass; and these the three grilled on pointed sticks that Lady Barbara had had him cut from a nearby tree.

"How long will it take to cook them?" demanded Smith. "I could eat mine raw. I could eat the whole kid raw, for that matter, in one sitting and have room left for the old nanny I missed."

"We'll eat only enough to keep us going," said Lady Barbara; "then we'll wrap the rest in the skin and take it with us. If we're careful, this should keep us alive for three or four days."

"Of course you're right," admitted Lafayette. "You always are."

"You can have a big meal this time," she told him, "because you've been longer without food than we."

"You have had nothing for a long time, Barbara," said Jezebel. "I am the one who needs the least."

"We all need it now," said Lafayette. "Let's have a good meal this time, get back our strength, and then ration the balance so that it will last several days. Maybe I will sit on something else before this is gone."

They all laughed; and presently the chops were done, and the three fell to upon them. "Like starving Armenians," was the simile Smith suggested.

Occupied with the delightful business of appeasing wolfish hunger, none of them saw Eshbaal halt behind a tree and observe them. Jezebel he recognized for what she was, and a sudden fire lighted his blue eyes. The others were enigmas to him—especially their strange apparel.

Of one thing Eshbaal was convinced. He had found his lost kid and there was wrath in his heart. For just a moment he watched the three; then he glided back into the forest until he was out of their sight, when he broke into a run.

The meal finished, Smith wrapped the remainder of the carcass in the skin of the kid; and the three again took up their search for the fissure.

An hour passed and then another. Still their efforts were not crowned with success. They saw no opening in the stern, forbidding face of the escarpment, nor did they see the slinking figures creeping steadily nearer and nearer—a score of stocky, yellow haired men led by Eshbaal, the Shepherd.

"We must have passed it," said Smith at last. "It just cannot be this far south," yet only a hundred yards farther on lay the illusive opening into the great fissure.

"We shall have to hunt for some other way out of the valley then," said Lady Barbara. "There is a place farther south that Jezebel and I used to see from the mouth of our cave where the cliff looked as though it might be scaled."

"Let's have a try at it then," said Smith. "Say, look there!" he pointed toward the north.

"What is it? Where?" demanded Jezebel.

"I thought I saw a man's head behind that rock," said Smith. "Yes, there he is again. Lord, look at 'em. They're all around."

Eshbaal and his fellows, realizing that they were discovered, came into the open, advancing slowly toward the three.

"The men of North Midian!" exclaimed Jezebel. "Are they not beautiful!"

"What shall we do?" demanded Lady Barbara. "We must not let them take us."

"We'll see what they want," said Smith. "They may not be unfriendly. Anyway, we couldn't escape them by running. They would overtake us in no time. Get behind me, and if they show any signs of attacking I'll shoot a few of them."

"Perhaps you had better go out and sit on them," suggested Lady Barbara, wearily.

"I am sorry," said Smith, "that my marksmanship is so poor; but, unfortunately perhaps, it never occurred to my parents to train me in the gentle art of murder. I realize now that they erred and that my education has been sadly neglected. I am only a school teacher, and in teaching the young intellect to shoot I have failed to learn to do so myself."

"I didn't intend to be nasty," said Lady Barbara, who detected in the irony of the man's reply a suggestion of wounded pride. "Please forgive me."

The North Midians were advancing cautiously, halting occasionally for brief, whispered conferences. Presently one of them spoke, addressing the three. "Who are you?" he demanded. "What do you in the land of Midian?"

"Can you understand him?" asked Smith, over his shoulder.

"Yes," replied both girls simultaneously.

"He speaks the same language as Jezebel's people," explained Lady Barbara. "He wants to know who we are and what we are doing here."

"You talk to him, Lady Barbara," said Smith.

The English girl stepped forward. "We are strangers in Midian," she said. "We are lost. All we wish is to get out of your country."

"There is no way out of Midian," replied the man. "You have killed a kid belonging to Eshbaal. For that you must be punished. You must come with us."

"We were starving," explained Lady Barbara. "If we could pay for the kid we would gladly do so. Let us go in peace."

The Midians held another whispered conference, after which their spokesman addressed the three again. "You must

come with us," he said, "the women at least. If the man will
go away we will not harm you, we do not want him; we want
the women."

"What did he say?" demanded Smith, and when Lady
Barbara had interpreted he shook his head. "Tell them no,"
he directed. "Also tell them that if they molest us I shall
have to kill them."

When the girl delivered this ultimatum to the Midians
they laughed. "What can one man do against twenty?" demanded their leader, then he advanced followed by his retainers. They were brandishing their clubs now, and some
of them raised their voices in a savage war cry.

"You will have to shoot," said Lady Barbara. "There
are at least twenty. You cannot miss them all."

"You flatter me," said Smith, as he raised his .32 and
levelled it at the advancing Midians.

"Go back!" shouted Jezebel, "or you will be killed," but
the attackers only came forward the faster.

Then Smith fired. At the sharp crack of the pistol the Midians halted, surprised; but no one fell. Instead, the leader
hurled his club, quickly and accurately, just as Smith was
about to fire again. He dodged; but the missile struck his
pistol hand a glancing blow, sending the weapon flying—
then the North Midians were upon them.

16
Trailing

TARZAN of the Apes had made a kill. It was only a small
rodent, but it would satisfy his hunger until the morrow.
Darkness had fallen shortly after he had discovered
the spoor of the missing American, and he was forced to
abandon the search until daylight came again. The first
sign of the spoor had been very faint—just the slightest
imprint of one corner of a boot heel, but that had been
enough for the ape-man. Clinging to a bush nearby was
the scarcely perceptible scent spoor of a white man, which
Tarzan might have followed even after dark; but it would
have been a slow and arduous method of tracking which the
ape-man did not consider the circumstances warranted. Therefore he made his kill, ate, and curled up in a patch of tall
grass to sleep.

Wild beasts may not sleep with one eye open, but often it seems that they sleep with both ears cocked. The ordinary night sounds go unnoticed, while a lesser sound, portending danger or suggesting the unfamiliar, may awaken them on the instant. It was a sound falling into the latter category that awoke Tarzan shortly after mid-night.

He raised his head and listened, then he lowered it and placed an ear against the ground. "Horses and men," he soliloquized as he rose to his feet. Standing erect, his great chest rising and falling to his breathing, he listened intently. His sensitive nostrils, seeking to confirm the testimony of his ears, dilated to receive and classify the messages that Usha, the wind, bore to them. They caught the scent of Tongani, the baboon, so strong as almost to negate the others. Tenuous, from a great distance came the scent spoor of Sabor, the lioness, and the sweet, heavy stench of Tantor, the elephant. One by one the ape-man read these invisible messages brought by Usha, the wind; but only those interested him that spoke of horses and men.

Why did horses and men move through the night? Who and what were the men? He scarcely needed to ask himself that latter question, and only the first one interested him.

It is the business of beasts and of men to know what their enemies do. Tarzan stretched his great muscles lazily and moved down the slope of the foot hills in the direction from which had come the evidence that his enemies were afoot.

The "Gunner" stumbled along in the darkness. Never in his twenty odd years of life had he even approximated such utter physical exhaustion. Each step he was sure must be his last. He had long since become too tired even to curse his captors as he plodded on, now almost numb to any sensation, his mind a chaos of dull misery.

But even endless journeys must ultimately end; and at last the cavalcade turned into the gateway of the village of Dominic Capietro, the raider; and the "Gunner" was escorted to a hut where he slumped to the hard earth floor after his bonds had been removed, positive that he would never rise again.

He was asleep when they brought him food; but aroused himself long enough to eat, for his hunger was fully as great as his fatigue. Then he stretched out again and slept, while a tired and disgusted *shifta* nodded drowsily on guard outside the entrance to the hut.

Tarzan had come down to the cliff above the village as the raiders were filing through the gateway. A full moon cast her revealing beams upon the scene, lighting the figures of horses and men. The ape-man recognized Capietro and Stabutch, he saw Ogonyo, the headman of the safari of the young American geologist; and he saw the "Gunner" stumbling painfully along in bonds.

The ape-man was an interested spectator of all that transpired in the village below. He noted particularly the location of the hut into which the white prisoner had been thrust. He watched the preparation of food, and he noted the great quantities of liquor that Capietro and Stabutch consumed while waiting for the midnight supper being prepared by slaves. The more they drank the better pleased was Tarzan.

As he watched them, he wondered how supposedly rational creatures could consider the appellation *beast* a term of reproach and *man* one of glorification. The beasts, as he knew, held an opposite conception of the relative virtues of these two orders, although they were ignorant of most of man's asininities and degredations, their minds being far too pure to understand them.

Waiting with the patience of the unspoiled primitive nervous system, Tarzan watched from the cliff top until the village below seemed to have settled down for the night. He saw the sentries in the banquette inside the palisade, but he did not see the guard squatting in the shadow of the hut where the "Gunner" lay in heavy slumber.

Satisfied, the ape-man rose and moved along the cliff until he was beyond the village; and there, where the escarpment was less precipitous, he made his way to its base. Noiselessly and cautiously he crept to the palisade at a point that was hidden from the view of the sentries. The moon shone full upon him, but the opposite side of the palisade he knew must be in dense shadow. There he listened for a moment to assure himself that his approach had aroused no suspicion. He wished that he might see the sentries at the gate, for when he topped the palisade he would be in full view for an instant. When last he had seen them they had been squatting upon the banquette, their backs to the palisade, and apparently upon the verge of sleep. Would they remain thus?

Here, however, was a chance he must take, and so he gave the matter little thought and few regrets. What was, was; and if he could not change it he must ignore it; and so, leaping lightly upward, he seized the top of the palisade and drew himself up and over. Only a glance he threw in the direction of the sentries as he topped the barrier, a glance that told him they had not moved since he had last looked.

In the shadow of the palisade he paused to look about.

There was nothing to cause him apprehension; and so he moved quickly, keeping ever in the shadows where he could, toward the hut where he expected to find the young white man. It was hidden from his view by another hut which he approached and had circled when he saw the figure of the guard sitting by the doorway, his rifle across his knees.

This was a contingency the ape-man had not anticipated, and it caused a change in his immediate plans. He drew back out of sight behind the hut he had been circling, lay down flat upon the ground, and then crawled forward again until his head protruded beyond the hut far enough to permit one eye to watch the unconscious guard. Here he lay waiting —a human beast watching its quarry.

For a long time he lay thus trusting to his knowledge of men that the moment for which he waited would arrive. Presently the chin of the *shifta* dropped to his chest; but immediately it snapped back again, erect. Then the fellow changed his position. He sat upon the ground, his legs stretched before him, and leaned his back against the hut. His rifle was still across his knees. It was a dangerous position for a man who would remain awake.

After a while his head rolled to one side. Tarzan watched him closely, as a cat watches a mouse. The head remained in the position to which it had rolled, the chin dropped, and the mouth gaped; the tempo of the breathing changed, denoting sleep.

Tarzan rose silently to his feet and as silently crept across the intervening space to the side of the unconscious man. There must be no outcry, no scuffle.

As strikes Histah, the snake, so struck Tarzan of the Apes. There was only the sound of parting vertebrae as the neck broke in the grip of those thews of steel.

The rifle Tarzan laid upon the ground; then he raised the corpse in his arms and bore it into the darkness of the hut's interior. Here he groped for a moment until he had located the body of the sleeping white, and knelt beside him. Cautiously he shook him, one hand ready to muffle any outcry the man might make, but the "Gunner" did not awaken. Tarzan shook him again more roughly and yet without results, then he slapped him heavily across the face.

The "Gunner" stirred. "Geeze," he muttered "can't you let a guy sleep? Didn't I tell you you'd get your ransom?"

Tarzan permitted a faint smile to touch his lips. "Wake up," he whispered. "Make no noise. I have come to take you away?"

"Who are you?"

"Tarzan of the Apes."

"Geeze!" The "Gunner" sat up.

"Make no noise," cautioned the ape-man once more.

"Sure," whispered Danny as he raised himself stiffly to his feet.

"Follow me," said Tarzan, "and no matter what happens stay very close to me. I am going to toss you to the top of the palisade. Try not to make any noise as you climb over, and be careful when you drop to the ground on the other side to alight with your knees flexed—it is a long drop."

"You say you're going to toss me to the top of the palisade, guy?"

"Yes."

"Do you know what I weigh?"

"No, and I don't care. Keep still and follow me. Don't stumble over this body." Tarzan paused in the entrance and looked about; then he passed out, with the "Gunner" at his heels, and crossed quickly to the palisade. Even if they discovered him now he still had time to accomplish what he had set out to do, before they could interfere, unless the sentries, firing on them, chanced to make a hit; but on that score he felt little apprehension.

As they came to the palisade the "Gunner" glanced up, and his skepticism increased—a fat chance any guy would have to toss his one hundred and eighty pounds to the top of that!

The ape-man seized him by the collar and the seat of his breeches. "Catch the top!" he whispered. Then he swung the "Gunner" backward as though he had been a fifty pound sack of meal, surged forward and upward; and in the same second Danny Patrick's outstretched fingers clutched the top of the palisade.

"Geeze," he muttered, "if I'd missed I'd of gone clean over."

Catlike, the ape-man ran up the barrier and dropped to the ground on the outside almost at the instant that the "Gunner" alighted, and without a word started toward the cliff, where once again he had to assist the other to reach the summit.

Danny "Gunner" Patrick was speechless, partly from shortness of breath following his exertions, but more, by far, from astonishment. Here was a guy! In all his experience of brawny men, and it had been considerable, he had never met, nor expected to meet, such a one as this.

"I have located the spoor of your friend," said Tarzan.

"The what?" asked the "Gunner." "Is he dead?"

"His tracks," explained the ape-man, who was still leading the way up the slope toward the higher mountains.

"I gotcha," said the "Gunner." "But you ain't seen him?"

"No, it was too dark to follow him when I found them. We will do so in the morning."

"If I can walk," said the "Gunner."

"What's the matter with you?" demanded Tarzan. "Injured?"

"I ain't got no legs from the knees down," replied Danny. "I walked my lousy dogs off yesterday."

"I'll carry you," suggested Tarzan.

"Nix!" exclaimed Danny. "I can crawl, but I'll be damned if I'll let any guy carry me."

"It will be a hard trip if you're exhausted now," the ape-man told him. "I could leave you somewhere near here and pick you up after I find your friend."

"Nothing doing. I'm going to look for old Smithy if I wear 'em off to the hips."

"I could probably travel faster alone," suggested Tarzan.

"Go ahead," agreed the "Gunner" cheerfully. "I'll tail along behind you."

"And get lost."

"Let me come along, mister. I'm worried about that crazy nut."

"All right. It won't make much difference anyway. He may be a little hungrier when we find him, but he can't starve to death in a couple of days."

"Say," exclaimed Danny, "how come you knew them guys had taken me for a ride?"

"I thought you walked."

"Well, what's the difference? How did you know I was in that lousy burgh of theirs?"

"I was on the cliff when they brought you in. I waited until they were asleep. I am not ready to deal with them yet."

"What you goin' to do to them?"

Tarzan shrugged but made no reply; and for a long time they walked on in silence through the night, the ape-man timing his speed to the physical condition of his companion, whose nerve he was constrained to admire, though his endurance and knowledge he viewed with contempt.

Far up in the hills, where he had bedded down earlier in the night, Tarzan halted and told the "Gunner" to get what rest he could before dawn.

"Geeze, them's the pleasantest words I've heard for years," sighed Danny, as he lay down in the high grass. "You may think you've seen a guy pound his ear, but you ain't seen nothin'. Watch me," and he was asleep almost before the words had left his mouth.

Tarzan lay down at a little distance; and he, too, was soon asleep, but at the first suggestion of dawn he was up. He saw that his companion still slept, and then he slipped silently away toward a water hole he had discovered the previous day in a rocky ravine near the cliff where he had met the tribe of Zugash, the tongani.

He kept well down the slope of the foot hills, for with the coming of dawn the wind had changed, and he wished to come up wind toward the water hole. He moved as silently as the disappearing shadows of the retreating night, his nostrils quivering to catch each vagrant scent borne upon the bosom of the early morning breeze.

There was deep mud at one edge of the water hole, where the earth had been trampled by the feet of drinking beasts; and near here he found that which he sought, the sticky sweetness of whose scent had been carried to his nostrils by Usha.

Low trees grew in the bottom of the ravine and much underbrush, for here the earth held its moisture longer than on the ridges that were more exposed to Kudu's merciless rays. It was a lovely sylvan glade, nor did its beauties escape the appreciative eyes of the ape-man, though the lure of the glade lay not this morning in its aesthetic charms, but rather in the fact that it harbored Horta, the boar.

Silently to the edge of the underbrush came the ape-man as Horta came down to the pool to drink. Upon the opposite side stood Tarzan, his bow and arrows ready in his hands; but the high brush precluded a fair shot, and so the hunter stepped out in full view of the boar. So quickly he moved that his arrow sped as Horta wheeled to run, catching the boar in the side behind the left shoulder—a vital spot.

With a snort of rage Horta turned back and charged. Straight through the pool he came for Tarzan; and as he came three more arrows shot with unbelievable accuracy and celerity, buried themselves deep in the breast of the great beast. Bloody foam flecked his jowls and his flashing tusks, fires of hate shot from his wicked little eyes as he sought to reach the author of his hurts and wreak his vengeance before he died.

Discarding his bow the ape-man met the mad charge of Horta with his spear, for there was no chance to elude the swift rush of that great body, hemmed, as he was, by the thick growth of underbrush. His feet braced, he dropped the point of his weapon the instant Horta was within its range, that they might have no opportunity to dodge it or strike it aside with his tusks. Straight through the chest it drove, deep into the savage heart, yet the beast still strove to reach the man-thing that held it off with a strength almost equal to its own.

But already as good as dead on his feet was Horta, the boar. His brief, savage struggles ended; and he dropped in the shallow water at the edge of the pool. Then the ape-man placed a foot upon his vanquished foe and screamed forth the hideous challenge of his tribe.

The "Gunner" sat suddenly erect, awakened out of a sound sleep. "Geeze!" he exclaimed. "What was that?" Receiving no answer he looked about. "Wouldn't that eat you?" he murmured. "He's went. I wonder has he run out on me? He didn't seem like that kind of a guy. But you can't never tell—I've had pals to double-cross me before this."

In the village of Capietro a dozing sentry snapped suddenly alert, while his companion half rose to his feet. "What was that?" demanded one.

"A hairy one has made a kill," said the other.

Sheeta, the panther, down wind, stalking both the man and the boar, stopped in his tracks; then he turned aside and loped away in easy, graceful bounds; but he had not gone far before he stopped again and raised his nose up-wind. Again the scent of man; but this time a different man, nor was there any sign of the feared thunder stick that usually accompanied the scent spoor of the tarmangani. Belly low, Sheeta moved slowly up the slope toward Danny "Gunner" Patrick.

"What to do?" mused the "Gunner." "Geeze, I'm hungry! Should I wait for him or should I go on? On, where? I sure got myself in a jam all right. Where do I go? How do I eat? Hell!"

He arose and moved about, feeling out his muscles. They were lame and sore, but he realized that he was much rested. Then he scanned the distances for a sight of Tarzan and, instead, saw Sheeta, the panther, a few hundred yards away.

Danny Patrick, hoodlum, racketeer, gangster, gunman, killer, trembled in terror. Cold sweat burst from every pore, and he could feel the hair rise on his scalp. He felt a mad impulse to run; but, fortunately for Danny, his legs refused to move. He was literally, in the vernacular to which he was accustomed, scared stiff. The "Gunner," without a gun, was a very different man.

The panther had stopped and was surveying him. Caution and an hereditary fear of man gave the great cat pause, but he was angry because he had been frightened from his prey after hunting futilely all night, and he was very, very hungry. He growled, his face wrinkled in a hideous snarl; and Danny felt his knees giving beneath him.

Then, beyond the panther, he saw the high grass moving to the approach of another animal, which the "Gunner" promptly assumed was the beast's mate. There was just a single, narrow strip of this high grass; and when the animal had crossed it he, too, would see Danny, who was confident that this would spell the end. One of them might hesitate to attack a man—he didn't know—but he was sure that two would not.

He dropped to his knees and did something that he had not done for many years—he prayed. And then the grasses parted; and Tarzan of the Apes stepped into view, the carcass of a boar upon one broad shoulder. Instantly the ape-man took in the scene that his nostrils had already prepared him for.

Dropping the carcass of Horta he voiced a sudden, ferocious growl that startled Sheeta no more than it did Danny Patrick. The cat wheeled, instantly on the defensive. Tarzan charged, growls rumbling from his throat; and Sheeta did exactly what he had assumed he would do—turned and fled. Then Tarzan picked up the carcass of Horta and came up the slope to Danny, who knelt open-mouthed and petrified.

"What are you kneeling for?" asked the ape-man.

"I was just tying my boot lace," explained the "Gunner."

"Here is breakfast," said Tarzan, dropping the boar to the ground. "Help yourself."

"That sure looks good to me," said Danny. "I could eat it raw."

"That is fine," said Tarzan; and, squatting, he cut two strips from one of the hams. "Here," he said, offering one to the "Gunner."

"Quit your kidding," remonstrated the latter.

Tarzan eyed him questioningly, at the same time tearing off a mouthful of the meat with his strong teeth. "Horta is a little bit tough," he remarked, "but he is the best I could do without losing a great deal of time. Why don't you eat? I thought you were hungry."

"I got to cook mine," said the "Gunner."

"But you said you could eat it raw," the ape-man reminded him.

"That's just a saying," explained the "Gunner." "I might at that, but I ain't never tried it."

"Make a fire, then; and cook yours," said Tarzan.

"Say," remarked Danny a few minutes later as he squatted before his fire grilling his meat, "did you hear that noise a little while ago?"

"What was it like?"

"I never heard nothing like it but once before—say I just took a tumble to myself! That was you killin' the pig. I heard you yell like that the night you killed the lion in our camp."

"We will be going as soon as you finish your meat," said Tarzan. He was hacking off several pieces, half of which he handed to the "Gunner" while he dropped the balance into his quiver. "Take these," he said. "You may get hungry before we can make another kill." Then he scraped a hole in the loose earth and buried the remainder of the carcass.

"What you doin' that for?" asked the "Gunner." "Afraid it will smell?"

"We may come back this way," explained Tarzan. "If we do Horta will be less tough."

The "Gunner" made no comment; but he assured himself, mentally, that he "wasn't no dog," to bury his meat and then dig it up again after it had rotted. The idea almost made him sick.

Tarzan quickly picked up the trail of Lafayette Smith and followed it easily, though the "Gunner" saw nothing to indicate that human foot had ever trod these hills.

"I don't see nothing," he said.

"I have noticed that," returned Tarzan.

"That," thought Danny Patrick, "sounds like a dirty crack;" but he said nothing.

"A lion picked up his trail here," said the ape-man.

"You ain't spoofin' me are you?" demanded Danny. "There ain't no sign of nothin' on this ground."

"Nothing that you can see perhaps," replied Tarzan; "but then, though you may not know it, you so-called civilized men are almost blind and quite stone deaf."

Soon they came to the fissure, and here Tarzan saw that the man and the lion had both gone in, the lion following the man, and that only the lion had come out.

"That looks tough for old Smithy, doesn't it?" said the "Gunner" when Tarzan had explained the story of the spoor.

"It may," replied the ape-man. "I'll go on in and look for him. You can wait here or follow. You can't get lost if you stay inside this crack."

"Go ahead," said Danny. "I'll follow."

The fissure was much longer than Tarzan had imagined; but some distance from the entrance he discovered that the lion had not attacked Smith, for he could see where Numa had turned about and that the man had continued on. Some recent scars on the sides of the fissure told him the rest of the story quite accurately.

"It's fortunate he didn't hit Numa," soliloquized the ape-man.

At the end of the fissure Tarzan had some difficulty in wriggling through the aperture that opened into the valley of the Land of Midian; but once through he picked up the trail of Smith again and followed it down toward the lake, while Danny, far behind him, stumbled wearily along the rough floor of the fissure.

Tarzan walked rapidly for the spoor was plain. When he came to the shore of Chinnereth he discovered Smith's tracks intermingled with those of a woman wearing well worn European boots and another shod with sandals.

When he had first entered the valley he had seen the village of the South Midians in the distance and now he drew the false conclusion that Smith had discovered a friendly people and other whites and that he was in no danger.

His curiosity piqued by the mystery of this hidden valley, the ape-man determined to visit the village before continuing on Smith's trail. Time had never entered greatly into his calculations, trained, as he had been, by savage apes to whom time meant less than nothing; but to investigate and to know every detail of his wilderness world was as much a part of the man as is his religion to a priest.

And so he continued rapidly on toward the distant village while Danny Patrick still crawled and stumbled slowly along the rocky floor of the fissure.

Danny was tired. Momentarily he expected to meet Tarzan returning either with Smith or with word of his death; so he stopped often to rest, with the result that when he had reached the end of the fissure and crawled through to behold the mystifying sight of a strange valley spread before him, Tarzan was already out of sight.

"Geeze!" exclaimed the "Gunner." "Who would have thought that hole led into a place like this? I wonder which way that Tarzan guy went?"

This thought occupied the "Gunner" for a few minutes. He examined the ground as he had seen Tarzan do, mistook a few spots where some little rodent had scratched up the earth, or taken a dust bath, for the footprints of a man, and set forth in the wrong direction.

17
She Is Mine!

THE stocky, blond warriors of Elija, the son of Noah, quickly surrounded and seized Lafayette Smith and his two companions. Elija picked up Smith's pistol and examined it with interest; then he dropped it into a goat skin pouch that was suspended from the girdle that held his single garment about him.

"This one," said Eshbaal, pointing to Jezebel, "is mine."

"Why?" asked Elija, the son of Noah.

"I saw her first," replied Eshbaal.

"Did you hear what he said?" demanded Jezebel of Lady Barbara.

The English girl nodded apathetically. Her brain was numb with disappointment and the horror of the situation, for in some respects their fate might be worse with these men than with those of South Midian. These were lusty, primitive warriors, not half-witted creatures whose natural passions had been weakened by generations of hereditary disease of nerve and brain.

"He wants me," said Jezebel. "Is he not beautiful?"

Lady Barbara turned upon the girl almost angrily, and then suddenly she remembered that Jezebel was little more than a child in experience and that she had no conception of the fate that might await her at the hands of the North Midians.

In their narrow religious fanaticism the South Midians denied even the most obvious phases of procreation. The subject was absolutely taboo and so hideous had ages of training and custom made it appear to them that mothers often killed their first born rather than exhibit these badges of sin.

"Poor little Jezebel," said Lady Barbara.

"What do you mean, Barbara?" asked the girl. "Are you not happy that the beautiful man wants me?"

"Listen, Jezebel," said Lady Barbara. "You know I am your friend, do you not?"

"My only friend," replied the girl. "The only person I ever loved."

"Then believe me when I say that you must kill yourself,

131

as I shall kill myself, if we are unable to escape from these creatures."

"Why?" demanded Jezebel. "Are they not more beautiful than the South Midians?"

"Forget their fatal beauty," replied Lady Barbara, "but never forget what I have told you."

"Now I am afraid," said Jezebel.

"Thank God for that," exclaimed the English girl.

The North Midians marched loosely and without discipline. They seemed a garrulous race, and their arguments and speeches were numerous and lengthy. Sometimes so intent did they become on some point at argument, or in listening to a long winded oration by one of their fellows, that they quite forgot their prisoners, who were sometimes amongst them, sometimes in advance and once behind them.

It was what Lady Barbara had been awaiting and what she had to some extent engineered.

"Now!" she whispered. "They are not looking." She halted and turned back. They were among the trees of the forest where some concealment might be found.

Smith and Jezebel had stopped at Lady Barbara's direction; and for an instant the three paused, breathless, watching the retreating figures of their captors.

"Now run!" whispered Lady Barbara. "We'll scatter and meet again at the foot of the cliff."

Just what prompted Lady Barbara to suggest that they separate Lafayette Smith did not understand. To him it seemed a foolish and unnecessary decision; but as he had a great deal more confidence in Lady Barbara's judgment in practical matters than in his own he did not voice his doubts, though he accepted her plan with certain mental reservations, which guided his subsequent acts.

The English girl ran in a southeasterly direction, while Jezebel, obeying the commands of her friend, scurried off toward the southwest. Smith, glancing to the rear, discovered no indication that their captors had, as yet, missed them. For a moment he was hesitant as to what course to pursue. The conviction still gripped him that he was the natural protector of both girls, notwithstanding the unfortunate circumstances that had nullified his efforts to function successfully in that rôle; but he saw that it was going to be still more difficult to protect them both now that they had elected to run in different directions.

However, his decision was soon made, difficult though it was. Jezebel was in her own world; contemplation of her capture by the North Midains had, so far from alarming her, appeared rather to have met with enthusiastic anticipation on her part; she could not be worse off with them than the only other people she knew.

Lady Barbara, on the other hand, was of another world —his own world—and he had heard her say that death would be preferable to captivity among these semi-savages. His duty, therefore, was to follow and protect Lady Barbara; and so he let Jezebel take her way unprotected back toward the cliff, while he pursued the English girl in the direction of Chinnereth.

Lady Barbara Collis ran until she was out of breath. For several minutes she had distinctly heard the sounds of pursuit behind her—the heavy footfalls of a man. Frantic from hopelessness, she drew her pocket knife from a pocket of her jacket and opened the blade as she ran.

She wondered if she could destroy herself with this inadequate weapon. She was positive that she could not inflict either fatal or disabling injuries upon her pursuer with it. Yet the thought of self-destruction revolted her. The realization was upon her that she had about reached the limit of her endurance, and that the fatal decision could not be long averted, when her heritage of English fighting blood decided the question for her. There was but one thing it would permit—she must stand and defend herself. She stopped then, suddenly, and wheeled about, the little knife clutched in her right hand—a tigress at bay.

When she saw Lafayette Smith running toward her she collapsed suddenly and sank to the ground, where she sat with her back against the bole of a tree. Lafayette Smith, breathing hard, came and sat down beside her. Neither had any breath for words.

Lady Barbara was the first to regain her power of speech. "I thought I said we would scatter," she reminded him.

"I couldn't leave you alone," he replied.

"But how about Jezebel? You left her alone."

"I couldn't go with both of you," he reminded her, "and you know Jezebel is really at home here. It means much more to you to escape than it means to her."

She shook her head. "Capture means the same thing to either of us," she said, "But of the two I am better able to take care of myself than Jezebel—she does not understand the nature of her danger."

"Nevertheless," he insisted, "you are the more important. You have relatives and friends who care for you. Poor little Jezebel has only one friend, and that is you, unless I may consider myself a friend, as I should like to do."

"I imagine we three have the unique distinction of being the closest corporation of friends in the world," she replied, with a wan smile, "and there doesn't seem to be anyone who wants to buy in."

"The Friendless Friends Corporation, Limited," he suggested.

"Perhaps we'd best hold a directors' meeting and decide what we should do next to conserve the interests of the stockholders."

"I move we move," he said.

"Seconded." The girl rose to her feet.

"You're terribly tired, aren't you?" he asked. "But I suppose the only thing we can do is to get as far away from the territory of the North Midians as possible. It's almost certain they will try to capture us again as soon as they discover we are missing."

"If we can only find a place to hide until night," she said. "Then we can go back to the cliffs under the cover of darkness and search for Jezebel and the place that she and I thought might be scaled."

"This forest is so open that it doesn't afford any good hiding places, but at least we can look."

"Perhaps we shall find a place near the lake," said Lady Barbara. "We ought to come to it soon."

They walked on for a considerable distance without talking, each occupied with his own thoughts; and as no sign of pursuit developed their spirits rose.

"Do you know," he said presently, "that I can't help but feel that we're going to get out of this all right in the end?"

"But what a terrible experience! It doesn't seem possible that such things could have happened to me. I can't forget Jobab." It was the first time mention had been made of the tragedy at the southern village.

"You must not give that a thought," he said. "You did the only thing possible under the circumstances. If you had not done what you did both you and Jezebel would have been recaptured, and you know what that would have meant."

"But I've killed a human being," she said. There was an awed tone in her voice.

"I killed one, too," he reminded her, "but I don't regret it in the least, notwithstanding the fact that I never killed anyone before. If I were not such a terrible marksman I should have killed another today, perhaps several. My regret is that I didn't."

"It's a strange world," he continued after a moment's reflective silence. "Now, I always considered myself rather well educated and fitted to meet the emergencies of life; and I suppose I should be, in the quiet environment of a college town; but what an awful failure I have proved to be when jolted out of my narrow little rut. I used to feel sorry for the boys who wasted their time in shooting galleries and in rabbit hunting. Men who boasted of their marksmanship merited only my contempt, yet within the last twenty-four hours I would have traded all my education along other lines for the ability to shoot straight."

"One should know something of many things to be truly educated," said the girl, "but I'm afraid you exaggerate the value of marksmanship in determining one's cultural status."

"Well, there's cooking," he admitted. "A person who cannot cook is not well educated. I had hoped one day to be an authority on geology; but with all I know of the subject, which of course isn't so much at that, I would probably starve to death in a land overrunning with game, because I can neither shoot nor cook."

Lady Barbara laughed. "Don't develop an inferiority complex at this stage," she cried. "We need every ounce of self-assurance that we can muster. I think you are top hole. You may not be much of a marksman—that I'll have to admit, and perhaps you cannot cook; but you've one thing that covers a multitude of shortcomings in a man—you are brave."

It was Lafayette Smith's turn to laugh. "That's mighty nice of you," he said. "I'd rather you thought that of me than anything else in the world; and I'd rather you thought it than any one else, because it would mean so much to you now; but it isn't true. I was scared stiff in that village last night and when those fellows came at us today, and that's the truth."

"Which only the more definitely justifies my statement," she replied.

"I don't understand."

"Cultured and intelligent people are more ready to realize and appreciate the dangers of a critical situation than are ignorant, unimaginative types. So, when such a person stands his ground determinedly in the face of danger, or voluntarily walks into a dangerous situation from a sense of duty, as you did last night, it evidences a much higher quality of courage than that possessed by the ignorant, physical lout who hasn't brains enough to visualize the contingencies that may result from his action."

"Be careful," he warned her, "or you'll make me believe all that—then I'll be unbearably egotistical. But please don't try to convince me that my inability to cook is a hallmark of virtue."

"I—listen! What was that?" she halted and turned her eyes toward the rear.

"They have found us," said Lafayette Smith. "Go on— go as fast as you can! I'll try to delay them."

"No," she replied, "there is no use. I'll remain with you, whatever happens."

"Please!" he begged. "Why should I face them if you won't take advantage of it."

"It wouldn't do any good," she said. "They'd only get me later, and your sacrifice would be useless. We might as well give ourselves up in the hope that we can persuade them to free us later, or, perhaps, find the opportunity to escape after dark."

"You had better run," he said, "because I am going to fight. I am not going to let them take you without raising a hand in your defense. If you get away now, perhaps I can get away later. We can meet at the foot of the cliffs—but don't wait for me if you can find a way out. Now, do as I tell you!" His tone was peremptory—commanding.

Obediently she continued on toward Chinnereth, but presently she stopped and turned. Three men were approaching Smith. Suddenly one of the three swung his club and hurled it at the American, at the same instant dashing forward with his fellows.

The club fell short of its mark, dropping at Smith's feet. She saw him stoop and seize it, and then she saw another detachment of the Midians coming through the woods in the wake of the first three.

Smith's antagonists were upon him as he straightened up with the club in his hand, and he swung it heavily upon the skull of the man who had hurled it at him and who had rushed forward in advance of his fellows with hands outstretched to seize the stranger.

Like a felled ox the man dropped; and then Lady Barbara saw Smith carry the unequal battle to the enemy as, swinging the club above his head, he rushed forward to meet them.

So unexpected was his attack that the men halted and turned to elude him, but one was too slow and the girl heard the fellow's skull crush beneath the heavy blow of the bludgeon.

Then the reinforcements, advancing at a run, surrounded and overwhelmed their lone antagonist, and Smith went down beneath them.

Lady Barbara could not bring herself to desert the man who had thus bravely, however hopelessly, sought to defend her; and when the North Midians had disarmed and secured Smith they saw her standing where she had stood during the brief engagement.

"I couldn't run away and leave you," she explained to Smith, as the two were being escorted toward the village of the North Midians. "I thought they were going to kill you, and I couldn't help you— Oh, it was awful. I couldn't leave you then, could I?"

He looked at her for a moment. "No," he answered. "*You* couldn't."

18
A Guy and A Skirt

DANNY "Gunner" Patrick was tired and disgusted. He had walked for several hours imagining that he was following a spoor, but he had seen nothing of his erstwhile companion. He was thirsty, and so cast frequent glances in the direction of the lake.

"T'ell!" he muttered. "I ain't goin' to tail that guy no longer till I get me a drink. My mouth feels like I'd been eating cotton for a week."

He turned away from the cliffs and started down in the direction of the lake, the inviting waters of which sparkled alluringly in the afternoon sun; but the beauties of the scene were wasted upon the "Gunner," who saw only a means of quenching his thirst.

The way led through a field of scattered boulders fallen from the towering rim above. He had to pick his way carefully among the smaller ones, and his eyes were almost constantly upon the ground. Occasionally he was compelled to skirt some of the larger masses, many of which towered above his head obstructing his view ahead.

He was damning Africa in general and this section of it in particular as he rounded the corner of an unusually large fragment of rock, when suddenly he stopped and his eyes went wide.

"Geeze!" he exclaimed aloud. "A broad!"

Before him, and coming in his direction, was a golden

haired girl attired in a single, scant piece of rough material. She saw him simultaneously and halted.

"Oh," exclaimed Jezebel with a happy smile. "Who art thou?" but as she spoke in the language of the land of Midian the "Gunner" failed to understand her.

"Geeze," he said. "I knew I must of come to Africa for something, and I guess you're it. Say kid, you're about all right. I'll tell the world you *are* all right."

"Thank you," said Jezebel in English. "I am so glad that you like me."

"Geeze," said Danny. "You talk United States, don't you? Where you from?"

"Midian," replied Jezebel.

"Ain't never heard of it. What you doin' here? Where're your people?"

"I am waiting for Lady Barbara," replied the girl, "and Smith," she added.

"Smith! What Smith?" he demanded.

"Oh, he is beautiful," confided Jezebel.

"Then he ain't the Smith I'm lookin' for," said the "Gunner." "What's he doin' here, and who's this Lady Barbara dame?"

"Abraham, the son of Abraham, would have killed Lady Barbara and Jezebel if Smith had not come and saved us. He is very brave."

"Now I know it ain't my Smith," said Danny, "though I ain't sayin' he ain't got guts. What I mean is he wouldn't know how to save no one—he's a geologist."

"Who are you?" demanded Jezebel.

"Call me Danny, Kid."

"My name is not kid," she explained sweetly. "It is Jezebel."

"Jezebel! Geeze, what a monicker! You look like it ought to be Gwendolyn."

"It is Jezebel," she assured him. "Do you know who I hoped you'd be?"

"No. Now just tell me, kid, who you supposed I was. Probably President Hoover or Big Bill Thompson, eh?"

"I do not know them," said Jezebel. "I hoped that you were the 'Gunner.' "

"The 'Gunner'? What do you know about the 'Gunner,' kid?"

"My name is not kid, it is Jezebel," she corrected him, sweetly.

"Oke, Jez," conceded Danny, "but tell me who wised you up to the 'Gunner' bozo."

"My name is not Jez, it is——"

"Oh, sure kid, it's Jezebel—that's oke by me; but how about the 'Gunner'?"

"What about him?"

"I just been a-askin' you."

"But I don't understand your language," explained Jezebel. "It sounds like English, but it is not the English Lady Barbara taught me."

"It ain't English," Danny assured her, seriously; "it's United States."

"It is quite like English though, isn't it?"

"Sure," said the "Gunner." "The only difference is we can understand English but the English don't never seem to understand all of ours. I guess they're dumb."

"Oh, no, they're not dumb," Jezebel assured him. "Lady Barbara is English, and she can talk quite as well as you."

Danny scratched his head. "I didn't say they was dummies. I said they was dumb. Dummies can't talk only with their mits. If a guy's dumb, he don't know nothing."

"Oh," said Jezebel.

"But what I asked you is, who wised you up to this 'Gunner' bozo?"

"Can you say it in English, please," asked Jezebel.

"Geeze, what could be plainer? I asked who told you about the 'Gunner' and what did they tell you?" Danny was waxing impatient.

"Smith told us. He said the 'Gunner' was a friend of his; and when I saw you I thought you must be Smith's friend, hunting for him."

"Now, what do you know about that!" exclaimed Danny.

"I have just told you what I know about it," explained the girl; "but perhaps you did not understand me. Perhaps you are what you call dumb."

"Are you trying to kid me, kid?" demanded the "Gunner."

"My name is not——"

"Oh, all right, all right. I know what your name is."

"Then why do you not call me by my name? Do you not like it?"

"Sure, kid—I mean Jezebel—sure I like it. It's a swell handle when you get used to it. But tell me, where is old Smithy?"

"I do not know such a person."

"But you just told me you did."

"Oh, I see," cried Jezebel. "Smithy is the United States for Smith. But Smith is not old. He's quite young."

"Well, where is he?" demanded Danny, resignedly.

"We were captured by the beautiful men from North Midian," explained Jezebel; "but we escaped and ran away. We ran in different directions, but we are going to meet tonight farther south along the cliffs."

"Beautiful men?" demanded the "Gunner." "Did old Smithy let a bunch of fairies hoist him?"

"I do not understand," said Jezebel.

"*You* wouldn't," he assured her; "but say, kid——"

"My name——"

"Aw, forget it—you know who I mean. As I was saying, let's me and you stick together till we find old Smithy. What say?"

"That would be nice, the 'Gunner,'" she assured him.

"Say, call me Danny, k— Jezebel."

"Yes, Danny."

"Geeze, I never knew Danny was such a swell monicker till I heard you say it. What say we beat it for the big drink down there? I got me such a thirst my tongue's hanging out. Then we can come back to this here rock pile and look for old Smithy."

"That will be nice," agreed Jezebel. "I, too, am thirsty." She sighed. "You can not know how happy I am, Danny."

"Why?" he asked.

"Because you are with me."

"Geeze, k—Jezebel, but you're sure a fast worker."

"I do not know what you mean," she replied, innocently.

"Well just tell me why you're happy because I'm with you."

"It is because I feel safe with you after what Smith told us. He said he always felt safe when you were around."

"So that's it? All you want is a protection guy, eh? You don't like me for myself at all, eh?"

"Oh, of course I like you, Danny," cried the girl. "I think you are beautiful."

"Yeah? Well, listen, sister. You may be a swell kidder —I dunno—or you may be just a dumb egg—but don't call me no names. I know what my pan looks like; and it ain't beautiful, and I ain't never wore a béret."

Jezebel, who only caught the occasional high-spots of Danny's conversation, made no reply, and they walked on in the direction of the lake, in silence, for some time. The forest was some little distance away, on their left, and they had no knowledge of what was transpiring there, nor did any sound reach their ears to acquaint them with the misfortune that was befalling Lady Barbara and Lafayette Smith.

At the lake they quenched their thirst, after which the

"Gunner" announced that he was going to rest for a while before he started back toward the cliffs. "I wonder," he said, "just how far a guy can walk, because in the last two days I've walked that far and back again."

"How far is that?" inquired Jezebel.

He looked at her a moment and then shook his head. "It's twice as far," he said, as he stretched himself at full length and closed his eyes. "Geeze, but I'm about all in," he murmured.

"In what?"

He deigned no reply, and presently the girl noted from his altered breathing that he was asleep. She sat with her eyes glued upon him, and occasionally a deep sigh broke from her lips. She was comparing Danny with Abraham, the son of Abraham, with Lafayette Smith and with the beautiful men of North Midian; and the comparison was not uncomplimentary to Danny.

The hot sun was beating down upon them, for there was no shade here; and presently its effects, combined with her fatigue, made her drowsy. She lay down near the "Gunner" and stretched luxuriously. Then she, too, fell asleep.

The "Gunner" did not sleep very long; the sun was too hot. When he awoke he raised himself on an elbow and looked around. His eyes fell on the girl and there they rested for some time, noting the graceful contours of the lithe young body, the wealth of golden hair, and the exquisite face.

"The kid's sure some looker," soliloquized Danny. "I seen a lotta broads in my day, but I ain't never seen nothin' could touch her. She'd sure be a swell number dolled up in them Boul Mich rags. Geeze, wouldn't she knock their lamps out! I wonder where this Midian burgh is she says she comes from. If they's all as swell lookin' as her, that's the burgh for me."

Jezebel stirred and he reached over and shook her on the shoulder. "We'd better be beatin' it," he said. "We don't want to miss old Smithy and that dame."

Jezebel sat up and looked about her. "Oh," she exclaimed, "you frightened me. I thought something was coming."

"Why? Been dreaming?"

"No. You said we'd have to beat something."

"Aw, cheese it! I meant we'd have to be hittin' the trail for the big rocks."

Jezebel looked puzzled.

"Hike back to them cliffs where you said old Smithy and that Lady Barbara dame were going to meet you."

"Now I understand," said Jezebel. "All right, come on."

But when they reached the cliffs there was no sign of Smith or Lady Barbara, and at Jezebel's suggestion they walked slowly southward in the direction of the place where she and the English girl had hoped to make a crossing to the outer world.

"How did you get into the valley, Danny?" asked the girl.

"I come through a big crack in the mountain," he replied.

"That must be the same place Smith came through," she said. "Could you find it again?"

"Sure. That's where I'm headed for now."

It was only mid-afternoon when Danny located the opening into the fissure. They had seen nothing of Lady Barbara and Smith, and they were in a quandary as to what was best to do.

"Maybe they come along and made their getaway while we was hittin' the hay," suggested Danny.

"I don't know what you are talking about," said Jezebel, "but what I think is that they may have located the opening while we were asleep and gone out of the valley."

"Well ain't that what I said?" demanded Danny.

"It didn't sound like it."

"Say, you trying to high hat me?"

"High hat?"

"Aw, what's the use?" growled the "Gunner," disgustedly. "Let's you and me beat it out of this here dump and look for old Smithy and the skirt on the other side. What say?"

"But suppose they haven't gone out?"

"Well, then we'll have to come back again; but I'm sure they must have. See this foot print?" he indicated one of his own, made earlier in the day, which pointed toward the valley. "I guess I'm getting good," he said. "Pretty soon that Tarzan guy won't have no edge on me at all."

"I'd like to see what's-on the other side of the cliffs," said Jezebel. "I have always wanted to do that."

"Well, you won't see nothin' much," he assured her. "Just some more scenery. They ain't even a hot dog stand or a single speakeasy."

"What are those?"

"Well, you might call 'em filling stations."

"What are filling stations?"

"Geeze, kid, what do you think I am, a college perfessor? I never saw anyone who could ask so many questions in my whole life."

"My name——"

"Yes, I know what your name is. Now come on and we'll

crawl through this hole-in-the-wall. I'll go first. You follow right behind me."

The rough going along the rocky floor of the fissure taxed the "Gunner's" endurance and his patience, but Jezebel was all excitement and anticipation. All her life she had dreamed of what might lie in the wonderful world beyond the cliffs.

Her people had told her that it was a flat expanse filled with sin, heresy, and iniquity, where, if one went too far he would surely fall over the edge and alight in the roaring flames of an eternal hades; but Jezebel had been a doubter. She had preferred to picture it as a land of flowers and trees and running water, where beautiful people laughed and sang through long, sunny days. Soon she was to see for herself, and she was much excited by the prospect.

And now at last they came to the end of the great fissure and looked out across the rolling foot hills toward a great forest in the distance.

Jezebel clasped her hands together in ecstacy. "Oh, Danny," she cried, "how beautiful it is!"

"What?" asked the "Gunner."

"Oh, everything. Don't you think it is beautiful, Danny?"

"The only beautiful thing around here, k—Jezebel, is you," said Danny.

The girl turned and looked up at him with her great blue eyes. "Do you think I am beautiful, Danny?"

"Sure I do."

"Do you think I am *too* beautiful?"

"There ain't no such thing," he replied, "but if they was you're it. What made you ask?"

"Lady Barbara said I was."

The "Gunner" considered this for some moments. "I guess she's right at that kid."

"You like to call me Kid, don't you?" asked Jezebel.

"Well, it seems more friendly-like," he explained, "and it's easier to remember."

"All right, you may call me Kid if you want to, but my name is Jezebel."

"That's a bet," said Danny. "When I don't think to call you Jezebel, I'll call you kid, Sister."

The girl laughed. "You're a funny man, Danny. You like to say everything wrong. I'm not your sister, of course."

"And I'm damn glad you ain't, kid."

"Why? Don't you like me?"

Danny laughed. "I never seen a kid like you before," he said. "You sure got me guessin'. But at that," he added, a little seriously for him, "they's one thing I ain't guessin' about and that's that you're a good little kid."

"I don't know what you are talking about," said Jezebel.

"And at that I'll bet you don't," he replied; "and now kid, let's sit down and rest. I'm tired."

"I'm hungry," said Jezebel.

"I ain't never see a skirt that wasn't, but why did you have to bring that up? I'm so hungry I could eat hay."

"Smith killed a kid and we ate some of that," said Jezebel. "He wrapped the rest up in the skin and I suppose he lost it when the North Midians attacked us. I wish——"

"Say," exclaimed Danny, "what a dumb-bell I am!" He reached down into one of his pockets and brought out several strips of raw meat. "Here I been packin' this around all day and forgets all about it—and me starvin' to death."

"What is it?" asked Jezebel, leaning closer to inspect the unsavory morsels.

"It's pig," said Danny as he started searching for twigs and dry grass to build a fire, "and I know where they is a lot more that I thought I couldn't never eat but I know now I could—even if I had to fight with the maggots for it."

Jezebel helped him gather wood, which was extremely scarce, being limited to dead branches of a small variety of artemisia that grew on the mountain side; but at length they had collected quite a supply, and presently they were grilling pieces of the boar meat over the flames. So preoccupied were they that neither saw three horsemen draw rein at the top of a ridge a mile away and survey them.

"This is like housekeeping, ain't it?" remarked the "Gunner."

"What is that?" asked Jezebel.

"That's where a guy and his girl friend get hitched and go to doin' their own cooking. Only in a way this is better—they ain't goin' to be no dishes to wash."

"What is hitched, Danny?" asked Jezebel.

"Why—er," Danny flushed. He had said many things to many girls in his life, many of them things that might have brought a blush to the cheek of a wooden Indian; but this was the first time, perhaps, that Danny had felt any embarrassment.

"Why—er," he repeated, "hitched means married."

"Oh," said Jezebel. She was silent for a while, watching the pork sizzling over the little flames. Then she looked up at Danny. "I think housekeeping is fun," she said.

"So do I," agreed Danny; "with you," he added and his voice was just a trifle husky. His eyes were on her; and there was a strange light in them, that no other girl had ever seen there. "You're a funny little kid," he said presently. "I never seen one like you before," and then the neglected pork fell off the end of the sharpened twig, with which he had been holding it, and tumbled into the fire.

"Geeze!" exclaimed Danny. "Look at that!" He fished the unsavory looking morsel from the ashes and flames and surveyed it. "It don't look so good, but I'm goin' to fool it. I'm goin' to eat it anyway. I wouldn't care if a elephant had sat on it for a week—I'd eat it, and the elephant, too."

"Oh, look!" cried Jezebel. "Here come some men and they are all black. What strange beasts are they sitting on? Oh, Danny, I am afraid."

At her first exclamation the "Gunner" had turned and leaped to his feet. A single look told him who the strangers were—no strangers to him.

"Beat it, kid!" he cried. "Duck back into the crack, and hit the trail for the valley. They can't follow you on gee-gees."

The three *shiftas* were already close; and when they saw that they had been discovered they spurred forward at a gallop, and yet Jezebel stood beside the little fire, wide eyed and frightened. She had not understood the strange argot that the "Gunner" employed in lieu of English. "Beat it" and "duck" and "hit the trail" had not been included in the English idiom she had gleaned from Lady Barbara Collis. But even had she understood him it would have made no difference, for Jezebel was not of the clay that is soft in the face of danger, her little feet not of the kind that run away, leaving a companion in distress.

The "Gunner" glanced behind him and saw her. "For God's sake run, kid," he cried. "These are tough guys. I know 'em," then the *shiftas* were upon him.

To conserve ammunition, which was always scarce and difficult to obtain, they tried to ride him down, striking at him with their rifles. He dodged the leading horseman; and as the fellow reined in to wheel his mount back to the attack, the "Gunner" leaped to his side and dragged him from the saddle. The mount of a second *shifta* stumbled over the two men and fell, unhorsing its rider.

The "Gunner" seized the long rifle that had fallen from the hands of the man he had dragged down and scrambled to his feet. Jezebel watched him in wide eyed wonder and admiration. She saw him swing the rifle like a club and strike at the third horseman, and then she saw the one he had first grappled lunge forward and, seizing him around the legs, drag him down, while the second to be unhorsed ran in now and leaped upon him just as the remaining *shifta* struck him a heavy blow on the head.

As she saw him fall, the blood gushing from an ugly wound in his head, Jezebel ran forward to him; but the *shiftas* seized her. She was thrown to the back of a horse in front of one of them, the others mounted, and the three galloped away with their prisoner, leaving Danny "Gunner" Patrick lying motionless in a welter of his own blood.

19

In the Village of Elija

AS TARZAN approached the village of Abraham, the son of Abraham, he was seen by a watcher who immediately warned his fellows, with the result that when the apeman arrived the huts were deserted, the villagers having taken refuge in the caves in the face of the towering cliff.

Abraham, the son of Abraham, from the safety of the highest cave, exhorted his people to repel the advance of this strange creature, whose partial nakedness and strange armament filled him with alarm, with the result that when Tarzan came near the base of the cliff the villagers, with much shouting, rolled rocks down the steep declivity in an effort to destroy him.

The Lord of the Jungle looked up at the howling creatures above him. Whatever his emotions his face did not reveal them. Doubtless contempt was predominant, for he read in their reception of him only fear and cowardice.

As naught but curiosity had prompted his visit to this strange village, since he knew that Smith already had quitted it, he remained only long enough for a brief survey of the people and their culture, neither of which was sufficiently attractive to detain him; and then he turned and retraced his steps toward the place on the shore of Chinnereth where he had picked up the northbound spoor of Smith and Lady Barbara and Jezebel.

He made his way in a leisurely manner, stopping beside the lake to quench his thirst and eat from his small store of boar meat; and then he lay down to rest, after the manner of beasts who have fed and are not hurried.

In the village he had quitted Abraham, the son of Abraham, gave thanks to Jehovah for their deliverance from the barbarian, though reserving proper credit to himself for his masterly defense of his flock.

And how fared it with Lady Barbara and Lafayette Smith? Following their recapture they were permitted no second opportunity to escape, as, heavily guarded, they were conducted northward toward the village of Elija, the son of Noah.

The girl was much depressed; and Smith sought to reassure her, though upon what grounds he himself could scarcely explain.

"I cannot believe that they intend to harm us," he said. "We have done nothing worse than kill one of their goats and that only because we were starving. I can pay them whatever price they name for the animal, and thus they will be recompensed and have no further cause for complaint against us."

"With what will you pay them?" asked Lady Barbara.

"I have money," replied Smith.

"Of what good would it be to them?"

"Of what good would it be to them! Why they could buy another goat if they wanted to," he replied.

"These people know nothing of money," she said. "It would be worthless to them."

"I suppose you are right," he admitted. "I hadn't thought of that. Well, I could give them my pistol, then."

"They already have it."

"But it's mine," he exclaimed. "They'll have to give it back to me."

She shook her head. "You are not dealing with civilized people guided by the codes and customs of civilization or responsible to the law-enforcing agencies with which we are familiar and which, perhaps, are all that keep us civilized."

"We escaped once," he ventured; "perhaps we can escape again."

"That, I think, is our only hope."

The village of the North Midians, where they presently arrived, was more pretentious than that of the people at the southern end of the valley. While there were many crude huts there were also several of stone, while the entire appearance of the village was more cleanly and prosperous.

Several hundred villagers came to meet the party as soon as it was sighted, and the prisoners noted that there was no evidence of the degeneracy and disease which were such marked characteristics of the South Midians. On the contrary, these people appeared endowed with abundant health, they looked intelligent and, physically, they were a splendid race, many of them being handsome. All were golden haired and blue eyed. That they were descended from the same stock that had produced Abraham, the son of Abraham, and his degraded flock would have appeared impossible, yet such was the fact.

The women and children pushed and jostled one another and the men in their efforts to get close to the prisoners. They jabbered and laughed incessantly, the clothing of the prisoners seeming to arouse the greatest wonder and mirth.

Their language being practically the same as that of the South Midians Lady Barbara had no difficulty in understanding what they were saying, and from scraps of their conversation which she overheard she realized that her worst fears might be realized. However, the crowd offered them no personal injury; and it was apparent that in themselves they were not inherently a cruel people, though their religion and their customs evidently prescribed harsh treatment for enemies who fell into their hands.

Upon arrival in the village Lady Barbara and Smith were separated. She was taken to a hut and put in charge of a young woman, while Smith was confined, under guard of several men, in another.

Lady Barbara's jailer, far from being ill favored, was quite beautiful, bearing a strong resemblance to Jezebel; and she proved to be quite as loquacious as the men who had captured them.

"You are the strangest looking South Midian I ever saw," she remarked, "and the man does not look at all like one. Your hair is neither the color of those they keep nor of those they destroy—it is just between, and your garments are such as no one ever saw before."

"We are not Midians," said Lady Barbara.

"But that is impossible," cried the woman. "There are none but Midians in the land of Midian and no way to get in or out. Some say there are people beyond the great cliffs, and some say there are only devils. If you are not a Midian perhaps you are a devil; but then, of course, you are a Midian."

"We come from a country beyond the cliffs," Lady Barbara told her, "and all we want is to go back to our own country."

"I do not think Elija will let you. He will treat you as we always treat South Midians."

"And how is that?"

"The men are put to death because of their heresy; and the women, if they are good looking, are kept as slaves. But being a slave is not bad. I am a slave. My mother was a slave. She was a South Midian who was captured by my father who owned her. She was very beautiful. After a while the South Midians would have killed her, as you do to all your beautiful women just before their first child is born.

"But we are different. We kill the bad looking ones, both boys and girls, and also any who become subject to the strange demons which afflict the South Midians. Do you have these demons?"

"I am not a Midian, I told you," said Lady Barbara.

The woman shook her head. "It is true that you do not look like them, but if Elija ever believes you are not you are lost."

"Why?" asked Lady Barbara.

"Elija is one of those who believe that the world beyond the cliffs is inhabited by demons; so, if you are not a South Midian, you must be a demon; and he would certainly destroy you as he will destroy the man; but for my part I am one of those who say they do not know. Some say that perhaps this world around Midian is inhabited by angels. Are you an angel?"

"I am not a demon," replied Lady Barbara.

"Then you must be a South Midian or an angel."

"I am no South Midian," insisted the English girl.

"Then you are an angel," reasoned the woman. "And if you are you will have no difficulty in proving it."

"How?"

"Just perform a miracle."

"Oh," said Lady Barbara.

"Is the man an angel?" demanded the woman.

"He is an American."

"I never heard of that—is it a kind of angel?"

"Europeans do not call them that."

"But really I think Elija will say he is a South Midian, and he will be destroyed."

"Why do your people hate the South Midians so?" asked Lady Barbara.

"They are heretics."

"They are very religious," said Lady Barbara; "they pray all the time to Jehovah and they never smile. Why do you think them heretics?"

"They insist that Paul's hair was black, while we know that it was yellow. They are very wicked, blasphemous people. Once, long before the memory of man, we were all one people; but there were many wicked heretics among us who had black hair and wished to kill all those with yellow hair; so those with yellow hair ran away and came to the north end of the valley. Ever since, the North Midians have killed all those with black hair and the South Midians all those with yellow hair. Do you think Paul had yellow hair?"

"Certainly I do," said Lady Barbara.

"That will be a point in your favor," said the woman. Just then a man came to the door of the hut and summoned Lady Barbara. "Come with me," he commanded.

The English girl followed the messenger, and the woman who had been guarding her accompanied them. Before a large stone hut they found Elija surrounded by a number of the older men of the village, while the remainder of the population was grouped in a semi-circle facing them. Lafayette Smith stood before Elija, and Lady Barbara was conducted to the side of the American.

Elija, the Prophet, was a middle aged man of not unprepossessing appearance. He was short and stocky, extremely muscular in build, and his face was adorned with a wealth of blond whiskers. Like the other North Midians he was garbed in a single garment of goat skin, his only ornament being the pistol he had taken from Smith, which he wore on a leather thong that encircled his neck.

"This man," said Elija, addressing Lady Barbara, "will not talk. He makes noises, but they mean nothing. Why will he not talk?"

"He does not understand the language of the land of Midian," replied the English girl.

"He must understand it," insisted Elija; "every one understands it."

"He is not from Midian," said Lady Barbara.

"Then he must be a demon," said Elija.

"Perhaps he is an angel," suggested Lady Barbara; "he believes that Paul's hair was yellow."

This statement precipitated a wordy argument and so impressed Elija and his apostles that they withdrew into the interior of the hut for a secret conference.

"What's it all about, Lady Barbara?" asked Smith, who, of course, had understood nothing of what had been said.

"You believe Paul's hair was yellow, don't you?" she asked.

"I don't know what you are talking about."

"Well, I told them you were a firm believer in the yellowness of Paul's hair."

"Why did you tell them that?" demanded Smith.

"Because the North Midians prefer blonds," she replied.

"But who is Paul?"

"Was, you mean. He is dead."

"Of course I'm sorry to hear that, but who *was* he?" insisted the American.

"I am afraid you have neglected the scriptures," she told him.

"Oh, the apostle; but what difference does it make what color his hair was?"

"It doesn't make any difference," she explained. "What does make a difference is that you have stated, through me, that you believe he had yellow hair; and that may be the means of saving your life."

"What nonsense!"

"Of course—the other fellow's religion is always nonsense; but not to him. You are also suspected of being an angel. Can you imagine!"

"No! Who suspects me?"

"It was I; or at least I suggested it, and I am hoping Elija will now suspect it. If he does we are both safe, provided that, in your celestial capacity, you will intercede for me."

"You are as good as saved then," he said, "for inasmuch as I cannot speak their language you can put any words you wish into my mouth without fear of being called to account."

"That's a fact, isn't it?" she said, laughing. "If our emergency were not so critical I could have a lot of fun, couldn't I?"

"You seem to find fun in everything," he replied, admiringly; "even in the face of disaster."

"Perhaps I am whistling in the dark," she said.

They talked a great deal while they waited for Elija and the apostles to return, for it helped them to tide over the anxious minutes of nervous strain that slowly dragged into hours. They could hear the chatter and buzz of conversation within the hut, as Elija and his fellows debated, while, outside, the villagers kept up a constant babel of conversation.

"They like to talk," commented Smith.

"And perhaps you have noticed an idiosyncrasy of the North Midians in this respect?" she asked.

"Lots of people like to talk."

"I mean that the men gabble more than the women."

"Perhaps in self-defense."

"Here they come!" she exclaimed as Elija appeared in the doorway of the hut, fingering the pistol he wore as an ornament.

Darkness was already falling as the Prophet and the twelve apostles filed out to their places in the open. Elija raised his hands in a signal for silence and when quiet had been restored he spoke.

"With the aid of Jehovah," he said, "we have wrestled with a mighty question. There were some among us who contended that this man is a South Midian, and others that he is an angel. Mighty was the weight of the statement that he believes that Paul had yellow hair, for if such is the turth then indeed he is not a heretic; and if he is no heretic he is not a South Midian, for they, as all the world knows, are heretics. Yet again, it was brought forth that if he is a demon he might still claim that he believed in the yellowness of Paul, in order that he might deceive us.

"How were we to know? We must know lest we, through our ignorance, do sin against one of His angels and bring down the wrath of Jehovah upon our heads.

"But at last I, Elija, the son of Noah, True Prophet of Paul, the son of Jehovah, discovered the truth. The man is no angel! The revelation descended upon me in a burst of glory from Jehovah Himself—the man cannot be an angel because he has no wings!"

There was an immediate burst of "Amens" and "Hallelujahs" from the assembled villagers, while Lady Barbara went cold with dread.

"Therefore," continued Elija, "he must be either a South Midian or a demon, and in either case he must be destroyed."

Lady Barbara turned a pale face toward Lafayette Smith—pale even through its coating of tan. Her lip trembled, just a little. It was the first indication of a weaker, feminine emotion that Smith had seen this remarkable girl display.

"What is it?" he asked. "Are they going to harm you?"

"It is you, my dear friend," she replied. "You must escape."

"But how?" he asked.

"Oh, I don't know; I don't know," she cried. "There is only one way. You will have to make a break for it—now. It is dark. They will not expect it. I will do something to engage their attention, and then you make a dash for the forest."

He shook his head. "No," he said. "We shall go together, or I do not go."

"Please," she begged, "or it will be too late."

Elija had been talking to one of his apostles, and now he raised his voice again so that all might hear. "Lest we have mistaken the divine instructions of Jehovah," he said, "we shall place this man in the mercy of Jehovah and as Jehovah wills so shall it be. Make ready the grave. If he is indeed an angel he will arise unharmed."

"Oh, go; please go!" cried Lady Barbara.

"What did he say?" demanded Smith.

"They are going to bury you alive," she cried.

"And you," he asked; "what are they going to do to you?"

"I am to be held in slavery."

With sharpened sticks and instruments of bone and stone a number of men were already engaged in excavating a grave in the center of the village street before the hut of Elija, who stood waiting its completion surrounded by his apostles. The Prophet was still toying with his new found ornament, concerning the purpose and mechanism of which he was wholly ignorant.

Lady Barbara was urging Smith to attempt escape while there was yet an opportunity, and the American was considering the best plan to adopt.

"You will have to come with me," he said. "I think if we make a sudden break right back through the village toward the cliffs we shall find our best chance for success. There are fewer people congregated on that side."

From the darkness beyond the village on the forest side a pair of eyes watched the proceedings taking place before the hut of Elija. Slowly, silently the owner of the eyes crept closer until he stood in the shadow of a hut at the edge of the village.

Suddenly Smith, seizing Lady Barbara's hand, started at a run toward the north side of the village; and so unexpected was his break for liberty that, for a moment, no hand was raised to stay him; but an instant later, at a cry from Elija, the entire band leaped in pursuit, while from the shadow of the hut where he had stood concealed the watcher slipped forward into the village where he stood near the hut of Elija watching the pursuit of the escaped prisoners. He was alone, for the little central compound of the village had emptied as by magic, even the women and children having joined in the chase.

Smith ran swiftly, holding tightly to the girl's hand; and close on their heels came the leaders of the pursuit. No longer did the village fires light their way; and only darkness loomed ahead, as the moon had not yet risen.

Gradually the American bore to the left, intending to swing in a half circle toward the south. There was yet a chance that they might make good their escape if they could outdistance the nearer of their pursuers until they reached the forest, for their strait gave them both speed and endurance far above normal.

But just as success seemed near they entered a patch of broken lava rock, invisible in the darkness; and Smith stumbled and fell dragging Lady Barbara down with him. Before they could scramble to their feet the leading Midian was upon them.

The American freed himself for a moment and struggled to his feet; and again the fellow sought to seize him, but Smith swung a heavy blow to his chin and felled him.

Brief, however, was this respite, for almost immediately both the American and the English girl were overwhelmed by superior numbers and once again found themselves captives, though Smith fought until he was overpowered, knocking his antagonists to right and left.

Miserably dejected, they were dragged back to the village compound, their last hope gone; and again the Midians gathered around the open grave to witness the torture of their victim.

Smith was conducted to the edge of the excavation, where he was held by two stalwart men, while Elija raised his voice in prayer, and the remainder of the assemblage knelt, bursting forth occasionally with hallelujahs and amens.

When he had concluded his long prayer the Prophet paused. Evidently there was something on his mind which vexed him. In fact it was the pistol which dangled from the thong about his neck. He was not quite sure of its purpose, and he was about to destroy the only person who might tell him.

To Elija the pistol was quite the most remarkable possession that had ever fallen into his hands, and he was filled with a great curiosity concerning it. It might be, he argued, some magic talisman for averting evil, or, upon the other hand, it might be the charm of a demon or a sorcerer, that would work evil upon him. At that thought he quickly removed the thong from about his neck, but he still held the weapon in his hand.

"What is this?" he demanded, turning to Lady Barbara and exhibiting the pistol.

"It is a weapon," she said. "Be careful or it will kill some one."

"How does it kill?" asked Elija.

"What is he saying?" demanded Smith.

"He is asking how the pistol kills," replied the girl.

A brilliant idea occurred to the American. "Tell him to give it to me, and I will show him," he said.

But when she translated the offer to Elija he demurred. "He could then kill me with it," he said, shrewdly.

"He wont give it to you," the girl told Smith. "He is afraid you want to kill him."

"I do," replied the man.

"Tell him," said Elija, "to explain to me how I may kill some one with it."

"Repeat my instructions to him very carefully," said Smith, after Lady Barbara had translated the demand of the prophet. "Tell him how to grasp the pistol," and when Lady Barbara had done so and Elija held the weapon by the grip in his right hand, "now tell him to place his index finger through the guard, but warn him not to pull the trigger."

Elija did as he was bid. "Now," continued Smith, "explain to him that in order to see how the weapon operates he should place one eye to the muzzle and look down the barrel."

"But I can see nothing," expostulated Elija when he had done as Lady Barbara directed. "It is quite dark down the little hole."

"He says it is too dark in the barrel for him to see anything," repeated Lady Barbara to the American.

"Explain to him that if he pulls the trigger there will be a light in the barrel," said Smith.

"But that will be murder," exclaimed the girl.

"It is war," said Smith, "and in the subsequent confusion we may escape."

Lady Barbara steeled herself. "You could see nothing because you did not press the little piece of metal beneath your index finger," she explained to Elija.

"What will that do?" demanded the prophet.

"It will make a light in the little hole," said Lady Barbara. Elija again placed his eye against the muzzle; and this time he pulled the trigger; and as the report cracked the tense silence of the watching villagers Elija, the son of Noah, pitched forward upon his face.

Instantly Lady Barbara sprang toward Smith, who simultaneously sought to break away from the grip of the men who held him; but they, although astonished at what had occurred, were not to be caught off their guard, and though he struggled desperately they held him.

For an instant there was a hushed silence; and then pandemonium broke loose as the villagers realized that their prophet was dead, slain by the wicked charm of a demon; but at the very outset of their demands for vengeance their attention was distracted by a strange and remarkable figure that sprang from the hut of Elija, stooped and picked up the pistol that had fallen from the hands of the dead man, and leaped to the side of the prisoner struggling with his guards.

This was such a man as none of them had ever seen—a

giant white man with a tousled shock of black hair and with grey eyes that sent a shiver through them, so fierce and implacable were they. Naked he was but for a loin cloth of skin, and the muscles that rolled beneath his brown hide were muscles such as they never had seen before.

As the newcomer sprang toward the American one of the men guarding Smith, sensing that an attempt was being made to rescue the prisoner, swung his club in readiness to deal a blow against the strange creature advancing upon him. At the same time the other guard sought to drag Smith from the compound.

The American did not at first recognize Tarzan of the Apes, yet, though he was not aware that the stranger was bent upon his rescue, he sensed that he was an enemy of the Midians, and so struggled to prevent his guard from forcing him away.

Another Midian seized Lady Barbara with the intention of carrying her from the scene, for all the villagers believed that the strange giant was a friend of the prisoners and had come to effect their release.

Smith was successful in tearing himself free from the man who held him, and immediately sprang to the girl's assistance, felling her captor with a single blow, just as Tarzan levelled the American's pistol at the guard who was preparing to cudgel him.

The sound of this second shot and the sight of their fellow dropping to the ground, as had Elija, filled the Midians with consternation; and for a moment they fell back from the three, leaving them alone in the center of the compound.

"Quick!" called Tarzan to Smith. "You and the girl get out of here before they recover from their surprise. I will follow you. That way," he added, pointing toward the south.

As Lafayette Smith and Lady Barbara hurried from the village Tarzan backed slowly after them, keeping the little pistol in full view of the frightened villagers, who, having seen two of their number die beneath its terrifying magic, were loath to approach it too closely.

Until out of range of a thrown club Tarzan continued his slow retreat; then he wheeled and bounded off into the night in pursuit of Lafayette Smith and Lady Barbara Collis.

THOUGH Jezebel was terrified by the black faces of her captors and by the strange beasts they bestrode, the like of which she had never even imagined, her fear for herself was outweighed by her sorrow. Her one thought was to escape and return to the side of the "Gunner," even though she believed him dead from the terrific blow that his assailant had struck him.

She struggled violently to free herself from the grasp of the man in front of whom she rode; but the fellow was far too powerful; and, though she was difficult to hold, at no time was there the slightest likelihood that she might escape. Her efforts, however, angered him and at last he struck her, bringing to the girl a realization of the futility of pitting her puny strength against his. She must wait, then, until she could accomplish by stealth what she could not effect by force.

The village of the raiders lay but a short distance from the point at which she had been captured, and but a few minutes had elapsed since that event when they rode up to its gates and into the central compound.

The shouts that greeted the arrival of a new and beautiful prisoner brought Capietro and Stabutch to the doorway of their hut.

"Now what have the black devils brought in?" exclaimed Capietro.

"It looks like a young woman," said Stabutch.

"It is," cried Capietro, as the *shiftas* approached the hut with their prisoner. "We shall have company, eh, Stabutch? Who have you there, my children?" he demanded of the three who were accompanying Jezebel.

"The price of a chief's ransom, perhaps," replied one of the blacks.

"Where did you find her?"

"Above the village a short distance, when we were returning from scouting. A man was with her. The man who escaped with the help of the ape-man."

"Where is he! Why did you not bring him, also?" demanded Capietro.

"He fought us, and we were forced to kill him."

"You have done well," said Capietro. "She is worth two of

him—in many ways. Come girl, hold up your head, let us have a look at that pretty face. Come, you need not fear anything—if you are a good girl you will find Dommic Capietro a good fellow."

"Perhaps she does not understand Italian," suggested Stabutch.

"You are right, my friend; I shall speak to her in English." Jezebel had looked up at Stabutch when she heard him speak a language she understood. Perhaps this man would be a friend, she thought; but when she saw his face her heart sank.

"What a beauty!" ejaculated the Russian.

"You have fallen in love with her quickly, my friend," commented Capietro. "Do you want to buy her?"

"How much do you want for her?"

"Friends should not bargain," said the Italian. "Wait, I have it! Come, girl," and he took Jezebel by the arm and led her into the hut, where Stabutch followed them.

"Why was I brought here?" asked Jezebel. "I have not harmed you. Let me go back to Danny; he is hurt."

"He is dead," said Capietro; "but don't you grieve, little one. You now have two friends in place of the one you have lost. Soon you will forget him; it is easy for a woman to forget."

"I shall never forget him," cried Jezebel. "I want to go back to him—perhaps he is not dead." Then she broke down and cried.

Stabutch stood eyeing the girl hungrily. Her youth and her beauty aroused a devil within him, and he made a mental vow that he would possess her. "Do not cry," he said, kindly. "I am your friend. Everything will be all right."

The new tone in his voice gave hope to Jezebel, and she looked up at him gratefully. "If you are my friend," she said, "take me away from here and back to Danny."

"After a while," replied Stabutch, and then to Capietro, "How much?"

"I shall not sell her to my good friend," replied the Italian. "Let us have a drink, and then I shall explain my plan."

The two drank from a bottle standing on the earth floor of the hut. "Sit down," said Capietro, waving Jezebel to a seat on the dirty rug. Then he searched for a moment in his duffle bag and brought out a deck of soiled and grimy cards. "Be seated, my friend," he said to Stabutch. "Let us have another drink, and then you shall hear my plan."

Stabutch drank from the bottle and wiped his lips with the back of his hand. "Well," he said, "what is it?"

"We shall play for her," exclaimed the Italian, shuffling the deck, "and whoever wins, keeps her."

"Let us drink to that," said Stabutch. "Five games, eh, and the first to win three takes her?"

"Another drink to seal the bargain!" exclaimed the Italian. "The best three out of five!"

Stabutch won the first game, while Jezebel sat looking on in ignorance of the purpose of the bits of pasteboard, and only knowing that in some way they were to decide her fate. She hoped the younger man would win, but only because he had said that he was her friend. Perhaps she could persuade him to take her back to Danny. She wondered what kind of water was in the bottle from which they drank, for she noticed that it wrought a change in them. They talked much louder now and shouted strange words when the little cards were thrown upon the rug, and then one would appear very angry while the other always laughed immoderately. Also they swayed and lurched in a peculiar manner that she had not noticed before they had drunk so much of the water from the bottle.

Capietro won the second game and the third. Stabutch was furious, but now he became very quiet. He exerted all his powers of concentration upon the game, and he seemed almost sober as the cards were dealt for the fourth game.

"She is as good as mine!" cried Capietro, as he looked at his hand.

"She will never be yours," growled the Russian.

"What do you mean?"

"I shall win the next two games."

The Italian laughed loudly. "That is good!" he cried. "We should drink to that." He raised the bottle to his lips and then passed it to Stabutch.

"I do not want a drink," said the Russian, in a surly tone, pushing the bottle aside.

"Ah, ha! My friend is getting nervous. He is afraid he is going to lose and so he will not drink. Sapristi! It is all the same to me. I get the brandy and the girl, too."

"Play!" snapped Stabutch.

"You are in a hurry to lose," taunted Capietro.

"To win," corrected Stabutch, and he did.

Now it was the Italian's turn to curse and rage at luck, and once again the cards were dealt and the players picked up their hands.

"It is the last game," said Stabutch.

"We have each won two," replied Capietro. "Let us drink to the winner—although I dislike proposing a toast to myself," and he laughed again, but this time there was an ugly note in his laughter.

In silence, now, they resumed their play. One by one the little pasteboards fell upon the rug. The girl looked on in wondering silence. There was a tenseness in the situation that she felt, without understanding. Poor little Jezebel, she understood so little!

Suddenly, with a triumphant oath, Capietro sprang to his feet. "I win!" he cried. "Come, friend, drink with me to my good fortune."

Sullenly the Russian drank, a very long draught this time. There was a sinister gleam in his eye as he handed the bottle back to Capietro. Leon Stabutch was a poor loser.

The Italian emptied the bottle and flung it to the ground. Then he turned toward Jezebel and stooping lifted her to her feet. "Come, my dear," he said, his coarse voice thick from drink, "Give me a kiss."

Jezebel drew back, but the Italian jerked her roughly to him and tried to draw her lips to his.

"Leave the girl alone," growled Stabutch. "Can't you see she is afraid of you?"

"What did I win her for?" demanded Capietro. "To leave her alone? Mind your own business."

"I'll make it my business," said Stabutch. "Take your hands off her." He stepped forward and laid a hand on Jezebel's arm. "She is mine by rights anyway."

"What do you mean?"

"You cheated. I caught you at it in the last game."

"You lie!" shouted Capietro and simultaneously he struck at Stabutch. The Russian dodged the blow and closed with the other.

Both were drunk and none too steady. It required much of their attention to keep from falling down. But as they wrestled about the interior of the hut a few blows were struck—enough to arouse their rage to fury and partially to sober them. Then the duel became deadly, as each sought the throat of the other.

Jezebel, wide eyed and terrified, had difficulty in keeping out of their way as they fought to and fro across the floor of the hut; and so centered was the attention of the two men upon one another that the girl might have escaped had she not been more afraid of the black men without than of the whites within.

Several times Stabutch released his hold with his right

hand and sought for something beneath his coat and at last he found it—a slim dagger. Capietro did not see it.

They were standing in the center of the hut now, their arms locked about one another, and resting thus as though by mutual consent. They were panting heavily from their exertions, and neither seemed to have gained any material advantage.

Slowly the Russian's right hand crept up the back of his adversary. Jezebel saw, but only her eyes reflected her horror. Though she had seen many people killed she yet had a horror of killing. She saw the Russian feel for a spot on the other's back with the point of his thumb. Then she saw him turn his hand and place the dagger point where his thumb had been.

There was a smile upon Stabutch's face as he drove the blade home. Capietro stiffened, screamed, and died. As the body slumped to the ground and rolled over on its back the murderer stood over the corpse of his victim, a smile upon his lips, and his eyes upon the girl.

But suddenly the smile died as a new thought came to the cunning mind of the slayer and his eyes snapped from the face of Jezebel to the doorway of the hut where a filthy blanket answered the purpose of a door.

He had forgotten the horde of cut-throats who had called this thing upon the floor their chief! But now he recalled them and his soul was filled with terror. He did not need to ask himself what his fate would be when they discovered his crime.

"You have murdered him!" cried the girl suddenly, a note of horror in her voice.

"Be quiet!" snapped Stabutch. "Do you want to die? They will kill us when they discover this."

"I did not do it," protested Jezebel.

"They will kill you just the same—afterwards. They are beasts."

Suddenly he stooped, seized the corpse by the ankles and, dragging it to the far end of the hut, he covered it with rugs and clothing.

"Now keep quiet until I come back," he said to Jezebel. "If you give an alarm I'll kill you myself before they have a chance to."

He rummaged in a dark corner of the hut and brought forth a revolver with its holster and belt, which he buckled about his hips, and a rifle which he leaned beside the doorway.

"When I return be ready to come with me," he snapped,

and raising the rug that covered the doorway, he stepped out into the village.

Quickly he made his way to where the ponies of the band were tethered. Here were several of the blacks loitering near the animals.

"Where is the headman?" he asked, but none of them understood English. He tried to tell them by means of signs, to saddle two horses, but they only shook their heads. If they understood him, as they doubtless did, they refused to take orders from him.

At this juncture the headman, attracted from a nearby hut, approached. He understood a little pidgin English, and Stabutch had no difficulty in making him understand that he wanted two horses saddled; but the headman wanted to know more. Did the chief want them?

"Yes, he wants them," replied Stabutch. "He sent me to get them. The chief is sick. Drink too much." Stabutch laughed and the headman seemed to understand.

"Who go with you?" asked the headman.

Stabutch hesitated. Well, he might as well tell him—everyone would see the girl ride out with him anyway. "The girl," he said.

The headman's eyes narrowed. "The Chief say?" he asked.

"Yes. The girl thinks the white man not dead. The Chief send me to look for him."

"You take men?"

"No. Man come back with us if girl say so. Be afraid of black men. No come."

The other nodded understandingly and ordered two horses saddled and bridled. "Him dead," he offered.

Stabutch shrugged. "We see," he replied, as he led the two animals toward the hut where Jezebel awaited him.

The headman accompanied him, and Stabutch was in terror. What if the man insisted on entering the hut to see his chief? Stabutch loosened the revolver in its holster. Now his greatest fear was that the shot might attract others to the hut. That would never do. He must find some other way. He stopped and the headman halted with him.

"Do not come to the hut yet," said Stabutch.

"Why?" asked the headman.

"The girl is afraid. If she sees you she will think we are deceiving her, and she may refuse to show me where the man is. We promised her that no black man would come."

The headman hesitated. Then he shrugged and turned back. "All right," he said.

"And tell them to leave the gates open till we have gone," called Stabutch.

At the hut door he called to the girl. "All ready," he said, "and hand me my rifle when you come out;" but she did not know what a rifle was and he had to step in and get it himself.

Jezebel looked at the horses with dismay.

At the thought of riding one of these strange beasts alone she was terrified. "I cannot do it," she told Stabutch.

"You will have to—or die," he whispered. "I'll lead the one you ride. Here, hurry."

He lifted her into the saddle and showed her how to use the stirrups and hold the reins. Then he put a rope about the neck of her horse; and, mounting his own, he led hers out through the village gateway while half a hundred murderers watched them depart.

As they turned upward toward the higher hills the setting sun projected their shadows far ahead, and presently night descended upon them and hid their sudden change of direction from any watchers there may have been at the village gates.

21

An Awakening

DANNY "GUNNER" PATRICK opened his eyes and stared up at the blue African sky. Slowly consciousness returned and with it the realization that his head pained severely. He raised a hand and felt of it. What was that? He looked at his hand and saw that it was bloody.

"Geeze!" he muttered. "They got me!" He tried to recall how it had happened. "I knew the finger was on me, but how the hell did they get me? Where was I?" His thoughts were all back in Chicago, and he was puzzled. Vaguely he felt that he had made his get-away, and yet they had "got" him. He could not figure it out.

Then he turned his head slightly and saw lofty mountains looming near. Slowly and painfully he sat up and looked around. Memory, partial and fragmentary, returned. "I must have fell off them mountains," he mused, "while I was lookin' for camp."

Gingerly he rose to his feet and was relieved to find that

he was not seriously injured—at least his arms and legs were intact. "My head never was much good. Geeze, it hurts, though."

A single urge dominated him—he must find camp. Old Smithy would be worrying about him if he did not return. Where was Obambi? "I wonder if he fell off too," he muttered, looking about him. But Obambi, neither dead nor alive, was in sight; and so the "Gunner" started upon his fruitless search for camp.

At first he wandered toward the northwest, directly away from Smith's last camp. Tongani, the baboon, sitting upon his sentinel rock, saw him coming and sounded the alarm. At first Danny saw only a couple of "monkeys" coming toward him, barking and growling. He saw them stop occasionally and place the backs of their heads against the ground and he mentally classified them as "nutty monks;" but when their numbers were swollen to a hundred and he finally realized the potential danger lying in those powerful jaws and sharp fangs, he altered his course and turned toward the southwest.

For a short distance the tongani followed him, but when they saw that he intended them no harm they let him proceed and returned to their interrupted feeding, while the man, with a sigh of relief, continued on his way.

In a ravine Danny found water, and with the discovery came a realization of his thirst and his hunger. He drank at the same pool at which Tarzan had slain Horta, the boar; and he also washed the blood from his head and face as well as he could. Then he continued on his aimless wandering. This time he climbed higher up the slope toward the mountains, in a southeasterly direction, and was headed at last toward the location of the now abandoned camp. Chance and the tongani had set him upon the right trail.

In a short time he reached a spot that seemed familiar; and here he stopped and looked around in an effort to recall his wandering mental faculties, which he fully realized were not functioning properly.

"That bat on the bean sure knocked me cuckoo," he remarked, half aloud. "Geeze, what's that?" Something was moving in the tall grass through which he had just come. He watched intently and a moment later saw the head of Sheeta, the panther, parting the grasses a short distance from him. The scene was suddenly familiar.

"I gotcha Steve!" exclaimed the "Gunner." "Me and that Tarzan guy flopped here last night—now I remember."

He also remembered how Tarzan had chased the panther

away by "running a bluff on him," and he wondered if he could do the same thing.

"Geeze, what a ornery lookin' pan! I'll bet you got a rotten disposition—and that Tarzan guy just growled and ran at you, and you beat it. Say, I don't believe it, if I did see it myself. Whyinell don't you go on about your business, you big stiff? You give me the heeby-jeebies." He stooped and picked up a fragment of rock. "Beat it!" he yelled, as he hurled the missile at Sheeta.

The great cat wheeled and bounded away, disappearing in the tall grass that the "Gunner" could now see waving along the path of the panther's retreat. "Well, what do you know about that?" ejaculated Danny. "I done it! Geeze, these lions aint so much."

His hunger now claimed his attention as his returning memory suggested a means of appeasing it. "I wonder could I do it?" he mused, as he hunted around on the ground until he had found a thin fragment of rock, with which he commenced to scrape away the dirt from a loose heap that rose a few inches above the contour of the surrounding ground. "I wonder could I!"

His digging soon revealed the remains of the boar Tarzan had cached against their possible return. With his pocket knife the "Gunner" hacked off several pieces, after which he scraped the dirt back over the body and busied himself in the preparation of a fire, where he grilled the meat in a sketchy fashion that produced culinary results which ordinarily would have caused him to turn up his nose in disgust. But today he was far from particular and bolted the partially cooked and partially charred morsels like a ravenous wolf.

His memory had returned now up to the point of the meal he had eaten at this same spot with Tarzan—from there on until he had regained consciousness a short time before, it was a blank. He knew now that he could find his way back to camp from the point above the raiders' village where he and Obambi had lunched, and so he turned his footsteps in that direction.

When he had found the place, he crept on down to the edge of the cliff where it overlooked the village; and here he lay down to rest and to spy upon the raiders, for he was very tired.

"The lousy bums!" he ejaculated beneath his breath, as he saw the *shiftas* moving about the village. "I wish I had my typewriter, I'd clean up that dump."

He saw Stabutch emerge from a hut and walk down to the horses. He watched him while he talked to the blacks there and to the headman. Then he saw the Russian leading two saddled horses back to the hut.

"That guy don't know it," he muttered, "but the finger is sure on him. I'll get him on the spot some day if it takes the rest of my natural life. Geeze, glom the broad!" Stabutch had summoned Jezebel from the hut. Suddenly a strange thing happened inside the head of Danny "Gunner" Patrick. It was as though someone had suddenly raised a window shade and let in a flood of light. He saw everything perfectly now in retrospection. With the sight of Jezebel his memory had returned!

It was with difficulty that he restrained an urge to call out and tell her that he was there; but caution stilled his tongue, and he lay watching while the two mounted and rode out of the gateway.

He rose to his feet and ran along the ridge toward the north, parallel to the course they were taking. It was already dusk. In a few minutes it would be dark. If he could only keep them in sight until he knew in what direction they finally went!

Exhaustion was forgotten as he ran through the approaching night. Dimly now he could see them. They rode for a short distance upward toward the cliffs; and then, just before the darkness swallowed them, he saw them turn and gallop away toward the northwest and the great forest that lay in that direction.

Reckless of life and limb, the "Gunner" half stumbled, half fell down the cliffs that here had crumbled away and spilled their fragments out upon the slope below.

"I gotta catch 'em, I gotta catch 'em," he kept repeating to himself. "The poor kid! The poor little kid! So help me God, if I catch 'em, what I won't do to that —— —— if he's hurt her!"

On through the night he stumbled, falling time and again only to pick himself up and continue his frantic and hopeless search for the little golden haired Jezebel who had come into his life for a few brief hours to leave a mark upon his heart that might never be erased.

Gradually the realization of it crept upon him as he groped blindly into the unknown, and it gave him strength to go on in the face of such physical exhaustion as he had never known before.

"Geeze," he muttered, "I sure must of fell hard for that kid."

22

By a Lonely Pool

NIGHT had fallen; and Tarzan of the Apes, leading Lady Barbara Collis and Lafayette Smith from the valley of the land of Midian, did not see the spoor of Jezebel and the "Gunner."

His two charges were upon the verge of exhaustion, but the ape-man led them on through the night in accordance with a plan he had decided upon. He knew that there were two more whites missing—Jezebel and Danny Patrick—and he wanted to get Lady Barbara and Smith to a place of safety that he might be free to pursue his search for these others.

To Lady Barbara and Smith the journey seemed interminable, yet they made no complaint, for the ape-man had explained the purpose of this forced march to them; and they were even more anxious than he concerning the fate of their friends.

Smith supported the girl as best he could; but his own strength was almost spent, and sometimes his desire to assist her tended more to impede than to aid her. Finally she stumbled and fell; and when Tarzan, striding in advance, heard and returned to them he found Smith vainly endeavoring to lift Lady Barbara.

This was the first intimation the ape-man had received that his charges were upon the verge of exhaustion, for neither had voiced a single complaint; and when he realized it he lifted Lady Barbara in his arms and carried her, while Smith, relieved at least of further anxiety concerning her, was able to keep going, though he moved like an automaton, apparently without conscious volition. Nor may his state be wondered at, when one considers what he had passed through during the preceding three days.

With Lady Barbara, he marvelled at the strength and endurance of the ape-man, which, because of his own weakened state, seemed unbelievable even as he witnessed it.

"It is not much farther," said Tarzan, guessing that the man needed encouragement.

"You are sure the hunter you told us of has not moved his camp?" asked Lady Barbara.

"He was there day before yesterday," replied the apeman. "I think we shall find him there tonight."

"He will take us in?" asked Smith.

"Certainly, just as you would, under similar circumstances, take in anyone who needed assistance," replied the Lord of the Jungle. "He is an Englishman," he added, as though that fact in itself were a sufficient answer to his doubts.

They were in a dense forest now, following an ancient game trail; and presently they saw lights flickering ahead.

"That must be the camp," exclaimed Lady Barbara.

"Yes," replied Tarzan, and a moment later he called out in a native dialect.

Instantly came an answering voice; and a moment later Tarzan halted upon the edge of the camp, just outside the circle of beast-fires.

Several askaris were on guard, and with them Tarzan conversed for a few moments; then he advanced and lowered Lady Barbara to her feet.

"I have told them not to disturb their bwana," the apeman explained. "There is another tent that Lady Barbara may occupy, and the headman will arrange to have a shelter thrown up for Smith. You will be perfectly safe here. The men tell me their bwana is Lord Passmore. He will doubtless arrange to get you out to rail head. In the meantime I shall try to locate your friends."

That was all—the ape-man turned and melted into the black night before they could voice any thanks.

"Why he's gone!" exclaimed the girl. "I didn't even thank him."

"I thought he would remain here until morning," said Smith. "He must be tired."

"He seems tireless," replied Lady Barbara. "He is a superman, if ever there was one."

"Come," said the headman, "your tent is over here. The boys are arranging a shelter for the bwana."

"Good night, Mr. Smith," said the girl. "I hope you sleep well."

"Good night, Lady Barbara," replied Smith. "I hope we wake up sometime."

And as they prepared for this welcome rest Stabutch and Jezebel were riding through the night, the man completely confused and lost.

Toward morning they drew rein at the edge of a great forest, after riding in wide circles during the greater part of the night. Stabutch was almost exhausted; and Jezebel was but little better off, but she had youth and health to give her the reserve strength that the man had undermined and wasted in dissipation.

"I've got to get some sleep," he said, dismounting.

Jezebel needed no invitation to slip from her saddle for she was stiff and sore from this unusual experience. Stabutch led the animals inside the forest and tied them to a tree. Then he threw himself upon the ground and was almost immediately asleep.

Jezebel sat in silence listening to the regular breathing of the man. "Now would be the time to escape," she thought. She rose quietly to her feet. How dark it was! Perhaps it would be better to wait until it became light enough to see. She was sure the man would sleep a long time, for it was evident that he was very tired.

She sat down again, listening to the noises of the jungle. They frightened her. Yes, she would wait until it was light; then she would untie the horses, ride one and lead the other away so that the man could not pursue her.

Slowly the minutes crept by. The sky became lighter in the east, over the distant mountains. The horses became restless. She noticed that they stood with ears pricked up and that they looked deeper into the jungle and trembled.

Suddenly there was the sound of crashing in the underbrush. The horses snorted and surged back upon their ropes, both of which broke. The noise awakened Stabutch, who sat up just as the two terrified animals wheeled and bolted. An instant later a lion leaped past the girl and the man, in pursuit of the two fleeing horses.

Stabutch sprang to his feet, his rifle in his hands. "God!" he exclaimed. "This is no place to sleep," and Jezebel's opportunity had passed.

The sun was topping the eastern mountains. The day had come. Soon the searchers would be ahorse. Now that he was afoot, Stabutch knew that he must not loiter. However, they must eat, or they would have no strength to proceed; and only by his rifle could they eat.

"Climb into that tree, little one," he said to Jezebel. "You will be safe there while I go and shoot something for our breakfast. Watch for the lion, and if you see him returning this way shout a warning. I am going farther into the forest to look for game."

Jezebel climbed into the tree, and Stabutch departed upon the hunt for breakfast. The girl watched for the lion, hoping it would return, for she had determined that she would give no warning to the man if it did.

She was afraid of the Russian because of things he had said

to her during that long night ride. Much that he had said she had not understood at all, but she understood enough to know that he was a bad man. But the lion did not return, and presently Jezebel dozed and nearly fell out of the tree.

Stabutch, hunting in the forest, found a water hole not far from where he had left Jezebel; and here he hid behind bushes waiting for some animal to come down to drink. Nor had he long to wait before he saw a creature appear suddenly upon the opposite side of the pool. So quietly had it come that the Russian had not dreamed that a creature stirred within a mile of his post. The most surprising feature of the occurrence, however, was that the animal thus suddenly to step into view was a man.

Stabutch's evil eyes narrowed. It was *the* man—the man he had travelled all the way from Moscow to kill. What an opportunity! Fate was indeed kind to him. He would fulfill his mission without danger to himself, and then he would escape with the girl—that wondrous girl! Stabutch had never seen so beautiful a woman in his life, and now he was to possess her—she was to be his.

But first he must attend to the business of the moment. What a pleasant business it was, too. He raised his rifle very cautiously and aimed. Tarzan had halted and turned his head to one side. He could not see the rifle barrel of his enemy because of the bush behind which Stabutch hid and the fact that his eyes were centered on something in another direction.

The Russian realized that he was trembling, and he cursed himself under his breath. The nervous strain was too great. He tensed his muscles in an effort to hold his hands firm and the rifle steady and immovable upon the target. The front sight of the rifle was describing a tiny circle instead of remaining fixed upon that great chest which offered such a splendid target.

But he must fire! The man would not stand there thus forever. The thought hurried Stabutch, and as the sight passed again across the body of the ape-man the Russian squeezed the trigger.

At the sound of the shot Jezebel's eyes snapped open. "Perhaps the lion returned," she soliloquized, "or maybe the man has found food. If it were the lion, I hope he missed it."

Also, as the rifle spoke, the target leaped into the air, seized a low hung branch and disappeared amidst the foliage of the trees above. Stabutch had missed—he should have relaxed his muscles rather than tensed them.

The Russian was terrified. He felt as must one who stands

upon the drop with the noose already about his neck. He turned and fled. His cunning mind suggested that he had better not return where the girl was. She was already lost to him, for he could not be burdened with her now in this flight, upon the success of which hung his very life. Accordingly he ran toward the south.

As he rushed headlong through the forest he was already out of breath when he felt a sudden sickening pain in his arm and at the same instant saw the feathered tip of an arrow waving beside him as he ran.

The shaft had pierced his forearm, its tip projecting from the opposite side. Sick with terror Stabutch increased his speed. Somewhere above him was his Nemesis, whom he could neither see nor hear. It was as though a ghostly assassin pursued him on silent wings.

Again an arrow struck him, sinking deep into the triceps of his other arm. With a scream of pain and horror Stabutch halted and, dropping upon his knees, raised his hands in supplication. "Spare me!" he cried. "Spare me! I have never wronged you. If you will spare——"

An arrow, speeding straight, drove through the Russian's throat. He screamed and clutched at the missile and fell forward on his face.

Jezebel, listening in the tree, heard the agonized shriek of the stricken man; and she shuddered. "The lion got him," she whispered. "He was wicked. It is the will of Jehovah!"

Tarzan of the Apes dropped lightly from a tree and warily approached the dying man. Stabutch, writhing in agony and terror, rolled over on his side. He saw the ape-man approaching, his bow and arrow ready in his hand, and, dying, reached for the revolver at his hip to complete the work that he had come so far to achieve and for which he was to give his life.

No more had his hand reached the grip of his weapon than the Lord of the Jungle loosed another shaft that drove deep through the chest of the Russian, deep through his heart. Without a sound Leon Stabutch collapsed; and a moment later there rang through the jungle the fierce, uncanny victory cry of the bull ape.

As the savage notes reverberated through the forest Jezebel slid to the ground and fled in terror. She knew not where nor to what fate her flying feet led her. She was obsessed by but a single idea—to escape from the terrors of that lonely spot.

23
Captured

WITH the coming of day the "Gunner" found himself near a forest. He had heard no sound of horses all during the night; and now that day had come, and he could see to a distance, he scanned the landscape for some sign of Stabutch and Jezebel but without success.

"Geeze," he muttered, "there aint no use, I gotta rest. The poor little kid! If I only knew where the rat took her; but I don't, and I gotta rest." He surveyed the forest. "That looks like a swell hideout. I'll lay up there and grab off a little sleep. Geeze, I'm all in."

As he walked toward the forest his attention was attracted to something moving a couple of miles to the north of him. He stopped short; and looked more closely as two horses, racing from the forest, dashed madly toward the foothills, pursued by a lion.

"Geeze!" exclaimed the "Gunner," "those must be their horses. What if the lion got her!"

Instantly his fatigue was forgotten; and he started at a run toward the north; but he could not keep the pace up for long; and soon he was walking again, his brain a turmoil of conjecture and apprehension.

He saw the lion give up the chase and turn away almost immediately, cutting up the slope in a northeasterly direction. The "Gunner" was glad to see him go, not for his own sake so much as for Jezebel, whom, he reasoned, the lion might not have killed after all. There was a possibility, he thought, that she might have had time to climb a tree. Otherwise, he was positive, the lion must have killed her.

His knowledge of lions was slight. In common with most people, he believed that lions wandered about killing everything so unfortunate as to fall into their pathways—unless they were bluffed out as he had bluffed the panther the day before. But of course, he reasoned, Jezebel wouldn't have been able to bluff a lion.

He was walking close to the edge of the forest, making the best time that he could, when he heard a shot in the distance. It was the report of Stabutch's rifle as he fired at Tarzan. The "Gunner" tried to increase his speed. There was too much doing there, where he thought Jezebel might be, to permit of loafing; but he was too exhausted to move rapidly.

Then, a few minutes later, the Russian's scream of agony was wafted to his ears and again he was goaded on. This was followed by the uncanny cry of the ape-man, which, for some reason, Danny did not recognize, though he had heard it twice before. Perhaps the distance and the intervening trees muffled and changed it.

On he plodded, trying occasionally to run; but his overtaxed muscles had reached their limit; and he had to give up the attempt, for already he was staggering and stumbling even at a walk.

"I aint no good," he muttered; "nothing but a lousy punk. Here's a guy beatin' it with my girl, and I aint even got the guts to work my dogs. Geeze, I'm a flop."

A little farther on he entered the forest so that he could approach the spot, where he had seen the horses emerge, without being seen, if Stabutch were still there.

Suddenly he stopped. Something was crashing through the brush toward him. He recalled the lion and drew his pocket knife. Then he hid behind a bush and waited, nor did he have long to wait before the author of the disturbance broke into view.

"Jezebel!" he cried, stepping into her path. His voice trembled with emotion.

With a startled scream the girl halted, and then she recognized him. "Danny!" It was the last straw—her over-wrought nerves went to pieces; and she sank to the ground, sobbing hysterically.

The "Gunner" took a step or two toward her. He staggered, his knees gave beneath him, and he sat down heavily a few yards from her; and then a strange thing happened. Tears welled to the eyes of Danny "Gunner" Patrick; he threw himself face down on the ground; and he, too, sobbed.

For several minutes they lay there, and then Jezebel gained control of herself and sat up. "Oh, Danny," she cried. "Are you hurt? Oh, your head! Don't die, Danny."

He had quelled his emotion and was roughly wiping his eyes on his shirt sleeve. "I aint dyin'," he said; "but I oughta. Some one oughta bump me off—a great big stiff like me, cryin'!"

"It's because you've been hurt, Danny," said Jezebel.

"Naw, it aint that. I been hurt before, but I aint bawled since I was a little kid—when my mother died. It was something else. I just blew up when I seen you, and knew that you was O. K. My nerves went blooey—just like that!" he snapped his fingers. "You see," he added, hesitantly, "I guess I like you an awful lot, kid."

"I like you, Danny," she told him. "You're top hole."

"I'm what? What does that mean?"

"I don't know," Jezebel admitted. "It's English, and you don't understand English, do you?"

He crawled over closer to her and took her hand in his. "Geeze," he said, "I thought I wasn't never goin' to see you again. Say," he burst out violently, "did that bum hurt you any, kid?"

"The man who took me away from the black men in the village, you mean?"

"Yes."

"No, Danny. After he killed his friend we rode all night. He was afraid the black men would catch him."

"What became of the rat? How did you make your getaway?"

She told him all that she knew, but they were unable to account for the sounds both had heard or to guess whether or not they had portended the death of Stabutch.

"I wouldn't be much good, if he showed up again," said Danny. "I gotta get my strength back some way."

"You must rest," she told him.

"I'll tell you what we'll do," he said. "We'll lay around here until we are rested up a bit; then we'll beat it back up toward the hills where I know where they's water and something to eat. It aint very good food," he added, "but it's better than none. Say, I got some of it in my pocket. We'll just have a feed now." He extracted some dirty scraps of half burned pork from one of his pockets and surveyed them ruefully.

"What is it?" asked Jezebel.

"It's pig, kid," he explained. "It don't look so hot, does it? Well, it don't taste no better than it looks; but it's food, and that's what we are needin' bad right now. Here, hop to it." He extended a handful of the scraps toward her. "Shut your eyes and hold your nose, and it aint so bad," he assured her. "Just imagine you're in the old College Inn."

Jezebel smiled and took a piece of the meat. "United States is a funny language, isn't it, Danny?"

"Why, I don't know—is it?"

"Yes, I think so. Sometimes it sound just like English and yet I can't understand it at all."

"That's because you aint used to it," he told her; "but I'll learn you if you want me to. Do you?"

"Oke, kid," replied Jezebel.

"You're learnin' all right," said Danny, admiringly.

They lay in the growing heat of the new day and talked together of many things, as they rested. Jezebel told him the story of the land of Midian, of her childhood, of the eventful coming of Lady Barbara and its strange effect upon her life; and Danny told her of Chicago, but there were many things in his own life that he did not tell her—things that, for the first time, he was ashamed of. And he wondered why he was ashamed.

As they talked, Tarzan of the Apes quitted the forest and set out upon his search for them, going upward toward the hills, intending to start his search for their spoor at the mouth of the fissure. If he did not find it there he would know that they were still in the valley; if he did find it, he would follow it until he located them.

At break of day a hundred *shiftas* rode out of their village. They had discovered the body of Capietro, and now they knew that the Russian had tricked them and fled, after killing their chief. They wanted the girl for ransom, and they wanted the life of Stabutch.

They had not ridden far when they met two riderless horses galloping back toward the village. The *shiftas* recognized them at once, and knowing that Stabutch and the girl were now afoot they anticipated little difficulty in overhauling them.

The rolling foothills were cut by swales and canyons; so that at times the vision of the riders was limited. They had been following downward along the bottom of a shallow canyon for some time, where they could neither see to a great distance nor be seen; and then their leader turned his mount toward higher ground, and as he topped the summit of a low ridge he saw a man approaching from the direction of the forest.

Tarzan saw the *shifta* simultaneously and changed his direction obliquely to the left, breaking into a trot. He knew that if that lone rider signified a force of mounted *shiftas* he would be no match for them; and, guided by the instinct of the wild beast, he sought ground where the advantage would be with him—the rough, rocky ground leading to the cliffs, where no horse could follow him.

With a yell to his followers, the *shifta* chieftain put spurs to his horse and rode at top speed to intercept the ape-man; and close behind him came his yelling, savage horde.

Tarzan quickly saw that he could not reach the cliffs ahead of them; but he maintained his steady, tireless trot that he might be that much nearer the goal when the attack came. Perhaps he could hold them off until he reached the sanctuary of the cliffs, but certainly he had no intention of giving up without exerting every effort to escape the unequal battle that must follow if they overtook him.

With savage yells the *shiftas* approached, their loose cotton garments fluttering in the wind, their rifles waving above their heads. The chief rode in the lead; and when he was near enough, the ape-man, who had been casting occasional glances rearward across a brown shoulder, stopped, wheeled and let an arrow drive at his foe; then he was away again as the shaft sank into the breast of the *shifta* chieftain.

With a scream, the fellow rolled from his saddle; and for a moment the others drew rein, but only for a moment. Here was but a single enemy, poorly armed with primitive weapons —he was no real menace to mounted riflemen.

Shouting their anger and their threats of vengeance, they spurred forward again in pursuit; but Tarzan had gained and the rocky ground was not far away.

Spreading in a great half circle, the *shiftas* sought to surround and head off their quarry, whose strategy they had guessed the moment that they had seen the course of his flight. Now another rider ventured too near, and for a brief instant Tarzan paused to loose another arrow. As this second enemy fell, mortally wounded, the ape-man continued his flight to the accompaniment of a rattle of musketry fire; but soon he was forced to halt again as several of the horsemen passed him and cut off his line of retreat.

The hail of slugs screaming past him or kicking up the dirt around him gave him slight concern, so traditionally poor was the marksmanship of these roving bands of robbers, illy equipped with ancient firearms with which, because of habitual shortage of ammunition, they had little opportunity to practice.

Now they pressed closer, in a rough circle of which he was the center; and, firing across him from all sides, it seemed impossible that they should miss him; but miss him they did, though their bullets found targets among their own men and horses, until one, who had supplanted the slain chief, took command and ordered them to cease firing.

Turning again in the direction of his flight, Tarzan tried to shoot his way through the cordon of horsemen shutting off his retreat; but, though each arrow sped true to its mark, the yelling horde closed in upon him until, his last shaft spent, he was the center of a closely milling mass of shrieking enemies.

Shrilly above the pandemonium of battle rose the cries of

the new leader. "Do not kill! Do not kill!" he screamed. "It is Tarzan of the Apes, and he is worth the ransom of a ras!"

Suddenly a giant black threw himself from his horse full upon the Lord of the Jungle, but Tarzan seized the fellow and hurled him back among the horsemen. Yet closer and closer they pressed; and now several fell upon him from their saddles, bearing him down beneath the feet of the now frantic horses.

Battling for life and liberty, the ape-man struggled against the over-powering odds that were being constantly augmented by new recruits who hurled themselves from their mounts upon the growing pile that overwhelmed him. Once he managed to struggle to his feet, shaking most of his opponents from him; but they seized him about the legs and dragged him down again; and presently succeeded in slipping nooses about his wrists and ankles, thus effectually subduing him.

Now that he was harmless many of them reviled and struck him; but there were many others who lay upon the ground, some never to rise again. The *shiftas* had captured the great Tarzan, but it had cost them dear.

Now some of them rounded up the riderless horses, while others stripped the dead of their weapons, ammunition, and any other valuables the living coveted. Tarzan was raised to an empty saddle, where he was securely bound; and four men were detailed to conduct him and the horses of the dead to the village, the wounded accompanying them, while the main body of the blacks continued the search for Stabutch and Jezebel.

24
The Long Night

THE sun was high in the heavens when Lady Barbara, refreshed by her long, undisturbed sleep, stepped from her tent in the camp of Lord Passmore. A smiling, handsome black boy came running toward her. "Breakfast soon be ready," he told her. "Lord Passmore very sorry. He have to go hunt."

She asked after Lafayette Smith and was told that he had just awakened, nor was it long before he joined her; and soon they were breakfasting together.

"If Jezebel and your friend were here," she said, "I

should be very happy. I am praying that Tarzan finds them."

"I am sure he will," Smith assured her, "though I am only worried about Jezebel. Danny can take care of himself."

"Doesn't it seem heavenly to eat a meal again?" the girl remarked. "Do you know it has been months since I have eaten anything that even vaguely approximated a civilized meal. Lord Passmore was fortunate to get such a cook for his safari. I had no such luck."

"Have you noticed what splendid looking fellows all his men are?" asked Smith. "They would make that aggregation of mine resemble fourth rate roustabouts with hookworm and sleeping sickness."

"There is another very noticeable thing about them," said Lady Barbara.

"What is that?"

"There is not a single piece of cast off European finery among them—their garb is native, pure and simple; and, while I'll have to admit there isn't much to it, it lends a dignity to them that European clothing would change to the absurd."

"I quite agree with you," said Smith. "I wonder why I didn't get a safari like this."

"Lord Passmore is evidently an African traveller and hunter of long experience. No amateur could hope to attract such men as these."

"I shall hate to go back to my own camp, if I stay here very long," said Smith; "but I suppose I'll have to; and that suggests another unpleasant feature of the change."

"And what is that?" she asked.

"I shan't see you any more," he said with a simple directness that vouched for the sincerity of his regret.

The girl was silent for a moment, as though the suggestion had aroused a train of thought she had not before considered. "That is true, isn't it?" she remarked, presently. "We shan't see each other any more—but not for always. I'm sure you'll stop and visit me in London. Isn't it odd what old friends we seem? And yet we only met two days ago. Or, maybe, it doesn't seem that way to you. You see I was so long without seeing a human being of my own world that you were quite like a long lost brother, when you came along so unexpectedly."

"I have the same feeling," he said—"as though I had known you forever—and—," he hesitated, "—as though I could never get along without you in the future." He flushed a little as he spoke those last words.

The girl looked up at him with a quick smile—a sympathetic, understanding smile. "It was nice of you to say that," she said. "Why it sounded almost like a declaration," she added, with a gay, friendly laugh.

He reached across the little camp table and laid a hand upon hers. "Accept it as such," he said. "I'm not very good at saying things—like that."

"Let's not be serious," she begged. "Really, we scarcely know each other, after all."

"I have known you always," he replied. "I think we were amœbas together before the first Cambrian dawn."

"Now you've compromised me," she cried, laughingly, "for I'm sure there were no chaperons way back there. I hope that you were a proper amœba. You didn't kiss me, did you?"

"Unfortunately for me amœbas have no mouths," he said, "but I've been profiting by several millions of years of evolution just to remedy that defect."

"Let's be amœbas again," she suggested.

"No," he said, "for then I couldn't tell you that I—I—" He choked and flushed.

"Please! Please, don't tell me," she cried. "We're such ripping friends—don't spoil it."

"Would it spoil it?" he asked.

"I don't know. It might. I am afraid."

"Can't I ever tell you?" he asked.

"Perhaps, some day," she said.

A sudden burst of distant rifle fire interrupted them. The blacks in the camp were instantly alert. Many of them sprang to their feet, and all were listening intently to the sounds of this mysterious engagement between armed men.

The man and the girl heard the headman speaking to his fellows in some African dialect. His manner showed no excitement, his tones were low but clear. It was evident that he was issuing instructions. The men went quickly to their shelters, and a moment later Lady Barbara saw the peaceful camp transformed. Every man was armed now. As by magic a modern rifle and a bandoleer of cartridges were in the possession of each black. White feathered headdresses were being adjusted and war paint applied to glossy hides.

Smith approached the headman. "What is the matter?" he asked. "Is something wrong?"

"I do not know, bwana," replied the black; "but we prepare."

"Is there any danger?" continued the white.

The headman straightened to his full, impressive height. "Are we not here?" he asked.

Jezebel and the "Gunner" were walking slowly in the direction of the distant water hole and the cached boar meat, following the bottom of a dip that was the mouth of a small canyon that led up into the hills.

They were stiff and lame and very tired; and the wound on the "Gunner's" head pained; but, notwithstanding, they were happy as, hand in hand, they dragged their weary feet toward water and food.

"Geeze, kid," said Danny, "it sure is a funny world. Just think, if I hadn't met old Smithy on board that ship me and you wouldn't never have met up. It all started from that," but then Danny knew nothing of Angustus the Ephesian.

"I got a few grand salted away, kid, and when we get out of this mess we'll go somewhere where nobody doesn't know me and I'll start over again. Get myself a garage or a filling station, and we'll have a little flat. Geeze, it's goin' to be great showin' you things. You don't know what you ain't seen—movies and railroads and boats! Geeze! You ain't seen nothin' and nobody ain't going to show you nothin', only me."

"Yes, Danny," said Jezebel, "it's going to be ripping," and she squeezed his hand.

Just then they were startled by the sound of rifle fire ahead.

"What was that?" asked Jezebel.

"It sounded like the Valentine Massacre," said Danny, "but I guess it's them toughs from the village. We better hide, kid." He drew her toward some low bushes; and there they lay down, listening to the shouts and shots that came down to them from where Tarzan fought for his life and liberty with the odds a hundred to one against him.

After awhile the din ceased, and a little later the two heard the thudding of many galloping hoofs. The sound increased in volume as it drew nearer, and Danny and Jezebel tried to make themselves as small as possible beneath the little bush in the inadequate concealment of which they were hiding.

At a thundering gallop the *shiftas* crossed the swale just above them, and all but a few had passed when one of the stragglers discovered them. His shout, which attracted the attention of others, was carried forward until it reached the new chief, and presently the entire band had circled back to learn what their fellow had discovered.

Poor "Gunner"! Poor Jezebel! Their happiness had been short lived. Their recapture was effected with humiliating ease. Broken and dejected, they were soon on their way to the village under escort of two black ruffians.

Bound, hands and feet, they were thrown into the hut formerly occupied by Capietro and left without food or water upon the pile of dirty rugs and clothing that littered the floor.

Beside them lay the corpse of the Italian which his followers, in their haste to overtake his slayer, had not taken the time to remove. It lay upon its back, the dead eyes staring upward.

Never before in his life had the spirits of Danny Patrick sunk so low, for the very reason, perhaps, that never in his life had they risen so high as during the brief interlude of happiness he had enjoyed following his reunion with Jezebel. Now he saw no hope ahead, for, with the two white men eliminated, he feared that he might not even be able to dicker with these ignorant black men for the ransom that he would gladly pay to free Jezebel and himself.

"There goes the garage, the filling station, and the flat," he said, lugubriously.

"Where?" asked Jezebel.

"Flooie," explained Danny.

"But you are here with me," said the golden one; "so I do not care what else there is."

"That's nice, kid; but I aint much help, all tied up like a Christmas present. They sure picked out a swell bed for me —feels like I was lyin' on a piece of the kitchen stove." He rolled himself to one side and nearer Jezebel. "That's better," he said, "but I wonder what was that thing I was parked on."

"Maybe your friend will come and take us away," suggested Jezebel.

"Who, Smithy? What would he take us with—that dinky toy pistol of his?"

"I was thinking of the other that you told me about."

"Oh, that Tarzan guy! Say kid, if he knew we was here he'd walk in and push all these nutty dumps over with one mitt and kick the whole gang over the back fence. Geeze, you bet I wish he was here. There is one big shot, and I don't mean maybe."

In a hut on the edge of the village was the answer to the "Gunner's" wish, bound hand and foot, as was the "Gunner," and, apparently, equally helpless. Constantly the ape-man was working on the thongs that confined his wrists—twisting, tugging, pulling.

The long day wore on and never did the giant captive cease his efforts to escape; the thongs were heavy and securely tied, yet little by little he felt that they were loosening.

Towards evening the new chief returned with the party that had been searching for Stabutch. They had not found him; but scouts had located the camp of Lord Passmore, and now the *shiftas* were discussing plans for attacking it on the morrow.

They had not come sufficiently close to it to note the number of armed natives it contained; but they had glimpsed Smith and Lady Barbara; and, being sure that there were not more than two white men, they felt little hesitation in attempting the raid, since they were planning to start back for Abyssinia on the morrow.

"We will kill the white man we now have," said the chief, "and carry the two girls and Tarzan with us. Tarzan should bring a good ransom and the girls a good price."

"Why not keep the girls for ourselves," suggested another.

"We shall sell them," said the chief.

"Who are you, to say what we shall do?" demanded the other. "You are no chief."

"No," growled a villanous looking black squatting beside the first objector.

He who would be chief leaped, catlike, upon the first speaker, before any was aware of his purpose. A sword gleamed for an instant in the light of the new made cook fires and fell with terrific force upon the skull of the victim.

"Who am I?" repeated the killer, as he wiped the bloody blade upon the garment of the slain man. "I am chief!" He looked around upon the scowling faces about him. "Is there any who says I am not chief?" There was no demur. Ntale was chief of the *shifta* band.

Inside the dark interior of the hut where he had lain bound all day without food or water the ape-man tugged and pulled until the sweat stood in beads upon his body, but not in vain. Gradually a hand slipped through the stretched thong, and he was free. Or at least his hands were, and it took them but a moment to loosen the bonds that secured his ankles.

With a low, inaudible growl he rose to his feet and stepped to the doorway. Before him lay the village compound. He saw the *shiftas* squatting about while slaves prepared the evening meal. Nearby was the palisade. They must see him as he crossed to it, but what matter?

He would be gone before they could gather their wits. Perhaps a few stray shots would be fired; but then, had they not fired many shots at him this morning, not one of which had touched him?

He stepped out into the open, and at the same instant a burly black stepped from the next hut and saw him. With a shout of warning to his fellows the man leaped upon the escaping prisoner. Those at the fires sprang to their feet and came running toward the two.

Within their prison hut Jezebel and Danny heard the commotion and wondered.

The ape-man seized the black who would have stopped him and wheeling him about to form a shield for himself, backed quickly toward the palisade.

"Stay where you are," he called to the advancing *shiftas*, in their own dialect. "Stay where you are, or I will kill this man."

"Let him kill him then," growled Ntale. "He is not worth the ransom we are losing," and with a shout of encouragement to his followers he leaped quickly forward to intercept the ape-man.

Tarzan was already near the palisade as Ntale charged. He raised the struggling black above his head and hurled him upon the advancing chief, and as the two went down he wheeled and ran for the palisade.

Like Manu the monkey he scaled the high barrier. A few scattered shots followed him, but he dropped to the ground outside unscathed and disappeared in the growing gloom of the advancing night.

The long night of their captivity dragged on and still the "Gunner" and Jezebel lay as they had been left, without food or drink, while the silent corpse of Capietro stared at the ceiling.

"I wouldn't treat nobody like this," said the "Gunner," "not even a rat."

Jezebel raised herself to one elbow. "Why not try it?" she whispered.

"What?" demanded Danny. "I'd try anything once."

"What you said about a rat made me think of it," said Jezebel. "We have lots of rats in the land of Midian. Sometimes we catch them—they are very good to eat. We make traps, but if we do not kill the rats soon after they are caught they gnaw their way to freedom—they gnaw the cords which bind the traps together."

"Well, what of it?" demanded Danny. "We ain't got no

rats, and if we had—well, I won't say I wouldn't eat 'em, kid; but I don't see what it's got to do with the mess we're in."

"We're like the rats, Danny," she said. "Don't you see? We're like the rats and—we can gnaw our way to freedom!"

"Well, kid," said Danny, "if you want to gnaw your way through the side of this hut, hop to it; but if I gets a chance to duck I'm goin' through the door."

"You do not understand, Danny," insisted Jezebel. "You are an egg that cannot talk. I mean that I can gnaw the cords that fasten your wrists together."

"Geeze, kid!" exclaimed Danny. "Dumb aint no name for it, and I always thought I was the bright little boy. You sure got a bean, and I don't mean maybe."

"I wish I knew what you are talking about, Danny," said Jezebel, "and I wish you would let me try to gnaw the cords from your wrist. Can't you understand what I'm talking about?"

"Sure, kid, but I'll do the gnawing—my jaws are tougher. Roll over, and I'll get busy. When you're free you can untie me."

Jezebel rolled over on her stomach and Danny wriggled into position where he could reach the thongs at her wrists with his teeth. He fell to work with a will, but it was soon evident to him that the job was going to be much more difficult than he had anticipated.

He found, too, that he was very weak and soon tired; but though often he was forced to stop through exhaustion, he never gave up. Once, when he paused to rest, he kissed the little hands that he was trying to liberate. It was a gentle, reverent kiss, quite unlike the "Gunner"; but then love is a strange force, and when it is aroused in the breast of a man by a clean and virtuous woman it makes him always a little tenderer and a little better.

Dawn was lifting the darkness within the hut, and still the "Gunner" gnawed upon the thongs that it seemed would never part. Capietro lay staring at the ceiling, his dead eyes rolled upward, just as he had lain there staring through all the long hours of the night, unseeing.

The *shiftas* were stirring in the village, for this was to be a busy day. Slaves were preparing the loads of camp equipment and plunder that they were to carry toward the north. The fighting men were hastening their breakfasts that they might look to their weapons and their horse gear before riding out on their last raid from this village, against the camp of the English hunter.

Ntale the chief was eating beside the fire of his favorite

wife. "Make haste, woman," he said. "I have work to do before we ride."

"You are chief now," she reminded him. "Let others work."

"This thing I do myself," replied the black man.

"What do you do that is so important that I must hasten the preparation of the morning meal?" she demanded.

"I go to kill the white man and get the girl ready for the journey," he replied. "Have food prepared for her. She must eat or she will die."

"Let her die," replied the woman. "I do not want her around. Kill them both."

"Shut thy mouth!" snapped the man. "I am chief."

"If you do not kill her, I shall," said the woman. "I shall not cook for any white bitch."

The man rose. "I go to kill the man," he said. "Have breakfast for the girl when I return with her."

25

The Waziri

"THERE!" gasped the "Gunner."

"I am free!" exclaimed Jezebel.

"And my jaws is wore out," said Danny.

Quickly Jezebel turned and worked upon the thongs that confined the "Gunner's" wrists before taking the time to loose her ankles. Her fingers were quite numb, for the cords had partially cut off the circulation from her hands; and she was slow and bungling at the work. It seemed to them both that she would never be done. Had they known that Ntale had already arisen from his breakfast fire with the announcement that he was going to kill the "Gunner," they would have been frantic; but they did not know it, and perhaps that were better, since to Jezebel's other handicaps was not added the nervous tension that surely would have accompanied a knowledge of the truth.

But at last the "Gunner's" hands were free; and then both fell to work upon the cords that secured their ankles, which were less tightly fastened.

At last the "Gunner" arose. "The first thing I do," he said, "is to find out what I was lyin' on yesterday. It had a familiar feel to it; and, if I'm right—boy!"

He rummaged among the filthy rags at the end of the hut, and a moment later straightened up with a Thompson sub-machine gun in one hand and his revolver, belt and holster in the other—a grin on his face.

"This is the first break I've had in a long time," he said. "Everything's jake now, sister."

"What are those things?" asked Jezebel.

"Them's the other half of 'Gunner' Patrick," replied Danny. "Now, bring on the dirty rats!"

As he spoke, Ntale the chief drew aside the rug at the doorway and looked in. The interior of the hut was rather dark, and at first glance he could not make out the figures of the girl and the man standing at the far side; but, silhouetted as he was against the growing morning light beyond the doorway, he was plainly visible to his intended victim; and Danny saw that the man carried a pistol ready in his hand.

The "Gunner" had already buckled his belt about him. Now he transferred the machine gun to his left hand and drew his revolver from its holster. He did these things quickly and silently. So quickly that, as he fired, Ntale had not realized that his prisoners were free of their bonds—a thing he never knew, as, doubtless, he never heard the report of the shot that killed him.

At the same instant that the "Gunner" fired, the report of his revolver was drowned by yells and a shot from a sentry at the gate, to whom the coming day had revealed a hostile force creeping upon the village.

As Danny Patrick stepped over the dead body of the chief and looked out into the village he realized something of what had occurred. He saw men running hastily toward the village gates and scrambling to the banquette. He heard a fusilade of shots that spattered the palisade, splintering the wood and tearing through to fill the village with a screaming, terror stricken mob.

His knowledge of such things told him that only high powered rifles could send their projectiles through the heavy wood of the palisade. He saw the *shiftas* on the banquette returning the fire with their antiquated muskets. He saw the slaves and prisoners cowering in a corner of the village that was freer from the fire of the attackers than other portions.

He wondered who the enemies of the *shiftas* might be, and past experience suggested only two possibilities—either a rival "gang" or the police.

"I never thought I'd come to it, kid," he said.

"Come to what, Danny?"

"I hate to tell you what I been hopin'," he admitted.

"Tell me, Danny," she said. "I won't be angry."

"I been hopin' them guys out there was cops. Just think o' that, kid! Me, 'Gunner' Patrick, a-hopin' the cops would come!"

"What are cops, Danny?"

"Laws, harness bulls—Geeze, kid, why do you ask so many questions? Cops is cops. And I'll tell you why I hope its them. If it aint cops its a rival mob, and we'd get just as tough a break with them as with these guys."

He stepped out into the village street. "Well," he said, "here goes Danny Patrick smearin' up with the police. You stay here, kid, and lie down on your bread basket, so none of them slugs'll find you, while I go out and push the smokes around."

Before the gate was a great crowd of *shiftas* firing through openings at the enemy beyond. The "Gunner" knelt and raised the machine gun to his shoulder. There was the vicious b-r-r-r as of some titanic rattle snake; and a dozen of the massed *shiftas* collapsed, dead or screaming, to the ground.

The others turned and, seeing the "Gunner," realized that they were caught between two fires, for they remembered the recent occasion upon which they had witnessed the deadly effects of this terrifying weapon.

The "Gunner" spied Ogonyo among the prisoners and slaves huddled not far from where he stood, and the sight of him suggested an idea to the white man.

"Hey! Big feller, you!" He waved his hand to Ogonyo. "Come here! Bring all them guys with you. Tell 'em to grab anything they can fight with if they want to make their getaway."

Whether or not Ogonyo understood even a small part of what the "Gunner" said, he seemed at least to grasp the main idea; and presently the whole mob of prisoners and slaves, except the women, had placed themselves behind Danny.

The firing from the attacking force had subsided somewhat since Danny's typewriter had spoken, as though the leader of that other party had recognized its voice and guessed that white prisoners within the village might be menaced by his rifle fire. Only an occasional shot, aimed at some specific target, was coming into the village.

The *shiftas* had regained their composure to some extent and were preparing their horses and mounting, with the evident intention of executing a sortie. They were leaderless and confused, half a dozen shouting advice and instructions at the same time.

It was at this moment that Danny advanced upon them with his motley horde armed with sticks and stones, an occasional knife and a few swords hastily stolen from the huts of their captors.

As the *shiftas* realized that they were menaced thus seriously from the rear, the "Gunner" opened fire upon them for the second time, and the confusion that followed in the village compound gave the attackers both within and without a new advantage.

The *shiftas* fought among themselves for the loose horses that were now stampeding in terror about the village; and as a number of them succeeded in mounting they rode for the village gates, overthrowing those who had remained to defend them. Some among them forced the portals open; and as the horsemen dashed out they were met by a band of black warriors, above whose heads waved white plumes, and in whose hands were modern high powered rifles.

The attacking force had been lying partially concealed behind a low ridge, and as it rose to meet the escaping *shiftas* the savage war cry of the Waziri rang above the tumult of the battle.

First to the gates was Tarzan, war chief of the Waziri, and while Muviro and a small detachment accounted for all but a few of the horsemen who had succeeded in leaving the village, the ape-man, with the remaining Waziri, charged the demoralized remnants of Capietro's band that remained within the palisade.

Surrounded by enemies, the *shiftas* threw down their rifles and begged for mercy, and soon they were herded into a corner of the village under guard of a detachment of the Waziri.

As Tarzan greeted the "Gunner" and Jezebel he expressed his relief at finding them unharmed.

"You sure come at the right time," Danny told him. "This old typewriter certainly chews up the ammunition, and that last burst just about emptied the drum; but say, who are your friends? Where did you raise this mob?"

"They are my people," replied Tarzan.

"Some gang!" ejaculated the "Gunner," admiringly; "but say, have you seen anything of old Smithy?"

"He is safe at my camp."

"And Barbara," asked Jezebel; "where is she?"

"She is with Smith," replied Tarzan. "You will see them both in a few hours. We start back as soon as I arrange for the disposal of these people." He turned away and commenced to make inquiries among the prisoners of the *shiftas*.

"Is he not beautiful!" exclaimed Jezebel.

"Hey, sister, can that 'beautiful' stuff," warned the "Gunner," "and from now on remember that I'm the only 'beautiful' guy you know, no matter what my pan looks like."

Quickly Tarzan separated the prisoners according to their tribes and villages, appointed headman to lead them back to their homes and issued instructions to them as he explained his plans.

The weapons, ammunition, loot and belongings of the *shiftas* were divided among the prisoners, after the Waziri had been allowed to select such trifles as they desired. The captured *shiftas* were placed in charge of a large band of Gallas with orders to return them to Abyssinia and turn them over to the nearest ras.

"Why not hang them here?" asked the Galla headman. "We shall then save all the food they would eat on the long march back to our country, besides saving us much trouble and worry in guarding them—for the ras will certainly hang them."

"Take them back, as I tell you," replied Tarzan. "But if they give you trouble do with them as you see fit."

It took little more than an hour to evacuate the village. All of Smith's loads were recovered, including Danny's precious ammunition and extra drums for his beloved Thompson; and these were assigned to Smith's porters, who were once again assembled under Ogonyo.

When the village was emptied it was fired in a dozen places; and, as the black smoke curled up toward the blue heavens, the various parties took their respective ways from the scene of their captivity, but not before the several headmen had come and knelt before the Lord of the Jungle and thanked him for the deliverance of their people.

26

The Last Knot Is Tied

Lafayette Smith and Lady Barbara had been mystified witnesses to the sudden transformation of the peaceful scene in the camp of Lord Passmore. All day the warriors had remained in readiness, as though expecting a summons; and when night fell they still waited.

Evidences of restlessness were apparent; and there was no singing and little laughter in the camp, as there had been before. The last that the two whites saw, as they retired for the night, were the little groups of plumed warriors squatting about their fires, their rifles ready to their hands; and they were asleep when the summons came and the sleek, black fighting men melted silently into the dark shadows of the forest, leaving only four of their number to guard the camp and the two guests.

When Lady Barbara emerged from her tent in the morning she was astonished to find the camp all but deserted. The *boy* who acted in the capacity of personal servant and cook for her and Smith was there and three other blacks. All were constantly armed; but their attitude toward her had not changed, and she felt only curiosity relative to the other altered conditions, so obvious at first glance, rather than apprehension.

When Smith joined her a few minutes later he was equally at a loss to understand the strange metamorphosis that had transformed the laughing, joking porters and askaris into painted warriors and sent them out into the night so surreptitiously, nor could they glean the slightest information from their *boy,* who, though still courteous and smiling, seemed by some strange trick of fate suddenly to have forgotten the very fair command of English that he had exhibited with evident pride on the previous day.

The long day dragged on until mid afternoon without sign of any change. Neither Lord Passmore nor the missing blacks returned, and the enigma was as baffling as before. The two whites, however, seemed to find much pleasure in one another's company; and so, perhaps, the day passed more rapidly for them than it did for the four blacks, waiting and listening through the hot, drowsy hours.

But suddenly there was a change. Lady Barbara saw her *boy* rise and stand in an attitude of eager listening. "They come!" he said, in his own tongue, to his companions. Now they all stood and, though they may have expected only friends, their rifles were in readiness for enemies.

Gradually the sound of voices and of marching men became distinctly audible to the untrained ears of the two whites, and a little later they saw the head of a column filing through the forest toward them.

"Why there's the 'Gunner!'" exclaimed Lafayette Smith. "And Jezebel, too. How odd that they should be together."

"With Tarzan of the Apes!" cried Lady Barbara. "He has saved them both."

A slow smile touched the lips of the ape-man as he witnessed the reunion of Lady Barbara and Jezebel and that between Smith and the "Gunner"; and it broadened a little, when, after the first burst of greetings and explanations, Lady Barbara said, "It is unfortunate that our host, Lord Passmore, isn't here."

"He is," said the ape-man.

"Where?" demanded Lafayette Smith, looking about the camp.

"I am 'Lord Passmore,'" said Tarzan.

"You?" exclaimed Lady Barbara.

"Yes. I assumed this rôle when I came north to investigate the rumors I had heard concerning Capietro and his band, believing that they not only would suspect no danger, but hoping, also, that they would seek to attack and plunder my safari as they have those of others."

"Geeze," said the "Gunner." "What a jolt they would of got!"

"That is why we never saw 'Lord Passmore,'" said Lady Barbara, laughing. "I thought him a most elusive host."

"The first night I left you here," explained Tarzan, "I walked into the jungle until I was out of sight, and then I came back from another direction and entered my tent from the rear. I slept there all night. The next morning, early, I left in search of your friends—and was captured myself. But everything has worked out well, and if you have no other immediate plans I hope that you will accompany me back to my home and remain a while as my guests while you recover from the rather rough experiences Africa has afforded you. Or, perhaps," he added, "Professor Smith and his friend wish to continue their geological investigations."

"I, ah, well, you see," stammered Lafayette Smith; "I have about decided to abandon my work in Africa and devote my life to the geology of England. We, or, er—you see, Lady Barbara——"

"I am going to take him back to England and teach him to shoot before I let him return to Africa. Possibly we shall come back later, though."

"And you, Patrick," asked Tarzan, "are you remaining to hunt, perhaps?"

"Nix, mister," said Danny, emphatically, "We're goin' to California and buy a garage and filling station."

"We?" queried Lady Barbara.

"Sure," said the "Gunner"; "me and Jez."

"Really?" exclaimed Lady Barbara. "Is he in earnest, Jezebel?"

"Oke, kid—isn't it ripping?" replied the golden one.